P9-DJU-871

RENNO—Unsurpassed as a warrior, his wisdom sharpened by the blades of betrayal and danger, the time has come for him to be Sachem of the Seneca . . . and the time has come to fight or die.

EMILY—Radiantly lovely, the new wife of Renno finds her love tested by the harsh challenges of Indian life, where danger lurks in the darkness and death may come with the dawn.

CAPTAIN ANDREW JACKSON—As dangerously hot-tempered as he was magnificently courageous, he must overcome his destructive prejudice against the Indian . . . or it will become his doom.

RANDY—Provocatively sensual, she grew up a wild child of the Tennessee mountains, skilled in fighting, undaunted by hardship, but dangerously innocent of the power of man's desires.

EL-I-CHI—Eager for scalps to prove his manhood, he joins Renno as a scout for Jackson's troops, but his heart hides a smouldering hatred . . . and a forbidden passion.

JAKE GENTRY—Treacherous and deadly, he is known as "The Ax" for the weapon he wields to kill, as he takes British gold to buy arms for renegades and feed the twisted hungers of his evil soul.

The White Indian Series
Ask your bookseller for the books you have missed

WHITE INDIAN—BOOK I
THE RENEGADE—BOOK II
WAR CHIEF—BOOK III
THE SACHEM—BOOK IV
RENNO—BOOK V
TOMAHAWK—BOOK VI
WAR CRY—BOOK VII
AMBUSH—BOOK VIII
SENECA—BOOK IX
CHEROKEE—BOOK X
CHOCTAW—BOOK XI
SEMINOLE—BOOK XII
WAR DRUMS—BOOK XIII

The White Indian Series
Book XIII

WAR DRUMS

Donald Clayton Porter

Created by the producers of
**Wagons West, Children of the Lion,
Stagecoach, and Saga of the Southwest.**

Chairman of the Board: Lyle Kenyon Engel

BANTAM BOOKS
TORONTO · NEW YORK · LONDON · SYDNEY · AUCKLAND

WAR DRUMS

*A Bantam Book / published by arrangement with
Book Creations, Inc.*

Bantam edition / September 1986

*Produced by Book Creations, Inc.
Chairman of the Board: Lyle Kenyon Engel.*

*All rights reserved.
Copyright © 1986 by Book Creations, Inc.
Cover art copyright © 1986 by Bantam Books, Inc.
This book may not be reproduced in whole or in part, by
mimeograph or any other means, without permission.
For information address: Bantam Books, Inc.*

ISBN 0-553-25868-0

Published simultaneously in the United States and Canada

---

*Bantam Books are published by Bantam Books, Inc. Its trademark,
consisting of the words "Bantam Books" and the portrayal of
a rooster, is Registered in U.S. Patent and Trademark Office
and in other countries. Marca Registrada. Bantam Books, Inc.,
666 Fifth Avenue, New York, New York 10103.*

PRINTED IN THE UNITED STATES OF AMERICA

O   0 9 8 7 6 5 4 3 2 1

This is a work of fiction. While the general outlines of history have been faithfully followed, certain details involving setting, characters, and events may have been simplified.

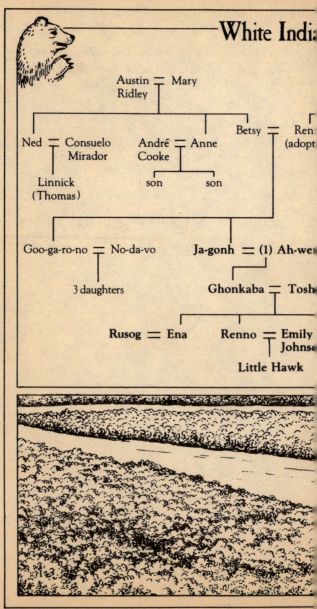

White Indi

Austin ≡ Mary
Ridley

Ned ≡ Consuelo
Mirador

Linnick
(Thomas)

André ≡ Anne
Cooke

son   son

Betsy ≡ Ren
(adopt

Goo-ga-ro-no ≡ No-da-vo

3 daughters

Ja-gonh ≡ (1) Ah-wer

Ghonkaba ≡ Tosh

Rusog ≡ Ena   Renno ≡ Emily
                        Johnse

Little Hawk

© 1986 BOOK CREATIONS INC.

mily Tree

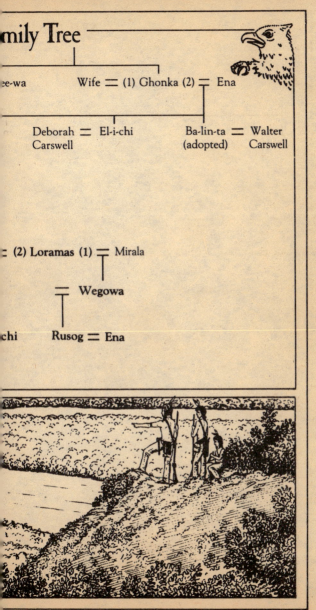

ee-wa   Wife = (1) Ghonka (2) = Ena

Deborah = El-i-chi   Ba-lin-ta = Walter
Carswell   (adopted)   Carswell

= (2) Loramas (1) = Mirala

= Wegowa

chi   Rusog = Ena

RON TOELKE '85

Chapter I

Renno awoke to the first light of a chill dawn. The fire had burned to embers, so he laid on dry kindling and topped it with small branches. The blaze lit the interior of the lodge and reflected off the smooth face of his wife, Emily. She made a sighing sound in her sleep and shifted her body under the warm coverings of hides and furs. Renno smiled as he noted the mound of her stomach. There was his son, his first child, and the time was near.

He stepped out into an iron-crisp winter morning, his breath making great clouds. He pulled his buffalo cloak together under his chin and listened to the morning sounds. An ax rang against wood, and although Renno did not consciously realize it at first, the sound was intrusive, a white man's sound.

The sun was edging over the hills to the east. He could see smoke piling upward from the lodgings of the other Seneca and their friends and allies, the Cherokee. His own sister, Ena, was married to a Cherokee warrior, the giant Rusog. There were more than a dozen stone chimneys among the traditional Cherokee lodges inside this walled town, and the chimneys were also a disturbance to him, even though he was not concentrating on the intrusion of the ways of the white men. He was smelling the air, noting the far flight of a crow, and watching the inquisitive nose of a squirrel, poked carefully around the trunk of a large tree near his lodge.

The first of the winter's snows had melted, leaving gray-white traces in deeper shadows. The sky was clean and blue, and Renno's heart leaped as a great hawk circled high, then lanced off to the west to disappear.

He was at peace. Soon he would have a son to carry on the tradition that had begun with his great-grandfather, who, taken as a baby during a successful raid on a white man's fort, had become the greatest and wisest leader ever known to the Seneca.

Renno was a man in his prime, lithe, and strongly built. He was made for action, for the challenges of the hunt and of war, and thus was restless with this period of peace, filled with a vague discontent that surfaced every now and then in a desire to be off and away. Even now the vast distances of the wilderness called to him, but thanks to his skill as a hunter, there was no real reason for a hunting trip. Plenty of meat was in the larder, and there were many deer-skins to be tanned and softened by the women for the making of clothing, and a store of nuts. The staples of Renno's customary Indian diet were further augmented by ground meal and sugar and other delicacies, all gifts from Emily's family. And a scouting trip was not necessary, since the land that Renno's band of Seneca now shared with their friends the Cherokee was secure and unthreatened.

He turned as Emily emerged to stand beside him. She had brushed her long wheat-colored hair and tossed it into a quick, loose braid resting on the back of her neck. She had adapted well to life in the Seneca village and had shown great courage during her captivity in the far southern lands of the Seminole. She put both hands in the small of her back and stretched, causing her belly to protrude even farther. A quick look of concern crossed Renno's face.

"Are you well?" he asked.

Emily laughed. Men, she had discovered, were all alike, be they white or Indian. She herself felt some trepidation as she anticipated the coming ordeal of birth, but of late, when she sighed with the weariness of carrying the child, she had noted that Renno's Seneca impassiveness was strained. This both pleased and amused her.

"I am well," she said. "We will eat now."

Not once had she ever regretted her decision to

leave her home in Knoxville to marry an Indian. At first she had missed a few of the luxuries she had grown used to as the daughter of a white settler, but there were compensations in the life she now led—such as standing beside her tall, handsome husband in the chill light of the early morning, the air a cold tonic in her nostrils.

"Come," Renno said, striding off, only to slow his pace to let her come alongside. She was carrying low and walked with a wide-legged waddle.

The house of Loramas, Grand Sachem of the Cherokee, was but a short walk away. Through habit and training, Renno moved silently, while Emily's moccasin-clad feet rustled the fading and deteriorating leaves of the past autumn. Loramas had not adopted the living style of the white men, as more and more of his people were doing. His was a traditional Cherokee dwelling, and the smell of food accompanied Loramas to the door as he greeted Renno and Emily.

Ah-wen-ga, Renno's grandmother, was kneeling beside the cooking fire. Married in her mature years to Loramas, thereby symbolizing the union of the Seneca and Cherokee, she still gave evidence of the beauty that had made Ja-gonh, Renno's grandfather, fall in love with her as a young woman. Renno took his place, sitting on a buffalo hide, while Emily, with a grunt of effort, lowered herself slowly by his side. One quick glance told Ah-wen-ga that Emily's time was still a matter of days away.

Renno and Emily often took meals with Ah-wen-ga and the strong Cherokee Grand Sachem. Today the older woman could see that her grandson had something on his mind, but she remained silent while serving the breakfast of venison stew and cornbread. The men ate heartily, while Emily picked at her food. The open fire had warmed the lodge, and Renno let his buffalo cloak fall from his shoulders.

"The signs were not wrong," Loramas said. "The fruits of fall ripened early. The brothers of the forest wear thick coats of fur."

"And yet it is warm," Renno replied, his mind on other things.

"The cold will come," Loramas said. "The wise men of your tribe say it is predicted by the manitous."

"Perhaps I will hunt," Renno said, "to prepare for the snows."

Ah-wen-ga laughed. "You and the young men have hunted until it strains the abilities of the women to preserve the meat. We have plenty."

Renno's face was expressionless. Ah-wen-ga laughed again. "But one might as well try to capture a moon-beam as to try to keep a warrior out of the forest. Hunt, then. A turkey roasted over the fire would be a welcome change."

Renno cast a quick look at Emily.

She smiled. "Yes, a turkey would be good."

"But something more than whether or not to hunt is bothering you," Ah-wen-ga said at last, her dark eyes carefully examining Renno's face.

"It is the matter of a name for my son," Renno admitted.

"Ah," Ah-wen-ga said, with a nod.

"I bear the name of a great man," Renno explained. "The name of my great-grandfather, the white Indian. I would like my son to have a name as honorable, and I pray to the manitous that he will live up to his ancestors. I have thought to name him for my father, Ghonkaba. And then again I thought to name him for my grandfather, Ja-gonh, but to choose one name dishonors the other."

"Your son will have one living grandfather," Ah-wen-ga said, speaking of Emily's father, Roy Johnson.

"My son is Seneca," Renno said, in a tone of voice that told them all that there was no possibility of giving any son of his a white man's name.

"Your son is many things," Ah-wen-ga reminded him gently. "In his blood runs the white vigor of the original Renno and his wife, Betsy, of the beautiful blond hair. I, his great-grandmother, am half-Seneca, half-Biloxi; and his grandmother Toshabe is half-French, half-Erie."

"My son is Seneca," Renno said calmly, "just as my father, Ghonkaba, and his father, Ja-gonh, and his father, Renno, were Seneca."

"As I am now Seneca," Emily added, earning an approving nod from Loramas, who had been listening to the discussion.

Renno turned his expressionless face to gaze at his white-skinned wife. She was one of those women who blossom in pregnancy. Her skin was flawless, and the fullness of her face, which came with her increase in weight, made her look younger and more beautiful.

"I will decide when it is fitting," Renno said. He rose and stalked out of the lodge, leaving his heavy buffalo cloak behind. Ah-wen-ga looked at Emily and shook her head with a smile as Emily started to rise.

"The strains of fatherhood affect even the boldest warriors," she said. "Stay, child. Let him walk off his restlessness alone."

Renno walked into the rising sun, quickly leaving the village behind him. The wilderness closed around him rapidly, the evergreens adding the only touch of color to the winter forest. To Renno it was not wilderness but a familiar and respected environment. He broke into a distance-eating trot, felt the muscles stretch in his legs, and began to breathe deeply. His body felt comfortably warm in his buckskins. He carried his bow in his left hand, quiver and arrows slung over his right shoulder for instant access, and his tomahawk and knife at his waist. As he crossed a glade his swift pace surprised a pair of red foxes, who dashed ahead of him for a short time and then faded into the trees.

He had run, perhaps, a mile, and his heart was pumping strongly, his lungs taking great drafts of the clean, crisp air. He froze almost in midstride, for he had heard a sound not in keeping with the quiet of the forest, a distant sound that sent him silently into a dense treed area, becoming invisible as he moved. There he bent and pressed his ear to the ground. The sound was clear, a horse moving at a comfortable canter.

Horses were rare in the lands of the Cherokee. The presence of a horse—and that meant, of course, a horseman—could mean only one thing: a white man was coming from the east, and although there was peace and friendship between the Cherokee and his own Seneca and the white men of the new state of Franklin, centered around Knoxville, Renno had known his share of dangerous white men. His own father had been murdered by the white man Ben Whipple, and there were white men who believed that all Indians were their natural enemies.

Now the sounds of the horse's hooves were clearly audible. The rider was following the trail toward the village. Renno readied his bow and selected an arrow. In the thick woods he would not be able to see the horseman until he was quite near. He saw the horse's breath first as it made a white cloud in the cold air. Then, with his bow half drawn, Renno nodded in pleasant surprise and returned the arrow to its quiver. He waited until the cantering horse was almost even with him before he leaped out into the trail. The horse, so suddenly reined in, reared, almost dislodging the rider, who was fumbling—as he tried to keep his seat—for his musket.

"Renno!" yelled Colonel Roy Johnson, Emily's father. "You scared me out of a year's growth."

"You travel too carelessly," Renno admonished, as Colonel Johnson threw himself out of the saddle and came forward, hand extended. Renno shook his father-in-law's hand briefly.

"Well, I'm supposed to be in friendly territory," Johnson said. "I wasn't expecting to be waylaid."

"The Choctaw range far," Renno said.

"You're right," Johnson admitted, "but this isn't the season for raiding." He grinned ruefully. "I know, Renno, you're just giving me a friendly warning. I guess I was so busy wondering whether my grandson had been born, I got careless."

"We still await his coming," Renno said, his face loosening up a bit to return his father-in-law's grin. "You are welcome."

They walked side by side back to the village, Johnson leading the horse. Emily displayed the reserve of a Seneca woman by nodding to her father, postponing throwing herself into his arms—as well as her protruding stomach would allow—until they were in the privacy of the lodge.

"You come alone?" Emily asked.

"Now, don't you start on me," Johnson said. "I've already had a lecture from Renno."

Emily took her father's hand and squeezed it. "I'm glad you came."

"Your mother wanted to be here, but she hasn't been feeling too well lately." He saw the look of quick concern on Emily's face. "Not anything serious, mind you, but we figured we'd save her visit till after the baby's born."

For the remainder of the morning and through the midday meal Emily eagerly asked questions about her mother, life in Knoxville, and people she had known.

The word of Roy Johnson's arrival had spread. Loramas and Ah-wen-ga came to pay their respects, followed by El-i-chi, Renno's fiery younger brother, and his mother, Toshabe. The lodge became quite crowded when Renno's sister, Ena, came in with her Cherokee husband, Rusog, and Rusog's father, Wegowa.

Wegowa, the senior war chief of the Cherokee, had been ill. The winter fevers had hit him hard. He had always been a man of controlled emotions, slow to be aroused, but a man to be valued in crisis. His tall slenderness had been accentuated by the illness so that he was gaunt. The folds of skin on his face made him look almost as old as Loramas, his father.

Johnson told all of them that Knoxville was growing, but that North Carolina, original owner of the territory west of the Smoky Mountains, was voicing opposition to the budding state of Franklin being admitted to the Union.

It was Loramas whose orders separated the gathering, leaving the women with Emily, the men going to Loramas's lodge. There they passed a pipe, drank heated herb tea brewed by Ah-wen-ga, and discussed the murderer Ben Whipple. The critical situation that Whipple had created by making it appear that Rusog had attacked Johnson, robbed him, and left him for dead had long since been smoothed over, but there were still hotheads in the white settlements who looked upon the Cherokee and their Seneca allies as enemies. Johnson assured them, however, that cooler heads would prevail. There was room, he said, for both peoples, and by working together they could make the western frontier safe for both Indian and white against marauding raids by warlike Indians from the west, south, and northwest.

The Seneca and the Cherokee knew that Roy Johnson spoke with authority, for he was the commander of the Franklin Frontier Regiment and had been appointed as a judge. His opinions were valued not only by John Sevier, governor of Franklin, but also by all who knew him, white or Indian.

When the informal gathering was over, Renno and his father-in-law returned to Renno's lodge. Only Ah-wen-ga was still with Emily, who was preparing the evening meal. During her time with the Seneca, she had become an accomplished cook, specializing in giving ordinary foods a more delicious taste by the addition of certain herbs that she had gathered and preserved.

It had been a good day, but as evening approached, Renno felt the return of his former restlessness. Waiting, he had learned, was a worrisome thing. Feeling the need to move, he paced, and Ah-wen-ga, helping Emily with the meal, had to step around him several times.

"Can you not find a place to sit down?" Ah-wen-ga asked fondly.

"He's been like that for days," Emily said with a loving smile. "I think it's harder on prospective fathers than on the mothers."

Ah-wen-ga turned to Roy Johnson. "In the name of the manitous," she pleaded, "take this warrior into the forest tomorrow."

"I wouldn't mind a hunting trip . . ." Johnson began.

Renno looked at Emily's swollen stomach.

Ah-wen-ga gave a gusty sigh. "My grandson," she told Renno, "go. Go into your forest. Let us women concern ourselves with birthing your son."

Renno said, "I will be here when my son is born."

"It will be days," Ah-wen-ga assured him. "You

will wear out your moccasins pacing. Go. Bring me a fat turkey hen."

Renno and his father-in-law left the village at first light, walking into a fog engendered by a flow of warm air from the south. The familiar forest took on a different aspect in the fog, the ghostly trees merging into a white nothingness. A silence, an almost ethereal quietness, caused both men to walk carefully, lest the sound of rustling leaves or breaking twigs disturb the peace. A mile from the village they walked within fifty feet of a buck with a regal set of antlers. The deer was standing serenely in a little glade and looked at them with big brown eyes. Johnson raised his musket. The buck, instead of hurrying away, merely turned and flipped a white tail. Johnson lowered his weapon, allowing the buck to disappear into the fog. Renno understood Johnson's reluctance to kill the deer: first, they had hardly left camp and their trip would have been cut far too short; second, the fog seemed to preclude killing of any kind, even for meat.

"Well," Johnson explained, shrugging, "I want to see some of the country."

"Then we will put some ground behind us," Renno said. He started at the easy, comfortable Seneca warrior's trot, and Johnson, slinging his musket over his shoulder, ran beside him. For an hour, then two, Renno set the pace. The fog had begun to lift, and as the morning warmed, Johnson had worked up a sweat, but still he ran beside his silent son-in-law. When the sun was at its zenith Renno halted beside a small, clear stream. Johnson dropped to his knees and drank thirstily. He estimated that by traveling steadily they had covered about twenty-five miles during the day.

"I kept up pretty good for an old man," he said when he had finished drinking.

Renno merely nodded, but now he did not run. He led the way through virgin forest, skirting areas of thick undergrowth, around trees that would not feel the bite of an ax blade for decades. He moved ever westward, angling slightly toward the south. Game signs were plentiful. In the early evening he used his bow to drop a yearling buck, then bled and dressed the carcass while Johnson gathered firewood. Roy Johnson carried salt, but Renno preferred his meat roasted naturally. Venison, with clear, cold water from a creek to wash it down, was, to Renno, a splendid repast.

Renno had chosen their campsite carefully, and Johnson accepted his son-in-law's caution as habitual. He threw up a brush shelter, using overlaid evergreen boughs to protect them from a cool wind that had risen out of the southwest; then he sat on a rock and lit a pipe, noticing that Renno was alert to every sound from the dark forest surrounding them.

The second day's march on a line roughly south of due west led them through some of the most beautiful country Johnson had ever seen, where virgin forest alternated with grassy meadows. They could have killed dozens of deer, but instead Renno complied with Johnson's stated desire to cover some country, so the main purpose was just to see what

was over the next hill, what was beyond the next
area of woodlands. In that wilderness there were no
boundaries. Johnson had a suspicion that he was the
first white man to penetrate that inland wilderness,
for white exploration had taken place along rivers,
mostly to the south and the north of the Cherokee
lands. There was little talk during the day. Johnson,
himself an experienced woodsman, was taking les-
sons, marveling at Renno's ability to move so silently, to become invisible among the growth at a
short distance. And he was pleased with his ability to
keep pace with Renno, for Renno was accustomed to
covering vast stretches of empty wilderness.

By the third day the Cherokee settlements were
far behind and Renno was traveling with more caution. Johnson felt that they were the only two men
within hundreds of miles, but his reason told him
otherwise; there were claims to all the land over
which they traveled, and after three days of hard
traveling, even he, who was not familiar with the
area, knew that they were nearing the western extent of the traditional Cherokee hunting grounds. To
the south the large and widespread tribe of the
Choctaw held dominion, and to the west, extending
onward to the big, muddy Mississippi, was Chickasaw
territory. Now he began to share Renno's caution,
for the Chickasaw especially had great renown as
warriors and were indeed considered to be among
the best fighting men in America.

With the morning of the fourth day, Renno turned
his face back toward the east. Although the days of
travel had done away with his feeling of restlessness,

Emily and the coming birth of his son had never been far from his mind. He had a strong desire to turn back now, to travel home with the same swiftness as he had traveled to the west and south.

"Mighty interesting country up there," Johnson said, pointing toward the west.

Renno had never been so far west; in him, as in Johnson, was an urge to see what was just over that far ridge on the horizon. This curiosity warred with his eagerness to return home. He decided to compromise.

"We will travel west until the sun is high," he said, leading off, but at midday there was another ridge and signs of plentiful game. Emily was now four days of travel behind them.

Johnson killed rabbits, wanting a change of diet. After the meal, he lit his pipe and leaned against a tree. "If there's any more beautiful country anywhere, I haven't seen it," he said.

"It is good country," Renno agreed.

"And there's more out there," Johnson said, waving his pipe toward the west.

"The land of the Chickasaw. Farther west, I have heard tell, are great plains, where Indians also live," Renno said.

"There are men who would kill for country like this," Johnson mused. "And the trouble is, they don't understand that there's plenty for everyone, Renno."

"When the white man comes, he breeds like the flies of summer," Renno said, a dark light coming into his blue eyes.

"But you and your ancestors have proven that we

can live and work together," Johnson said. "We're building a great nation here. Without getting into a discussion about whose ways are best, I think it's safe to say that we've got to keep open minds. We're all going to have to learn to live peacefully side by side."

"The Indian lives by the hunt," Renno reminded his father-in-law.

"Yes, and that's going to be a problem as time goes on," Johnson admitted. "You may have to change your ways. Look around you. We've been traveling for four days, and we haven't seen another man. That's a waste of good land. We've crossed enough good farmland to feed all thirteen states, but there's not so much as a potato or a row of corn planted."

"We've always had gardens, but they have been small," Renno said. "Planting corn for people we do not know is not our way."

"But your Seneca ancestors were willing to change with the times," Johnson countered. "Your ancestors went against an early treaty in order to fight against the British and for us colonists. You're a part of this country. As time goes on, your ties with us white settlers will become ever closer. We'll work together to make sure everyone has enough land and food."

"As you said, there is land for all," Renno stated. "You now have what you wanted. You have independence from England. You have settled lands that once were the hunting grounds of many tribes, and those tribes have either been exterminated or pushed to the west. You must learn to settle for what you have and stop the westward push."

"And let England and Spain take the entire midcontinent?"

Renno shrugged. "That is why we fought a war."

"The war is over," Johnson said, "but the struggle isn't. The war was fought on borrowed money. All the states have vast foreign and public debts. Some of them are unhappy with the terms of peace we made with England, and by no means have the British given up hope of keeping vast tracts of land here."

Johnson leaned forward and scratched a rough map of the eastern portion of the North American continent into the dirt beside the fire. "Look here. Here are the thirteen states. As you can see, we're right in the middle. In the north, in Canada, the British are waiting. They penetrate down into the midcontinent occasionally. The Spanish are down here, in the south, in Louisiana and Florida. The British and Spanish both are after one thing—the riches of this new continent. They're always bickering over fur-trading rights. Up north, off Vancouver Island, there's a dispute right now, with the Spanish claiming the areas around Nootka Sound. There could very well be another Spanish-English war, Renno, and if there is, we're going to be caught right smack dab in the middle of it."

Renno mused for a moment. "I have fought for the United States. I would fight again."

"I'm sure you would," Johnson responded. "But how about the others?"

"The Cherokee are friends of the white man. I cannot speak for them, however, nor can I speak for all my people. I believe they would follow me, but I would not force them to fight."

"So there you are," Johnson said, spreading his hands. "We're new at this business of being a nation, and we're caught between a rock and a hard place. The states have been bled dry from the War of Independence. We're dead broke. If it comes to war, we'll need friends like you."

Renno rose easily, walked to the nearby stream, and drank deeply. Around him the winter forest was silent, save for the rustle of a prowling small animal. He looked up at the stars and a field of glory, all in white, sparkling dots of light, and thought about the country and about his people. Roy Johnson's words caused him deep concern. His knowledge of the Americans, British, Spanish, and French told him that his best chance to preserve his people lay with the Americans. But, not unlike others, the Americans were land hungry, always ready to move west into Indian territory. It was, he decided, a problem too big for him to solve alone. But he would continue to do his best, using the wisdom passed down to him by his ancestors. Whether he had asked for it or not, he had indeed become a part of the new nation. Even though he lived outside its boundaries, his wife was an American. His son would have the blood of Roy Johnson in his veins, passed down through his daughter.

During the night, Renno thought he heard a sound not explained by normal activity of the night creatures of the forest, but as he lay in his blanket with all senses alert, he finally decided that he had dreamed the sound. He was awake with the sun and determined that they had gone far enough. He had no wish to encounter a hunting party of Chickasaw encroaching into the far western limits of Cherokee lands. He would have welcomed some action, but he had his father-in-law's safety in his hands.

"Now we will go back," he said, after carefully putting out the embers of the night's fire and concealing all signs of their presence in the tiny clearing.

"I guess it's time," Johnson agreed. "Wouldn't want to miss the big event."

They had not traveled two hundred yards when the silence of the virgin forest was broken by the sharp report of a musket. Renno froze. For a moment there was only silence, and then there came a sound that both thrilled and chilled him—the angry war cry of an adult bear. He motioned Johnson to be silent, then set off toward the sound at a trot, readying his musket, seeing to the placement of his other weapons. The sound of a musket shot in the forest could mean only one thing, the presence of an enemy, for the well-fed Cherokee would not have ventured so far to the west in the winter. Behind him, Johnson's foot cracked a twig, and Renno turned, again warning his father-in-law into silence.

The bear sounds had ceased as abruptly as they had begun. Renno moved like a wraith, using trees for cover, his feet not disturbing the detritus of the forest floor. Johnson, while not moving quite so silently, was doing well. Now there came into Renno's nostrils the scent of burned gunpowder and the rank, woodsy odor of a bear. He slowed, creeping forward, straining all his senses. The trees began to thin into a small glade. Renno moved into position, motioning Johnson to remain where he was.

In the center of the glade lay a man. The first impression was that of much blood, for the body was severely mauled, to the point of mutilation. Then Renno saw that the man was white, but dressed unlike any white man he had ever seen. For a long, long time Renno remained completely motionless, listening, sniffing the air, watching for the smallest movement of a leaf. It would be more than odd for a white man to be traveling alone in the vast forest.

He could hear Johnson's quiet breathing as his father-in-law exhibited Indian-like patience, remaining motionless. When Renno was certain that there was no other presence near the glade, he turned his head, gestured, and then waited until Johnson had come alongside before stepping out of the cover of the trees into the glade.

"Pretty damn odd," Johnson whispered as they walked toward the body.

When an arrow whistled past Renno's ear and the hiss of its passage was shattered by the discharge of a musket, Renno knew exactly how odd it was to think that the white man could have been alone. For one split second he castigated himself for his carelessness. He should have circled the glade to make certain there were no other men nearby. Instead, he and Johnson were caught in the open.

The musket ball had taken a bite out of the crown of Johnson's hat. Another arrow narrowly missed Renno as he gave a great war cry, as much a whoop of anger at himself as at whoever was trying to kill him. He and Johnson leaped forward, knowing that they had walked into a trap, but unwilling to turn their backs. Another musket ball sang angrily by Renno's ear, and an arrow slashed through Roy Johnson's buckskin, leaving an angry red wound on his upper arm. Then they were across the small glade, Renno leaping over the body of the dead white man and charging into the trees.

The sheer audacity of his attack, coupled with the ferocity of his anger, confused the four Indians who had waited patiently in ambush. Then, with war cries, they sprang to meet the assault.

Renno's strong right arm slashed horizontally, and the cutting edge of his tomahawk met flesh, almost severing the spinal column of the first of the enemy to come within his reach. Blood spurted from a severed jugular vein, and Renno, moving on even as the first man fell, felt a tug at his sleeve. He would see later that the musket ball had taken a bite of flesh from his arm. Johnson, yelling almost as fiercely as Renno, dispatched an Indian with his sword, but as he tried to pull the blade from the chest of his fallen enemy, the fourth Indian, the one who had shot Renno, now came at him, tomahawk raised, forcing Johnson to leave his sword impaled and meet the attack with nothing more than his knife.

The Indian facing Renno had an arrow nocked, the bow almost drawn, when Renno threw his tomahawk and watched it flash through the air and embed its sharp blade in the forehead of the enemy, crushing bone and taking life instantly.

Johnson managed to grab the wrist of his foe to forestall a fate like that of Renno's victim, but the Indian was a strong and skilled warrior. With a mighty jerk of his arm the Indian freed his tomahawk hand and danced back, and then it was an unequal battle, as the tomahawk came dangerously near, and Johnson was unable to get close enough to use his knife. But the match ended quickly, with one of Renno's arrows whistling through the air to stab deeply, with a sound like the dropping of a stone on hard earth.

"Stay. Watch," Renno ordered, even as the fourth Indian fell. He was unable to excuse himself for his carelessness. He had been too long at peace. He had been distracted, thinking of Emily and his son. But now he was in his element. He had battled against the odds and emerged alive and victorious. He scouted at a swift trot, circling the glade, moving silently among the trees. Once he crossed bear sign marked with blood. The animal he had heard had been wounded. As he circled to the south, he found the trail of five men, one of them a white man, his tracks showing the marks of heavy boots. When he was satisfied that there were no other enemies near, he rejoined his father-in-law, who was squatting beside one of the dead Indians.

"Take a look, Renno," he said. "This gets odder and odder."

It took Renno only a few moments to agree. Two of the dead were Choctaw, the other two Chickasaw. Although legend said they had once been members of the same tribe, the Choctaw and Chickasaw were traditional enemies. Their provisions were of the type carried on a long journey.

"Are you thinking what I'm thinking?" Johnson asked. "Why are Choctaw and Chickasaw traveling together?"

"Renegades, perhaps," Renno suggested, without convincing himself.

"That white man is an odd one, too," Johnson commented.

Renno walked into the glade. The dead man wore high leather boots with wide, flapping tops; tight black breeches; a frilly shirt under a serviceable warm woolen coat; and a rapier with a basket hilt.

"French?" Renno ventured.

"I don't think so," Johnson said. "I'd swear he's a Spaniard because of his sword. But why would a Spaniard be so far north, and traveling with a Choctaw-Chickasaw escort?"

The white man had not been killed by the Indians—his injuries were massive, the type that could have been inflicted only by the power in an adult bear's claws and teeth. Renno bent, sniffed the muzzle of the dead man's musket.

"Let's see what this fellow was carrying," Johnson said, but before he could bend over, his attention was seized, in a rather spectacular way, by the appearance on the far side of the glade of a huge black bear. The bear reared onto its hind legs, standing—it seemed to Johnson—treetop tall, and it loosed a challenging roar. Johnson lifted his musket hurriedly, but Renno put a staying hand on the barrel.

Johnson gave Renno an incredulous look. "That

bear's been shot," he said. "He's mad, and I don't think he cares who he's mad at."

"Hold," Renno said, taking a few steps toward the bear, lifting his hands to let his weapons fall to the ground, and extending his palms toward the growling animal.

"Nayah-wey Shapnoh!" Renno said. *"Gayah-da-sey."*

At the traditional Seneca greeting, the bear's low growls ceased. Johnson rubbed his eyes. It was no time, he felt, to carry on a friendly conversation with a wounded bear.

"We are brothers, you and I," Renno continued, stepping even closer. He clasped his hand over the talisman of the Bear Clan that he wore, always, around his neck. The talisman was extended toward the bear as Renno talked soothingly in his native language. The bear gave one roar, dropped to its feet, and swayed heavily toward Renno.

Johnson, watching in awe, saw a mature male black bear sit on its haunches. The ball from the dead man's musket had grazed the bear's shoulder, parting the fur. The bleeding had almost stopped. Renno gently examined the wound, went into the woods, gathered moss and herbs, and came back to pack the bear's injured shoulder. The bear, seeming to sense when Renno was finished, raised himself to his full height. Renno extended one hand upward in salute, his eyes locked into the small, closely set eyes of the animal.

Astounded and confused by what he had witnessed, Johnson wondered what kind of man this was to whom he had given his only child in marriage. He was aware that the Seneca Bear Clan felt a close kinship with the bear, but what he had just seen defied reason. He had always been aware that Renno was one of the bravest men he had ever known, and one of the most deadly warriors, but he had not until that moment realized what an extraordinary man Renno actually was.

Renno, acting as if nothing out of the ordinary had happened, turned his attention to the wounds he and his father-in-law had taken in the battle. Using the same methods as with the bear, he treated and bound both his own arm and Johnson's. Then Renno searched the dead white man and found a small leather pouch inside his pocket. This Renno handed to Johnson. Inside was an official-looking document written in a flourishing hand on thick parchment.

"I think this is written in Spanish," Johnson said. "I can't read a word of it."

Renno's attention was elsewhere. He had never seen hair as thick and as dark as that of the dead man. He drew his knife and quickly scalped the man and, in the process, noticed lying underneath the body a beautifully wrought leather scabbard. Upon close examination he saw delicate designs in gold beaten into the leather, and the scabbard held a long, thin stiletto, which was one of the most beautiful things Renno had ever seen. He knew weapons, but he had never seen a knife that looked so deadly and yet so beautiful at the same time. The handle of the stiletto was ivory, inlaid in gold. The blade was of the finest steel he had ever seen. It was a weapon to be prized. Remembering how his father-in-law had charged into unknown odds at his side, Renno extended the beautiful stiletto toward him.

"Keep it," Johnson said. "I think it will be of more use in your hands. I'll take the sword." He looked distastefully over at his own sword, which was still embedded in one of the dead Indians' chests.

Renno handed the sword to Johnson, then moved to where the brief battle had been fought and swiftly scalped his three fallen enemies. Johnson was, of course, familiar with the practice of scalping a fallen enemy but had never done so himself. However, he had always felt a great friendship for Renno. And after what Johnson had just witnessed—the swift charge, the heated but brief and deadly battle, the incredible scene involving the bear—Roy Johnson wanted Renno's approval more than ever. He therefore drew his knife and, with some concealed disgust, scalped the Indian he had killed.

"We will go now," Renno said.

Johnson was more than ready to be off. The skies were a dark, ominous gray, and he and Renno were days away from the Seneca village. Roy Johnson did not want to be the cause of Renno's absence when the baby was born. Also, he was eager to get back to Knoxville to find someone who could read Spanish. He had a feeling that the document carried by the dead man was going to be very important to those people—white and Indian—who lived on the frontier to the west of the great Smoky Mountains.

Chapter II

The signs had been right. Renno and Roy Johnson traveled through a snowstorm more typical of the traditional northern home of the Seneca in New York State than of the southern latitudes of the Cherokee, where so many of the Seneca had recently come to live. The snow had stopped by the time they reached the village to learn that Emily's preliminary labor had begun. They arrived with fresh meat slung over their shoulders, and both rushed to Renno's lodge upon hearing the news that birth was imminent.

Turned away by Ah-wen-ga, Roy Johnson began to pace in the fresh snow.

Renno felt a desire to be alone. He walked away from the village and to a high place where he stood with his eyes upcast silently, and the sky seemed to smile at him. In spite of the severe cold that had moved in behind the snowstorm, the sun was warm on his face, and he knew within himself that all would be right, that his child would be a son. He fervently prayed to the manitous and the spirits of his illustrious ancestors that they grant the child strength in both body and spirit.

From his vantage point he could see the village, his lodge, and Colonel Johnson as he paced, paused to speak to someone, and paced again. A half smile came to Renno's lips. True, he himself had been acting quite un-Seneca-like, perhaps even showing his concern, but his father-in-law was openly displaying his nervousness.

Renno found a leaning tree, blown over by some past wind, brushed away the snow, and sat. He absently fingered the hilt of the beautifully decorated stiletto, which had fascinated him ever since it had come into his possession. On the trip home, Renno had constantly toyed with it, admiring the delicate work of the handle, the sharpness of the blade. He had found the odd, apparently fragile weapon to be perfectly balanced. At first he had been fearful of using it as a throwing weapon lest it break, but Roy Johnson had pointed out a small imprint on the base of the blade, letters etched into the steel by a craftsman.

"That I can read," Johnson had said. "The word is 'Toledo,' and although I've not had the pleasure of owning a blade of such quality, Toledo steel is reputed to be the world's best."

Now Renno rose from the log and with a swift movement pivoted quickly and drew back his arm, throwing the stiletto. It rotated just once in the air before thudding into a tree trunk to bury its sharp point deeply. It was the best-balanced throwing knife Renno had ever held.

The day seemed endless. When Renno retrieved his knife and walked back to his lodge, his father-in-law was seated outside, smoking his pipe frantically, sending up a veritable cloud of smoke. There was only silence from within the lodge.

"Ah-wen-ga says soon," Johnson reported before getting up to pace.

Toshabe came out of the lodge, her face grim. Renno's impassive face hid his quick concern. Toshabe looked at him and said, with a movement of her shoulders, "It is her first, and it is difficult."

Just once Renno heard, from inside, the voice of his grandmother. "Now," Ah-wen-ga said gently, encouraging Emily, "push hard now."

He heard one muffled grunt from his wife, and in spite of his concern, he knew great pride. She had become a good Seneca wife; her silence during the painful ordeal of birth was expected by the attending women, for a Seneca woman is able to endure pain.

Roy Johnson gave a war whoop when the cold, still air was rent by the protesting cry of a newborn child. Renno went stiff for a moment, and then his father-in-

law was pounding him on the back, offering congratu-
lations.

Toshabe's head appeared momentarily in the doorway, just long enough for her to say, "You have a
son."

When the door opened once again, Johnson and
Renno tried to enter at the same time and bumped
shoulders. Johnson pulled back so that Renno could
enter first, then followed him into the dwelling.

Emily was pale but smiling. The look she saw in
Renno's eyes told her of his feelings, and she felt
happier than she had ever felt in her life. She had
kept her promise to give her husband a son, and the
joy and pride she saw in his usually impassive expression was her reward.

Ah-wen-ga held out a small, wriggling bundle
wrapped in a settler's blanket. "The manitous have
been kind, my grandson," she said.

Renno extended his hands, withdrew them, wiped
his palms on his buckskin trousers, then reached out
tentatively.

"The child will not break easily," Ah-wen-ga said
with a smile, and then Renno's son was in his hands
and he was looking down into a red face that quickly
screwed up into a look of discomfort as the baby
cried.

"Hey, give a fellow a chance," Roy Johnson said,
trying to take the baby from Renno's hands. "That's
my grandson."

Reluctantly Renno gave the boy to Johnson and
stood, head cocked, looking at the little face, the tiny
fingers, listening to the surprisingly loud wails.

"Got a set of lungs on him, hasn't he?" Johnson asked, handing the baby back to Ah-wen-ga.

"He will be a great warrior," Renno said, "as were his grandfathers before him."

"Now leave us," Ah-wen-ga said, "for we have work to do, and Emily needs her rest."

Outside, people were gathering to pay their respects to the infant who would one day wear the mantle of authority of the Seneca, the mantle of his illustrious fathers. Casno, the aging war chief who was the chief medicine man of the Seneca—and who had acted as regent since the murder of Renno's father, Ghonkaba—was on hand, waiting to be admitted to the lodge to give his blessings and work his good magic on the baby. El-i-chi, Ena, Rusog, and all the others were there, grinning broadly, and for a while Renno forgot the vague feeling of restlessness that had been plaguing him for so long. But when Roy Johnson reminded him of the document they had taken from the body of the dead man thought to be a Spaniard, Renno once again knew that feeling of disquiet, as if something were wrong.

"I hate to leave just now," Johnson said, frowning, "but I know you're as eager as I am to know what's written on that paper."

Renno agreed that getting the document translated was very important. He put his hand on his brother's shoulder and told El-i-chi to choose two warriors and escort Johnson back to Knoxville. El-i-chi, in the fire of youth, had been complaining bitterly that the extended period of peace was depriving him of the right of all young warriors, the right to build honor through war.

"I have no war to offer," Renno said with concealed amusement, "but a run through the snow will strengthen your muscles, my brother."

El-i-chi was more than willing. He quickly selected two strong young warriors to round out the escort party.

"I can make better time alone," Roy Johnson protested.

"Ride as fast as you like, Colonel," El-i-chi said. "We will be ahead of you or at your side."

Colonel Johnson grunted, realizing the futility of further protest. After all, he and Renno had seen and fought a mixed band of Choctaw and Chickasaw in Cherokee territory. Traveling alone would be foolhardy. He gathered his few belongings, and with El-i-chi already on the trail, he left the Seneca village at midafternoon, the two warriors running easily on either side of his horse.

Although the winter had been long in coming, the creatures of the forest needed their heavy furs to protect them against its cold, and the young ones of the village were kept busy gathering firewood. As the days passed, Renno's son, as yet unnamed, grew strong. It was a time of waiting. Snow and freezing rain weighted the limbs of the trees. In the still of the night a sudden crack, almost like a musket shot, told of the surrender of some limb to the weight.

El-i-chi and his warriors returned from Knoxville with tales of hardship among the white settlers there.

There had been no one in Knoxville who could read Spanish, but Johnson had sent word that he would pursue the matter diligently and send word to Renno the moment he knew the content of the document taken from the dead man in the forest.

Casno, nominal leader of the Seneca until Renno was of an age to assume leadership, noted when the sun reached its southernmost position in the midday sky. He had decreed that the first new moon after the sun had begun its slow return toward the north would be the proper time for Renno's son to become a Seneca.

When the day was at hand, Casno, with much ceremony, hovered by the baby boy, then engaged in traditional chants and dances as the father, dressed in his finest ceremonial togs, carried the infant, well bundled against the cold, to the frozen stream at the foot of the slope below the village. Emily, dressed properly as a Seneca woman, was not quite sure what the ceremony entailed and was concerned at having the baby exposed to the cold, but, she told herself, she had known before she married Renno that any child of hers would be reared as a Seneca, and she thought she was prepared for any eventuality.

Casno used a tomahawk to break the ice on the stream, took the baby in his hands, lifted his lined face, and chanted for blessings from the Seneca manitous. Renno then accepted the baby from Casno and removed the soft swaddling blanket.

Emily gasped and started to move forward as Renno denuded the baby. Toshabe, standing beside Emily, took her daughter-in-law's arm and held her.

The baby seemed to be unaffected by the cold. Naked, with fat legs and arms, he squirmed in his father's hands as Renno added his own prayers for his son's future before dunking the baby into the icy water exposed by the break in the frozen stream.

Emily shouted, "No!" but it was too late. The others ignored her protest.

It was over in an instant. The baby was submerged in a quick, decisive movement, lifted and bundled immediately into the blanket, and clutched to Renno's breast in pride, for the child had not cried when exposed to the numbing water.

"He is a little hawk," proclaimed Casno. "A true Seneca."

"Is it over now?" Emily asked Toshabe, who nodded. "Good," Emily said, running forward to take the baby from Renno's arms. She ran back to the lodge, rubbed her son's chilled limbs, wrapped him carefully, and placed his cradle near the fire. The boy showed no ill effects, but she feared the winter fevers, and for days she watched the child carefully, praying that he would not sicken. For the first time since she had come to the Seneca camp to be tutored in the ways of the Indians by Ah-wen-ga and Toshabe, she had doubts. What else, she wondered, would be required of her son as he grew to take his place in the Seneca way of life?

As the second moon after the winter solstice approached, a change could be sensed among the Seneca in the village. The winter had been severe, as predicted by all the signs, and seemingly endless.

Warriors longed for the greening newness of spring. Women talked of the coming pleasures of the new season and of good green things to eat. As medicine man, Casno was preparing for one of the Seneca's most important traditional ceremonies, the new-year festival. Members of the False Face Society, headed by Casno, polished and renewed carved wooden masks, among the ancient trappings brought by the Seneca from their home in the north. Or the members carved new ones and covered the false faces with human hair. The preparations went on for days, giving everyone in the village something to break the monotony of winter living.

With the new moon, the season of rejoicing began. To symbolize the newness, old fires were scattered and new ones made. In his own lodge, Renno had scattered the old fire, making certain that each ember was dead and all old embers and ash removed before he struck the new fire and coaxed it with the appropriate prayers.

Now was a time of fasting, of cleansing the body and soul, of prayer to the manitous—for although new life had always come after the winters, the evil enemy of the Master of Life was always present, as was the possibility that evil could prevail, that the cold would continue, that new life would never come.

During the winter, the evil spirits, the allies of the enemy, had appeared to several Seneca and brought sickness or death. Now it would be up to Casno and the members of the False Face Society to frighten away the evil spirits by wearing carved likenesses even more horrible than the evil spirits themselves.

The celebration began with the time-honored eagle dance of the Seneca, led by Renno. He had been carefully coached and trained by Casno, and he made a striking figure as he led the warriors in the dance inside the large warriors' lodge.

The highlight of the period was the False Face ceremony, during which Casno and his helpers thoroughly frightened the children as they danced and howled from behind the frightening masks. Casno's mask was outstandingly ugly, the mouth distorted and grimacing, a black face with snow-white hair; one exposed eye, bloody and without lids, dominated the mask, with the other eye glaring balefully.

Renno glanced at Emily to see how she was reacting to the ancient rites and suspected that she was suppressing a smile. Little Hawk—the formal naming of the infant had been postponed indefinitely, the temporary name being used as a matter of convenience—slept through the entire noisy affair.

It was at the height of the False Face ceremony that Renno received a private sign from the manitous. Casno's assistant, a huge man, his mask a cross-eyed, big-lipped horror, raised himself to his full height, extended his arms upward, and gave a roar, which, to Renno's ear, became the fighting challenge of an angry bear. As the white Indian shook his head in an effort to clear his suddenly misty vision, the shaman became that honorable totem of the Bear Clan and was, in Renno's eyes, for one brief moment, a living bear. The bear gazed at Renno for that instant, with a meaning in his eyes that escaped the Indian.

Casno, panting from the dance, announced that all the signs were favorable; once again, good was overcoming the forces of evil, and soon the healthy green things of spring and summer would sprout with renewed life.

Not long after the conclusion of the festival, on a beautifully clear and crisp winter night, with the heavens a field of glowing white and the new moon a weak but encouraging presence, Renno entered the forest and, listening to the night sounds, walked to a ridge where he built a fire in the shelter of a ledge of exposed rock. He had been troubled by his inability to read the private sign given to him during the False Face ceremony and hoped now to communicate with the manitous and learn what it was that the bear wanted him to know. In preparation for this night, he had fasted for two days. Now, in the light of the fire he quickly cut branches to build a shelter against the rocks, and then, with the moon down and the hush of predawn upon the world, Renno wrapped himself in his robe and sat motionless, beginning his vigil.

He had seen a sign, and he prayed to the manitous to reveal the meaning of it. He prayed for *orenda*, the sacred message of wisdom. In his mind were questions regarding the events that had happened during his hunting trip with his father-in-law. Somehow he saw a threat to his people and his allies from the presence of Choctaw and Chickasaw warriors and an unknown white man in Cherokee territory, and hoped the manitous would favor him with information about that.

He sat through the dawn and into the morning, his limbs being numbed by the cold creeping up from the frozen ground, moving only to replenish the fuel of the fire. He sought that state of being where dreams come to the worthy, but the day passed, and he sat stoically through another starred night, to see another dawn. Now he had been over seventy-two hours without food or water or sleep. Still there was no answer.

In the late afternoon, with the weak sun far to the west, he felt very tired and fought against sleep, although he felt his chin drop to his chest a couple of times. He made himself stare into the arch of the blue sky, and his heart lifted as he saw, far off, a speck, a dark dot soaring toward him. While Renno lingered in that foggy consciousness of near-sleep, the dark speck in the sky came near enough to be identified as a hawk, and it flew straight and true toward him. Then, directly overhead, and low enough so that Renno could see the swiveling of the head as its sharp eyes examined and saw everything below it, the hawk began a tight circle. It was indeed a favorable omen, but Renno's questions were not answered.

For a long, long time the hawk circled, and once Renno heard its sharp, distinctive cry. It was then that he noticed that the stiletto was in his hand, his fingers closed around the hilt. It felt good and natural in his grip, and once again he admired the balance of the weapon. He tossed it into the air, watched it make one slow, complete revolution, and, with quick reflex, plucked it from its downward fall, his hand closing unerringly around the handle. Once again he tossed the stiletto, almost as if something outside him were directing his seemingly idle play with the weapon, and he himself were watching.

On the third toss he flung the knife high, and his heart soared as the circling hawk folded its wings and dived like a plummeting stone to snatch the stiletto at the apex of its upward flight, seizing the weapon in its talons, beating powerful wings, and gaining altitude until, the stiletto held tightly, it was a considerable height directly above Renno. The white Indian seemed to float to a standing position and raised his arms in salute. He did not understand the meaning of the sign and was not even sure if this was a dream or reality. Since the stiletto was not a typical Indian weapon, was he being told by the manitous that he was not to have it?

He saw the weapon fall from the hawk's talons. Perfectly balanced as it was, it fell swiftly, turning slowly. His face was upturned, his arms raised, and he threw his chest out, for it seemed that the stiletto was aimed directly for his heart. He did not move. The manitous had sent him a powerful sign, and he would accept it, even if it meant his death. But the blade flashed past his upturned eyes, a handbreadth from his chest, and with a solid *thunk* of sound, buried itself to the hilt in the frozen ground. The hawk gave one harsh cry and arrowed off to disappear beyond the ridge.

Suddenly more alert, Renno found himself seated again. He pondered the meaning of the signs and whether they were a meaningless dream born out of his fatigue, or an all-important message from the manitous. Wrapping his robe around him, he studied the gold-inlaid hilt of the stiletto, stared at it until the sun sank below the horizon and quick winter darkness came over him.

At midnight it was cold, but the white Indian seemed to be immune to it. The fire held his eyes hypnotically. He seemed to see movement there, and his eyes widened as he prayed for a vision, a message to explain the events of the day. A great peace came to him, and as the fire burned low, leaving only glowing embers, he saw something deep within the fiery red glow that grew and towered over him, blotting out the dying light of the fire. The great bear stood in silence, its small staring eyes impaling Renno's calm blue ones.

He immediately recognized the voice that spoke to him. It was the voice of his father, Ghonkaba. "The danger comes from the west, but first by the Father of Waters."

"My father," Renno whispered, making a motion of respect. "What is this danger?"

But the great bear was slowly dissolving, becoming nothing more than a wisp of smoke from the dying fire. He was alone.

He sat there until another dawn broke, this time with a red glow. To the west a great cloud bank spoke of a coming weather change. There had been no further vision, no explanation of the danger that was to come from the west.

Now he felt the cold, felt the dizzy weakness of his fasting. He had had his message, and it was time to go, to do something, but he knew not what. He put his hand on the hilt of the stiletto, the blade still buried in hard earth, frozen there so that he could not pull it directly upward. He tried to loosen the earth's hold by moving the handle back and forth, and felt something give. Thinking that he had broken the fine weapon, Renno looked at the hilt, ivory and inlaid gold, that had come loose in his hand. He was saddened for a moment, but then he saw a small folded piece of parchment tucked into a carved cavity cunningly placed alongside the shaft for the shank of the blade. He plucked the paper out, unfolded it, and saw what looked to be the same written language that he had seen on the document taken from the dead man in the forest.

He knew that his brother the hawk had made it possible for him to find the secret message hidden in the hilt of the stiletto, knew that it had something to do with the danger from the west about which he had been warned by the spirit of his father.

His mind, cleansed by the fasting, was sharp, moving at lightning speed as he trotted back to the village and ate and drank prudently, lest he be sickened by a feast of plenty following his fast.

"I must go to Knoxville tomorrow," he told Emily.

"Oh, wonderful!" she said. "I do so want my mother to see Little Hawk."

"I must travel fast, and alone," he said, to her disappointment.

At dawn the next day he left the village, carrying his weapons and enough dried meat to prevent any loss of time in hunting for food. He ran in a cold, drizzling morning rain, rested briefly, then ran on into the night. It was a good feeling to be alone in the forest, to run until his legs were fire and his lungs ached with the intake of cold air. He was in his element—a man, a Seneca, covering distance as only a Seneca warrior can, competing against his human limitations.

His arrival in the white settlement was timely, for Roy Johnson had been making preparations to journey to the Seneca village the very next day. The winter fevers had struck hard at the settlement, and there were fresh graves in the growing cemetery. Johnson's wife, Nora, from whom Emily had inherited her blond hair, had been confined with the winter sickness but had survived, although she looked thin, with dark shadows under her eyes. However, she felt well enough to insist that Renno tell her all there was to tell about Emily and the baby. Then she led him to the table, for he had arrived just before suppertime.

"You men can leave your business until after we eat," she said, and Renno, not yet recovered fully from his fast and famished after his bracing run, was more than willing to let his mother-in-law's order stand.

After the meal, Roy Johnson led Renno into his study, where there were rude chairs and a fireplace giving off comfortable heat—an all-purpose room for reading, sitting, and living. During the meal, Johnson had managed to get in a word that he had found a traveling tinker who could read Spanish, for the language on the document was indeed that of the conquistadors. He pulled the parchment out of a drawer in a small desk and said, "It's bad business, Renno."

Renno, who had taken a place on the braided rug on the floor before the fire, long legs crossed under him, waited patiently as Johnson lit his pipe before speaking further.

"It's a copy of a treaty," Johnson said. "It was intended for Oklawahpa."

Renno's eyes went cold. There was no need for Johnson to explain who Oklawahpa was. Renno had never seen Oklawahpa, but he knew him by reputation as a fierce war leader of the Chickasaw. Oklawahpa led that portion of the Chickasaw nation concentrated around Chickasaw Bluffs, the great center on the big river to the west of Cherokee lands. He was thinking of the words of his father: "The danger comes from the west, but first by the Father of Waters."

"It's signed by the Spanish governor, Baron de Carondelet. And it's also signed by the great chiefs of the Choctaw, Chickasaw, and Creek nations."

Johnson paused to let the import of that statement sink in. Renno nodded grimly. Of the three tribes, the Choctaw, spread widely to the south of them, was the largest. But he was surprised most of all to learn that those old enemies, the Choctaw and the Chickasaw, had jointly entered into an agreement.

"The three tribes acknowledge themselves to be under the protection of Spain," Johnson continued. "They agree to exclude traders who do not have Spanish licenses."

That did not disturb Renno too much. "Is it, then, just a treaty for trade?"

"On the surface," his father-in-law said. "But you have to look at it this way: with this treaty, the Spanish have united three of the most powerful tribes in the south and southeast. We know that the Spanish have ambitions to extend their holdings. They're greedy, just like all the Europeans, and are not satisfied with holding just Louisiana and Florida. They're contesting the English for territory in the north. Wouldn't it make much more sense, instead of having to transport men and equipment all the way up north, to make a move here in the south, where they already have secure bases?"

"There is no mention of war or of expansion in the treaty?" Renno asked.

"No. As I said, it reads just like a typical trade treaty, and if that's all they want, just fur-trading rights in the lands of the three tribes, it won't have much effect on us. But what worries me is that this copy of the treaty was being sent out west for Oklawahpa's signature. They're warlike, Oklawahpa's Chickasaw. It might take time to organize a large army of Choctaw and Creek, but Oklawahpa's Chickasaw are always ready. And they're among the finest fighting men in America."

Renno started to bristle a bit, for he knew that his Seneca veterans and Wegowa's Cherokee would be a match for any enemy, but he was silent.

"I guess," Johnson said, "that the only thing we can do is wait and see what happens."

"Perhaps not," Renno said, taking the piece of

parchment from a pocket and handing it to Johnson.
"This was hidden in the hilt of the stiletto carried by
the Spanish messenger. When your tinker reads it,
perhaps we will know more."

Johnson muttered a curse. "The beggar left Knoxville two days ago. We'd have a devil of a time
finding him."

Renno was silent for a moment. "No war party will
move until after the floods of spring." He nodded to
himself. "Perhaps I will go myself to the big river
and look around."

"That would be very dangerous," Johnson warned.
"The Chickasaw are very protective of their territory."

Renno nodded. He was also protective, but of his
own lands, and of those of the Cherokee. He did not
intend to remain idle while waiting to see what would
happen, for the warning of his father still rang in his
ears: "The danger comes from the west, but first by
the Father of Waters."

Renno's return to his home was delayed by the
arrival of visitors to the small frontier settlement.
Visitors from east of the mountains were rare, a
cause for curiosity among all the settlers, and when it
was learned that these visitors were both official and
very important, Knoxville buzzed with excitement.

The two men, who had arrived on horseback, accompanied by a small force of trained soldiers, had
come to Knoxville to see Governor John Sevier. One,
Joseph Martin, a pudgy but powerfully built man
who looked almost like a clothed barrel, was a repre-
sentative of the governor of Georgia, and Georgia's

official agent to the Chickasaw and Cherokee nations. He was accompanied by Colonel Arthur Campbell, a distinguished, graying, spare man dressed in expensive and fine clothing, which almost instantly labeled him, to those who had knowledge, as being from Virginia. Since Roy Johnson was the commander of the would-be state of Franklin's military forces, the two agents to the Indians sought him out and requested a private conference. Johnson said that he would like to include a friend and ally, a warrior of the Seneca in the south. At first Arthur Campbell frowned, but then, hearing that the Seneca was the great Renno, Campbell spread his hands, smiled, and said, "Any friend of George Washington's is welcome at any parley I might hold."

Martin and Campbell already knew about the treaty among the three tribes and the Spanish. In fact, Martin was able to provide Johnson with some details: the treaty had been signed, with much feasting and gift-giving and ceremony, in Pensacola in the summer of 1784. He agreed that, in wording, the treaty dealt only with trading rights.

"But you, too, read intent between the lines?" asked Johnson.

"Colonel," Martin said, "the Spanish have the greatest highway on this continent in front of them, the Mississippi River. I'm just surprised that they haven't already used it. The whole midcontinent is open to them. We haven't got a thing to stop them from moving up the river. If the Indians allow them to establish forts on their lands, within a couple of years they can have a secure presence in an area larger than our thirteen states."

"Governor Henry of Virginia also sees the possibility of Spanish penetration up the Mississippi," said Colonel Campbell. "I'm going to suggest to Governor Sevier today that Franklin establish a fort at Muscle Shoals, on the Tennessee River, as a defensive post against the Choctaw. How we'll guard the river, I don't know."

Both Renno and Roy Johnson mused a bit about Campbell's suggestion. The shoals on the river were to the south, and a fort there would encroach on Choctaw lands, a sure provocation for war. But neither spoke.

"I believe that the presence here of two gentlemen of your stature speaks of the seriousness of the situation," Johnson said. "We'd welcome your help, gentlemen. I ask you to take word to your governors that the forces of Franklin would welcome an alliance with concerned men from Georgia and Virginia to meet this threat, if threat it is."

Campbell cleared his throat and looked at Martin of Georgia for a moment before speaking. "Colonel, Patrick Henry's goodwill is with you. He asked me to tell Governor Sevier that he's all for admitting Franklin to the union, but only if Franklin can defend its own borders."

"Are you saying, then, that we can expect no help from Virginia in the event of a war with the Spanish and the Indians?" Renno asked. He had once met the fiery little American patriot who was now governor of Virginia and had found him to be a man worthy of respect.

"My friend," Campbell said, "Virginia is deeply in debt from the war. She has obligations to the more northern states, which still face the military might of the British in Canada." He shook his head sadly. "At this time, gentlemen, Virginia can only promise moral support and our prayers."

"And Georgia?" Johnson asked Martin.

"Georgia is in the same position as Virginia. We borrowed to the hilt to finance the war. I don't think we could get the legislature to finance a war on the far western frontier."

Johnson sighed. "Well, gentlemen, we do appreciate your moral support and your prayers. We'll need them if we're right in thinking that the Spanish and their Indian allies are on the move. God knows we can't expect any help from North Carolina; they'd be happy to see us get into trouble. It would give them an excuse to say that the state of Franklin is a joke, and all this land is a part of North Carolina, after all."

"Well," Johnson said when he and Renno were alone, "if the fat's in the fire, we won't have any help in pulling it out."

"The Seneca will fight, and I'm certain that the Cherokee will fight. It is our land that must be protected," Renno said.

"We'll have to hang together, Son," Johnson said, using the word for the first time and feeling just a little bit uncomfortable about it, but Renno seemed to accept it.

"I will see the big river," Renno said, rising, eager to be off, already planning his strategy. He would use a small force of his most accomplished warriors, moving swiftly and silently, penetrating Chickasaw lands and seeing for himself whether any preparations for war were being made. This would have to be done without detection, avoiding armed conflict.

"I've always had a hankering to see it myself," Johnson said. "Give me an hour or two to get ready."

"You must stay," Renno said quickly. "Perhaps the translation of the stiletto paper will tell us more."

"That can wait," Johnson said. "It looks as if we're going to have to fight alone, your people and mine. As a citizen of Franklin, I will not allow you to be the only one to take the initial risk."

"We will be a small force, and we will move fast," Renno said.

Johnson chuckled, knowing what Renno was thinking. "I kept up with you once," he reminded his son-in-law.

Renno gave him a thin smile. He had come to know Roy Johnson as a brave man, a man of surprising stamina and strength. "So be it," he said.

The trip back to the village was made swiftly and, in deference to Johnson, on horseback. The arrival of the two cantering horsemen brought out the village en masse, and Renno gave a Seneca greeting to his brother, El-i-chi, swiftly telling him to convene a conference of the Seneca and Cherokee leaders. The gathering of warriors met in the warriors' lodge, and all faces were serious as Renno stood in the midst of them and in a quiet, serious voice explained the grave situation.

The ailing Wegowa, senior war chief, was granted the right to speak first. When he had finished, his son, Rusog, asked for the floor.

The outstanding Cherokee war leader and heir to leadership of his tribe through his father and grandfather, Rusog had once been accused unjustly of terrible crimes by white settlers. That event almost precipitated a war between the settlers and the Seneca and Cherokee, and it had left Rusog with a legacy of anger. "Are we to be in the forefront, fighting the white man's battles to keep other white men at a secure distance from the white settlements?" he demanded angrily.

A chorus of agreement sounded from a few warriors. Old Loramas, the Grand Sachem of the Cherokee, rose, drew himself to his full height. He had dressed ceremoniously for the conclave, and he was an impressive figure.

"We are in the forefront," he explained patiently, "because it is our lands that are adjacent to those of the Choctaw and the Chickasaw. Will we do nothing while our lands are invaded? There is a white man's saying about the one who cuts off his nose to spite his face. The white warriors of Franklin are few. Will we allow enemies to overrun our traditional hunting grounds to see the white men embarrassed?"

Renno looked at Loramas in approval, and there was a loud chorus of agreement. "As for me and mine," Renno said, steel in his back and in his voice, "we will protect that which is ours. We will welcome all who choose to join us."

A warrior began to beat an intense rhythm on the packed floor with his hands, the sounds of a war drum, muted. Others began to chant in low voices the ancient words of war.

Meanwhile, Rusog conferred quietly with his father, Wegowa, then nodded, stood, and strode to stand face-to-face with Renno. "We are brothers," Rusog said, extending his hands toward Renno. "I and the Cherokee will protect that which is ours."

There was a great whoop, and now a warrior was using a cooking pan for a drum, and the war chant was rising. Renno held up his hands for silence.

"I will see with my eyes what transpires to the west," he said. "We leave with the dawn. I name my brother El-i-chi to accompany me and to choose the eight mightiest Seneca warriors to come also. My brother Rusog will name the Cherokee, to total ten, making for a force of twenty warriors."

El-i-chi, still rankling at the lack of opportunity to build his honor and to seek advancement through war, gave a shrill war cry and leaped to his feet. He was a high-spirited young man just coming into his prime. The blood ran hot in his veins, and the long period of peace had galled him. He was feeling the mighty forces of nature in him, and he knew that soon it would be time for him to choose a mate. But before he did that, he wanted the chance to become a respected warrior, and without war there was no chance. He felt very happy and began to think whom he would pick as the balance of the Seneca half of the scouting party. He felt like dancing. His hand ached to swing a tomahawk. His blood cried out for the taking of enemy scalps. Renno, remembering his own fiery youth, and that not long passed, had to will his face to remain impassive, lest he smile at El-i-chi's eagerness. He knew that he had left himself open to question in appointing such a junior warrior to so important a task, but, after all, El-i-chi was not totally unproven, and he was Seneca and of the blood of the white Indian.

Spring is a sad time for a warrior to say good-bye to his wife and his new son, but a great time to do some traveling and, Renno hoped, enough fighting to test his band's readiness without risking a major encounter with a superior force of Chickasaw. Renno broke the news to Emily over the evening meal. Knowing her as her father's daughter, an intelligent woman, he explained it all to her—the treaty, the Spanish threat.

Although her heart was heavy to think of being separated from Renno, she recognized the importance of his mission and merely nodded, thus giving him her blessings. In her bed, she prayed to God to protect Renno.

Now there was no more restlessness in Renno. There were still questions, but he was going into action and felt confident that all the questions would soon be answered. No longer was he merely awaiting events, marking time. Instead, he would be the event maker. That, he felt, as he fell into quick, deep sleep, was as it was intended to be.

Elsewhere, one person did not sleep. In the lodge of the Cherokee Rusog, there was a slender, green-eyed Seneca woman who was not at all happy. She had just been told, for the third time, that she would not, under any circumstances, accompany the fast-moving party of warriors.

It was not that Ena wanted willfully to disobey the wishes of her husband; on the other hand, she knew her own worth, strong will, and proven ability. While it was not customary for a woman to be made a member of a war party, she felt she had earned the right by past performance and was not content to abide by Rusog's decision. She considered going to her brother Renno, but she knew what he would say. Although he knew that she was worth at least two warriors in battle, he was still her brother and, as such, would not want to put her at risk. That left her one avenue of appeal.

She waited until Rusog was sleeping soundly and slipped out into the night. It was not late. Darkness, however, was for sleeping, for the village would be awake with the morning sun.

As a bachelor, El-i-chi had chosen not to live with the other young warriors in a men's house, but had his own lodge, which he had constructed. It was there that Ena went, to tap lightly at his door. El-i-chi opened the door, and Ena put her fingers lightly on his mouth to indicate silence. She slipped in and closed the door behind her.

"And why does my sister sneak around in the dead of night?" El-i-chi asked.

El-i-chi was more than fond of his sister. While he

had been still a fledgling, Ena had earned honor by fighting and scouting as a man. It never ceased to amaze him that this willowy, beautiful woman, looking more white than Indian, could be a deadly force in battle. He was proud to be her brother, just as he was proud to be Renno's.

"You must help me, brother," Ena pleaded.

"Gladly."

"Speak, then, to our brother, Renno, that I may take my rightful place alongside my husband in the coming action," she said quickly.

"Ah, Ena," El-i-chi said. "You know—"

"I know that it is degrading to be treated as an ordinary woman," she hissed at him. "Will you speak for me?"

"I will," El-i-chi said. "But you and I both know what Renno will say." He took her arm. "Both Renno and I know your worth. It is not necessary for you—"

"I want to go. I must go," she interrupted impatiently.

"Ena, of all women I have known, I admire you most," El-i-chi said. "When it is time for me to take a wife, I pray that I will find one like you, a warrior maiden. Were I Rusog, I would consider myself fortunate, but still I would not allow you on this war party."

"Men," Ena spat. "You said you would speak to Renno."

"And what I say I will do, I will do," he promised.

"I will wait here," she said.

It was Emily who heard El-i-chi's soft tapping at the door. She got up quickly, and when she saw who was there, she said, "Renno is sleeping, El-i-chi."

"I *was* sleeping," Renno said from the darkness inside.

"I have come on behalf of our sister," El-i-chi said, stepping inside.

Renno sighed. "I can guess the intent."

"She can keep pace with the strongest warriors," El-i-chi said. "I promised I would speak for her, although I told her that if I were responsible, I myself would not allow her to accompany us."

Renno nodded. "Tell our sister that although her strength is not that of an ordinary woman, there is no place for her."

"She *is* the finest of scouts," El-i-chi said.

"She is a woman," Renno said, "and she will stay here, in her place."

"So be it, my chief," El-i-chi said.

Ena was waiting impatiently when he returned. She stood in the shadows of the lodge.

"He said what both of us expected him to say," El-i-chi told her.

Ena was silent for a moment; then she said, "Thank you for trying, brother."

He patted her shoulder. "At least one of us with the blood of the white Indian should stay here, to protect the women and children."

"Men," Ena said, but she returned El-i-chi's affectionate pat before she turned and disappeared into the darkness.

Yes, El-i-chi was thinking, *she is a woman among women, a pride to our family. Could there, anywhere in the world, be another like her? If so, I will find that woman, and she will be my wife.*

Chapter III

El-i-chi and the eight Seneca warriors he had chosen to make up the complement of ten awaited
Renno as he stepped out of his lodge. The morning
was just being born with a soft glow of dawn light.
El-i-chi stiffened in pride at the emergence of his
brother. Behind him, the warriors made a low, warlike hum of respect and greeting for their future
sachem. Each warrior carried the necessities of war
and travel. Muskets were grasped in strong hands.
Bows slanted across shoulders, and on each man's
back was his quiver, filled with arrows and a small

travel pack containing food. Each warrior had tomahawk and knife at his waist.

Game would, of course, be plentiful in the spring,
but Renno had given orders to be prepared to travel
fast and light, so there would not always be time for
the killing and cooking of game. In the food packs
there was a variety of travel rations: parched corn
and jerky, and the traditional Seneca pemmican. A
few of the warriors had acquired a taste for *canutchie*
and carried balls of it almost as large as a man's fist,
because ounce for ounce *canutchie*, made of roasted
and pounded hickory nuts, gave more filling food
value than parched corn, for example, and it lasted
well.

The village was turning out to bid the scouting
party a silent and respectful farewell. From within
his lodging, Renno heard Emily softly crooning to
Little Hawk as the infant suckled his breakfast. Their
farewells had been made, and good wife that Emily
was, she would not embarrass him by showing her
sadness in public.

Hearing the soft sounds of many running feet,
Renno turned and saw Rusog enter the central square,
followed by his chosen band of Cherokee. Roy Johnson emerged from the guest lodge and walked to
stand by Renno's side. Johnson was dressed in fringed
buckskins supplied by his daughter and, at first glance,
looked very much the Indian. His pale skin soon
belied that impression, and he did not carry bow and
arrow or tomahawk. Instead, he wore a brace of
pistols on a woven belt at his waist.

Loramas, Ah-wen-ga, Wegowa, Toshabe, and Casno

had been standing together nearby. They approached, and Loramas lifted his hand in blessing. "The manitous will be with you," he said.

Casno started to chant. A warrior began to pound his feet on the dirt, and the others joined him. It was time. Renno looked up at the eastern blue of the mountains and saw the first emerging rays of the sun. He turned.

"Renno," said a young, vibrant voice.

Renno turned back to face the square. A Cherokee lad of perhaps fifteen years had thrust himself between Renno and the body of warriors.

"Yes, Se-quo-i?"

Rusog grunted disapproval and made a motion of anger with his hand, telling the lad to go away, but the boy already had Renno's attention.

"I know you are generous, wise, and courageous," the Cherokee boy began. "Will you hear my petition?"

"It is not the time for that," Rusog growled, but the boy continued to stare into Renno's face with a pair of large, alert eyes, eyes as dark as the skies before morning.

"Quickly, then," Renno said, liking the boy's stance, his unblinking gaze.

"I ask to be allowed to accompany you," Se-quo-i stated.

Before Rusog could speak, Renno said, "The selection of Cherokee was Rusog's."

"I know," Se-quo-i responded, letting his eyes fall for only a moment, "but hear me. I feel that I can contribute to your mission."

Half-amused but impatient, Renno frowned.

"With this," Se-quo-i continued, raising a long tube in both hands.

Renno was familiar with the Cherokee blowgun. In fact, he had toyed with a blowgun and had found it to be an unsatisfactory weapon. His thoughts were voiced openly by El-i-chi.

"It is a toy for the young," El-i-chi scoffed, "for the taking of birds and squirrels."

"May I?" Se-quo-i asked Renno, holding the long blowgun in one hand, a dart in the other.

For the first time Renno looked closely at Se-quo-i's weapon. It was longer than the usual blowgun, and of larger diameter, obviously made from the largest of the native canes, a variety of bamboo. The dart was ten inches long, and one end was wrapped in thistledown so that the base of the dart would fit closely into the pipe and give the user something to blow against. The tube itself was decorated in blacks and reds in a symmetrical pattern, the work of a sensitive craftsman.

"Leave, boy," Rusog said, his voice deep to show his irritation.

"Wait," Renno said, hand lifted.

Se-quo-i carefully placed the dart in the pipe, took two deep breaths, and with lungs fully inflated, lifted the tube to his lips. Fifty feet away a dried gourd hung from the end of the ridgepole. With a huff that was clearly audible, Se-quo-i sent the dart winging, so swiftly that it was almost invisible, to pierce the dried gourd with a sharp *thunk*.

Se-quo-i smiled, satisfied. "My weapon is silent. It will kill not only small game."

"You are wasting our time," Rusog said. "We kill men, not rabbits."

"Renno?" Se-quo-i said, asking permission to continue, while fitting another dart into the tube. "Should it be necessary to kill a man silently—" He turned and nodded to a twelve-year-old Cherokee boy who lifted a flat board on which was painted a face, the eyes of the face emphasized. The boy stood a full thirty feet away as the dart huffed out and thunked into one painted eye. "Death is instantaneous and silent," Se-quo-i explained. He looked up at Renno hopefully. "There might also be a time when the taking of a rabbit would give you a quick and silent meal."

Renno grunted. He turned to Rusog. "The boy speaks with truth and merit, but I would not interfere. It is your choice."

Rusog, secretly a bit pleased by Se-quo-i's performance, lifted one hand. "It was you who set the number of warriors, my brother."

"Then I have just increased that number by one," Renno said. He clasped Se-quo-i's upper arm. "Prepare your rations and catch up to us. If you can do that—and we will be traveling swiftly—then you are welcome."

With a great whoop that brought chuckles from the people gathered to bid the scouting party farewell, the twelve-year-old boy who had held Se-quo-i's second target ran forward and handed him a small pack.

"I am prepared," Se-quo-i said, happiness reflecting in his dark eyes.

* * *

Without waiting for instructions, El-i-chi ran ahead of the main body of warriors. He set a swift pace, and by midmorning Roy Johnson found himself panting from the effort of keeping up with the strong young men. For an hour there had been a pain in his side and his lungs were on fire, but his pride was such that he maintained a stoic expression and vowed to himself that he would fall and perish before he asked for a halt. His stubbornness paid off, for just before Renno held up his hand to indicate a brief period of rest, the pain in the colonel's side went away, and his lungs seemed to have gained new capacity so that he was running easily.

As the scouting party ate quickly, El-i-chi came trotting silently back to report to Renno that the river ahead was not yet in flood and could be crossed at the usual ford. Johnson was chewing on pemmican. He noted the exchange with interest. Although the morning was cool, El-i-chi's light-complexioned face glistened with perspiration, testimony to the fact that the young warrior had covered much more ground than the main party during his scouting of the way ahead.

"I would like you to send another scout ahead, while you travel with us," Renno told El-i-chi.

At first El-i-chi seemed ready to protest, but then he nodded and pointed to one of Rusog's Cherokee, waving him down the trail ahead. The Cherokee vanished quickly, his moccasin-clad feet soundless.

"Renno," said Se-quo-i, who had been sitting cross-legged on the ground near the white Indian, "should you need my services as a scout, I am ready."

Johnson grinned behind the hand holding the pemmican. He had been surprised when Renno allowed the boy to come with the scouting party.

"Your time will come," Renno assured him, without expression. He had been watching the boy. Se-quo-i had kept the pace effortlessly. Renno had also noted that the boy's face was not that of a typical Cherokee. "Se-quo-i . . ." he said.

"Yes, Renno?"

"Who are your parents?"

Se-quo-i's dark eyes fell; then he looked Renno in the eye and said, "The same blood runs in our veins."

It was as Renno had suspected. It was evident that Se-quo-i had white blood. Renno did not press his questioning, for it obviously embarrassed the boy. Instead, he said, "For all its whiteness, my blood is Seneca."

"As mine is Cherokee," Se-quo-i responded.

Renno nodded in satisfaction. "You will pass the word that we are ready," he told Se-quo-i as he rose, and the boy bounded to his feet and ran among the seated warriors. Soon the group was moving again, at the same ground-covering pace.

The waters of the first river to be crossed were chilled by the snow runoff from the distant blue mountains. El-i-chi led the band into the virgin forest on the far bank, and as Renno trotted easily along, he noticed new growth budding on the hardwood trees—a fresh green paleness that was the fulfillment of the promises of the manitous. Through occasional breaks in the canopy of branches, the sky was a clean, brilliant blue. He had been running long enough for his body to be toned, to have his blood racing, his heart pumping swiftly. He felt so good that he had to stifle an impulse to yell out his well-being in one loud, yodeling whoop of sheer joy.

At the end of the third day Renno sat next to his father-in-law in a small clearing. There were no fires.

"From this point we will be in strange lands," Renno remarked.

"There, just down that slope, is where we found the Spaniard," Johnson commented.

Renno nodded, pleased that Johnson had been alert enough to recognize the area, but he said nothing for a long time. Around him the warriors had prepared their beds, some having cut fresh evergreen boughs, others content to sleep curled on the ground. Renno rose, and one by one the warriors looked up at him.

"Tomorrow," he said, "we will slow the pace in order to have total silence." That was all he needed to say. Each of the men knew that they were at the farthest boundary of Cherokee lands; danger would be everywhere.

Renno noted with some amusement that Se-quo-i had made his bed quite nearby. The boy was seated cross-legged, polishing his blowgun with a piece of cloth. Renno was not yet sleepy. He walked to Se-quo-i and squatted beside him. "Tomorrow you will march toward the rear of the column," he said.

Se-quo-i's eyes showed his disappointment, but he nodded. Renno put out a hand, and Se-quo-i handed him the blowgun, which he examined. "I will try this weapon," he said.

Se-quo-i reached into a pouch, took something out, then opened his fist to show Renno a palm covered with fire-hardened clay pellets. "For practice," he explained when Renno raised his eyebrows.

Renno dropped a pellet into the pipe and raised the blowgun to his lips. Some twenty feet away El-i-chi was already sleeping, curled on his side, his back toward Renno. Renno, not usually one for pranks, suppressed a grin and blew mightily. The pellet struck El-i-chi on the left buttock and galvanized him into instant action. He leaped to his feet in one swift motion, tomahawk raised, eyes darting around the clearing, which was dim in the last light of the day. When he saw Renno's chest heaving with silent laughter and saw the blowgun in Renno's hand, he lowered the tomahawk and said, "So, our leader has adopted not only a boy's weapon but also the ways of a boy." Renno could no longer contain his laughter. He rolled back on the ground. El-i-chi, disgust on his face, lay down again.

"It seems that you do not need practice," Se-quo-i said through his own silent laughter. He himself had often done the same thing, but never with a full-grown warrior as his target.

"I would advise you not to follow my example," Renno said gravely, controlling his laughter.

"I value my hide too much," Se-quo-i confessed. "When we find a canebrake, shall I make you a blowgun?"

"Your offer is generous," Renno said, "but I have my own weapons, with which I am more familiar."

Se-quo-i looked away, disappointed. He had long admired Renno, not only for his strength and bravery but also for his manner. To Se-quo-i, Renno was the perfect war chief, the kind of man who would be a great sachem.

"But perhaps the time will come when we will need your weapon."

"I will be ready," Se-quo-i vowed, brightening.

"A man is no better than his weapons in war," Renno said. "You must also know the bow, the knife, the tomahawk, the musket."

"Yes, Great Chief," Se-quo-i said. "For the use of those weapons, I follow your example."

Renno grunted.

"But it is more than weapons that make a people strong," Se-quo-i ventured, a bit surprised by his audacity.

"And what are those other qualities?" Renno asked.

"Why does the white man have superior weapons?" Se-quo-i asked. "Why does he bring such power and so many warriors from across the great waters? To match his power, we have to adopt his weapons." He patted the stock of Renno's musket. "The white man has more things—more deadly weapons, more wealth. Why?"

"Perhaps you want to tell me *your* reasoning," Renno said.

Se-quo-i's dark eyes seem to sparkle in the fading light. "Because no knowledge is ever lost with the white man," he said. "Because the knowledge of one becomes the knowledge of all."

"*Hmmm*," Renno said.

"The Indian can pass his knowledge along only by this," Se-quo-i continued, thrusting fingers toward his mouth. "The knowledge and skills of a great warrior are thus lost when he goes to join his ancestors, but the white man can leave his knowledge behind him, for anyone who can read the printed word. You, Great Chief, can read the words on paper, is that not true?"

"It is true," Renno confirmed.

"And because of that, you can accumulate great knowledge, the white man's knowledge."

Renno nodded, impressed by the wisdom of this young Cherokee. He himself had long known the desirability of communication by the written word. He had just recently encountered an instance where the inability to read had caused great question: he and Roy Johnson had had to wait to find someone who could read Spanish before knowing the message on the parchment taken from the dead Spaniard. And he still did not know the contents of the small paper he had taken from the hilt of the stiletto.

"I learned to read and write because of my white blood," Renno said, "and my wife continues to teach me."

"Not many of our people are so fortunate," Se-quo-i pointed out. "If we had a written language of our own—"

"Perhaps someday," Renno said, "a wise man will do that task, for there are many languages, and many have already been reduced to paper."

"Perhaps," Se-quo-i murmured thoughtfully.

"And now we sleep," Renno said, rising and handing the blowgun back to Se-quo-i.

But he did not sleep. His band numbered twenty-two, and it would be greatly outnumbered by almost any force it encountered in the hostile Chickasaw lands ahead. It would be vitally important to reach the big river undetected, to gather the needed information, and to return without fighting. It would be up to him to restrain his warriors, all of whom were eager to count coup on the hated Chickasaw and to carry home scalps to prove their bravery. He would have to be very alert and be everywhere at once to keep the zealous warriors from attacking the first enemy that was sighted.

The bright, warm spring days pleased Emily. These were quiet times, too early in the season for the women to begin the spring plantings. The bounties of nature had not begun to ripen, and although she was a bit tired of the stored foods of the winter, Emily's life was pleasant. She took endless delight in the health and good humor of her baby.

Little Hawk was thriving on the attentions of three generations of women—mother, grandmother, and great-grandmother—and was, Emily feared, in danger of becoming just a bit spoiled. Already it was evident that Little Hawk would have the strong facial characteristics of his father. His skin was so white that it belied the one-quarter of his blood that was Indian. He was a chubby, happy, active baby, and it was his natural energy, his mewling attempts at beginning to coordinate his movements, that reminded Emily once again that although he was mostly white, he was and would always be a Seneca baby.

Before leaving on the scouting expedition, Renno had put a gift for his son, a large necklace of bear claws, into Little Hawk's crib. This gift had more than sentimental meaning, since the bear was the chief totem of Renno's clan group within the tribe. The large claws rattled when the necklace was moved, thus attracting Little Hawk. Emily, fearing that the child would injure himself on the sharp claws, wanted to keep the necklace out of Little Hawk's crib. She asked permission of Toshabe and Ah-wen-ga, but both women felt it best for Emily to leave the talisman dangling over Little Hawk. Out of respect for her husband's mother and grandmother, Emily bent to their advice, even though it went against her own good judgment. A clash of cultures in the raising of her son was something she had anticipated, but she never realized how very difficult it would be for her actually to accept some of the Seneca traditions.

And then one day, just as Emily had feared, a too-energetic jerking movement by uncoordinated little hands thrust a claw into the soft skin next to Little Hawk's eye, narrowly missing the eye itself but causing bleeding.

"No more," Emily said flatly, jerking the necklace from Little Hawk's hand and hanging it on a peg high in the top of the lodge.

When Toshabe and Ah-wen-ga noticed the talisman's new location the next day, they were very concerned; when they asked Emily about it, she was quite unmoving in her decision to keep the necklace from her son.

Ah-wen-ga, although she disagreed, was silent. The manitous, she believed, would never permit the talisman to do real harm to the boy, and its medicine should be close to him.

That evening she told Loramas of the incident, concerned that Emily had inadvertently dishonored a powerful talisman of the Bear Clan.

Loramas shrugged his shoulders and tried to console his wife, since there was no way of getting word from Renno and his group to know if Emily's decision had caused her husband ill luck. The people of the combined Cherokee and Seneca village could only wait, pray to the spirits, and as the weeks passed, cast glances down the trail leading to the west, for the first news that they would receive of the absent warriors would be the sight of one of them trotting home, perhaps giving a whoop of triumph.

An annual event of rejoicing took the minds of the people off the absent warriors when two young boys ran into the village brandishing the first tender shoots of the *pocan*, or pokeweed. Now, it was felt, the new beginning had definitely arrived, for the *pocan* shoots were among the first of the delicate green things to raise their tender heads above the earth. The shoots were delicious, had a strong, pleasant flavor, and everyone was ready for a feast of fresh greens to add variety to the winter diet.

"Go," Toshabe urged Emily, as the women, children, and the young warriors who would guard them prepared for a day in the field to gather *pocan*. "I will gladly stay with the child."

Emily had been inside the lodge for the long winter, never more than a few feet from Little Hawk. She longed to stretch her legs, to walk and run through the greening meadows, and to see the new growth blossoming on the trees of the forest. "If you don't mind, mother, I will go," she said eagerly.

Emily disappeared from the square, surrounded by her friends and several children. She knew the name of every child in the village. The older, independent boys ran ahead. The older girls, as sturdy and as active as the boys, some with a beauty that lifted Emily's heart, chose to walk with the women. But her special favorite was the daughter of a senior warrior, a sunny little girl not yet six whose name was Wynema. Wynema's mother was with child, quite heavy, and had not come on the outing. It was natural for Wynema to attach herself to Emily. This pleased Emily, who dreamed of having her own little girl someday soon.

The village shared by Loramas's Cherokee and Renno's Seneca was located roughly in the center of Cherokee lands, in an area most thickly settled with Cherokee villages. It was a day's travel, at a warrior's pace, from the village to the beginnings of the foothills of the blue, distant mountains. Located as it was, the area was as safe as could be in a time when enemy tribes' war parties might travel hundreds of miles, but the young warriors remained alert even as they teased the unmarried girls and sometimes aided them in picking the tender *pocan* shoots. No one was too concerned about returning to the village; the mood of spring was upon them. Everyone had brought food, and there was pure, clear water, still chilled by the snows of the mountains, to be had from two small creeks that ran into a larger stream some distance from the village. The Indians were children of the wilderness, and distance meant little to them. Even with the younger children, they traveled a number of miles, headed toward the larger stream.

Emily and Wynema had quickly filled their leather bags with enough of the poke greens to feed two families, so Emily was taking advantage of the outing to search out both dried and newly green herbs. She had taken great interest in herb craft. She had known something of the healing powers of certain plants from her mother and had added to this knowledge by questioning the older Seneca and Cherokee women and Casno, the medicine man. Emily was gaining quite a reputation, and many people now came to her for potions and balms to ease the fevers of winter or the pain of small injuries.

The fastest walkers of the group had reached the banks of the large, rocky stream when Emily and Wynema arrived. They joined the others in resting or tossing rocks into the stream, which was swollen by the spring rains and the snowmelt. While the others were still eating and talking, Emily spotted a likely growth of green on the bank of the stream and left the group to walk toward it. Wynema followed her. One patch of green led to another, and to Emily's pleasure, she saw the fresh green leaves of watercress growing in an area where the force of the swiftly running water had been slowed by rocks.

She began to salivate, just seeing the watercress. She put aside her bag filled with *pocan* and stepped out onto an exposed rock to reach one particular bunch of the greens. As she bent over, her foot slipped on the moss of the rock, and with a gasp, she tumbled into the icy water. She was immediately seized by the swift current and swept downstream.

Wynema cried out when her friend fell into the water, but Emily was not frightened. It was an easy matter for her to avoid being swept into the exposed rocks, for she was a strong swimmer, and once the initial shock of cold was past, the water was delightfully refreshing. She knew that it was useless to battle the current head-on, so she swam easily, taking care to avoid the rocks, pushing herself off with her feet and hands, angling slowly toward the bank.

"Don't worry, I'm all right," Emily called back to the little girl.

As Emily was swept downstream toward the narrowing of the river, where white water crashed against huge, obstructing rocks, Wynema ran along the bank, falling slightly behind.

"Stay back!" Emily yelled, as she saw the little girl getting dangerously close to the slick, steep bank. But her warning came too late, for as Wynema leaped from stone to stone, her foot encountered wet moss, and she splashed into the water and was immediately pulled under by the roiling current.

Emily began to fight the current, desperate to reach the struggling little girl, whose head repeatedly went underwater. The manitous were with them, for the current swept Wynema directly into Emily's grasp. She seized the neck of Wynema's doeskin garment and used one arm to try to angle toward the bank. She saw immediately that she was not going to be able to reach the shore before the rapids began, so she concentrated on spotting the best way to float through the white water of the constricted area. She banged painfully against a rock but managed to hang on to the coughing, sputtering Wynema, and then her full attention was required to keep from being battered severely.

The two shot out of the last tumble of water into a narrow, swift-flowing, but smooth stretch of water. Emily started swimming strongly. The river had entered a rocky gorge, and she could hear the roar of a waterfall. She managed to reach the rocky bank but could not hold both herself and Wynema. She let the water take them while she looked desperately for a way to get out of the gorge. As she searched for a low, accessible area of the rocky bank, she failed to see that a thick limb from a fallen tree brushed the surface of the water directly ahead. Her head was turned to the side when the force of the current slammed her head into the limb. White light exploded in front of her eyes.

It was Ena who first missed Emily. The meal in the open had been enjoyed by everyone, especially the youngsters. In good spirits, no one really wanted to head for home but knew they must, lest darkness overtake them before they reached the village. Ena's inquiries revealed that some of the children had seen

Emily and Wynema going downstream. Not wanting to cause a general alarm, Ena called three of the young warriors aside and led them at a swift pace to the river, there to see the marks of Emily's moccasins along the bank. Ena's heart went cold when she reached the spot where Emily had fallen in, for the marks left in the wet moss told her exactly what had happened. She quickened her pace and found the spot where Wynema had slipped. Ena and the warriors set out at a run. A young woman in the prime of life, Ena had already proven her stamina while acting as scout in the War of Independence. The young warriors were hard put to keep up with her. She kept her eyes on the turbulent water, looking for any sign. She was not yet too worried because she knew that Emily was a good swimmer.

When the river entered the rocky gorge, she had to make her way along the top, through thick brush. This slowed her pace, which enabled her to spot a smear of blood on the low-hanging limb extending to the surface of the water. Ena stopped for a moment. She could hear the roar of the waterfall, not fifty yards downstream. A cold shiver went down her spine. Knowing that the swiftness of the current through the narrow gorge would carry anyone or anything to the falls, she broke out of the brush, ran to the bluff over which the water tumbled, heedlessly skidded, half standing, half sitting, down the rocks, and dived into the clear, deep pool at the foot of the falls, penetrating deeply, eyes straining.

One of the young warriors joined her in the water, and they dived time and time again, unable to reach the bottom of the pool. At last Ena surfaced and told the other two warriors to scout downstream. She followed quickly, soon catching them.

About a quarter of a mile below the waterfall, the river widened and became more calm. Ena reasoned that if Emily and Wynema had survived the tumble over the waterfall, they could have easily got out of the river at that point, so she and the young warriors carefully searched both banks for sign, but found none.

Ena sent one of the warriors back to tell the main group to return to the village and send help. The messenger came back soon, with two other young men, and the search continued as long as there was light and, with the aid of torches, into the night.

Ena could come to but one conclusion: Emily and the little girl were dead. Their bodies would surface in a day or two in the deep pool below the falls, unless they had been carried far, far downstream. A warrior woman, Ena did not weep, but her heart was aching as she summoned the most experienced of the young warriors.

"Nondaga," she said, her voice calm, not giving a hint of her sadness, "Renno must be told about this. I would like you to find him. Run hard, directly into the setting sun, and perhaps you will intercept him returning from the big river."

Chapter IV

Miguel Ibáñez, personal secretary to Baron de Carondelet, governor of Spain's southeastern possessions in the New World, waited until the baron had finished his hearty breakfast before climbing the wide stairs to the governor's office and entering after a respectful knock.

De Carondelet was still in his robe, a regal creation worthy of the king himself. He was sipping noisily at a cup of coffee, and when he looked up to see Ibáñez standing there, a sheaf of papers in his hands, he sighed.

"Ah, Miguel," the governor said, "you are my personal slave driver. You barely give me time to eat before you force work upon me."

"There is nothing pressing, Governor," Ibáñez said.

"Sit down, sit down," de Carondelet said. "Join me in a cup of coffee and tell me what you have for me."

Ibáñez poured, sweetened the dark brew with coarse sugar from the new fields of sugarcane, and opened his sheaf of papers. The matters at hand were routine, merely formalities of previous decisions, requiring the governor's signature. When the boring business was finished, Ibáñez stood, gathering the papers. De Carondelet waved him back to his seat.

"I have given you authority to select an emissary to the Chicksaw," the governor said. "Have you taken action on that matter?"

Ibáñez sighed before answering. The baron, a grandee of old Spain, was often a trial to him. Ibáñez did the work, and the governor received the glory and the riches that flowed from Spain's possessions in Florida and Louisiana. "I gave you a written report, your Excellency, over a month ago."

The governor waved a hand. "You know, Ibáñez, that I don't have time to read everything that crosses my desk. I am a busy man."

"Yes, your Excellency," Ibáñez said. He knew how busy the governor was, but it was not with affairs of government. Rather, the governor spent most of his time in the company of ladies of dubious virtue, many of them French.

"Whom did you select?" de Carondelet asked, his voice betraying his disinterest in the matter.

"Captain Guy de Rojas," Ibáñez said. "He has the experience."

"Por Dios!" de Carondelet exclaimed, the name having caught his attention. "De Rojas?"

"He knows the Indians," Ibáñez said.

"He is more Indian than Spanish," de Carondelet said in disapproval.

"That was one of the factors in his favor," Ibáñez explained. "Successful interaction with the savages requires a certain character, your Excellency, a certain strength and determination."

"And a total lack of scruples?" the governor shot back.

Ibáñez squirmed.

"I am not sure I approve," the governor said, looking at Ibáñez, dark brows gathered into a glower.

That is too bad, Ibáñez thought, but aloud he said, "De Rojas has lived with the Indians—"

"The English have a word for that. Squaw man."

Ibáñez smiled. "Not just one squaw, your Excellency. Nevertheless, he speaks the languages of the Indians. He knows how they think." He shrugged and smiled. "The very qualities that make de Rojas objectionable in civilized society are assets when dealing with the savages. He is a man who can be as treacherous as they, as cruel as they, and as heedless of the value of human life as they. He is a man the Indians can respect."

"I hope you are right, Ibáñez," the governor said. "Much depends on the success of his mission. In order to implement our plans, we must have an alliance with this . . . What is his name?"

"His name is Oklawahpa," Ibáñez answered. "He is the war chief of the western Chickasaw, whose main settlements are grouped around Chickasaw Bluffs on the Mississippi."

"Barbaric name for a barbaric man," de Carondelet growled. "You think de Rojas will be able to bring Oklawahpa into the fold?"

"I am confident," Ibáñez said.

"Then I will trust your decision," de Carondelet concluded, rising. "As soon as I am dressed, I will be going out. You can handle things today?"

"Yes, Excellency." He was thinking that he could handle things much better in the governor's absence than in his presence. "May I ask if there is a place where you can be reached in the event of emergency?"

"The usual place," de Carondelet said.

Ibáñez nodded. The usual place was the home of a certain French lady whose gay parties were the highlight of New Orleans society.

Captain Guy de Rojas sat on a skin blanket on the floor of a Chickasaw lodge, his legs crossed under him, a pipe in his hand. He sucked the bitter, harsh smoke and passed the pipe to his second in command, a bookish, genteel young man who had come to New Spain with visions of finding gold. So many had come with that false hope, and so many had died, that de Rojas had little respect for the type. Ramón de Vega, however, was not, in de Rojas's eyes, all that bad. On the surface, it seemed that de

Vega was an unlikely companion for a brawler and old wilderness hand like de Rojas, who felt that brute force solved most problems. But de Vega showed promise: on the long and arduous march from Louisiana, through the lands of the Choctaw, de Vega had kept the pace without complaint, even after the horses had died. And it had not taken de Vega long to discover that cold winter nights are made more pleasant by the presence of a warm, female body, even if that body has red skin and the flat, ugly features of a Choctaw. De Vega had not even been put off in the slightest when, as guests, they were forced to observe one of the more repulsive of Choctaw customs, the picking of rotting flesh from the bones of a dead warrior.

But now they were in Chickasaw territory, and across from de Rojas and de Vega sat the war chief of the western Chickasaw. Oklawahpa, a fierce man in his late thirties, wore the regalia of a chief, and his dark eyes never left those of de Rojas as the pipe was passed around the circle of Oklawahpa's advisers and warriors.

De Rojas knew how to be patient when dealing with Indians. He had more than one Choctaw wife in the south, and he spoke Choctaw like a native. Since the Choctaw and Chickasaw were of common racial stock, the languages were almost identical, so de Rojas had no problem communicating with Oklawahpa.

One did not rush a parley with an Indian. One smoked, then was silent, then waited. De Rojas knew that the less-experienced de Vega was getting restless, and he looked at de Vega with a thin smile touching his lips above his untrimmed black beard.

At last Oklawahpa spoke. "What has the great white chief in the south sent to his brother Oklawahpa?"

De Rojas nodded to de Vega, who rose, left the Chickasaw counsel house, and spoke in Spanish to the four young Choctaw who had been pressed into acting as bearers during the long march to the north. The Choctaw brought the large bundles in to the Spanish agent.

De Rojas did not rush the ceremony. He removed from the bales bolts of brightly dyed cloth, strings of glass beads, sugar, and coffee. With each addition to the growing heap in the center of the dirt floor of the counsel house, Oklawahpa merely grunted, but his eyes narrowed and he leaned forward in interest when de Rojas placed a pair of handsome pistols on the heap and followed them with knives and two muskets.

The old legends had it that at one time, far in the past, the Choctaw and the Chickasaw were brothers, of one tribe, that they migrated together, as a unit, from some unknown point in the southwest and then separated. The Choctaw adopted the ways of the woodland Indians, and some of these adopted customs caused contempt in the breast of every Chickasaw. The two Indian tribes shared a common language, but there the kinship ceased. To the Chicksaws' way of thinking, the Choctaw wore their hair long like women and had settled into the dull, sedentary life of the agriculturist.

Oklawahpa was a prime example of the difference

between Choctaw and Chickasaw. He was the war leader of a tribe that demanded total freedom to hunt at will through vast virgin areas. The Chickasaw claimed—and defended with a fierce joy in fighting—an area of land extending from the mountains to trackless forests, from the big river to wide prairies. Oklawahpa lived to fight. He was not and would never be a hoe farmer. He was a raider, and his most fanciful dreams were of victory and conquest. Within a year's time his warriors were likely to fight against Choctaw or Cherokee close to his own lands, or to raid and plunder the Illinois, the Kickapoo, the Osage, the Quapaw, or any other of the more minor tribes far to the north.

According to Oklawahpa, a Chickasaw warrior needed space. A Chickasaw warrior scorned the closely grouped villages of the Cherokee and Choctaw. Village living was not for the Chickasaw, no. From the Chickasaw Bluffs on the Mississippi, trails extended outward for well over a hundred and fifty miles, linking communities that were usually strung out for several miles along a stream.

During the early days of white exploration and colonization, the Chickasaw had sided with the French, so the English takeover of the eastern seaboard and then the victory of the colonists in the American War of Independence had hit them hard and brought many hardships and setbacks. Oklawahpa had no love for the white settlers on the far boundaries of Cherokee lands. He had no love for the Spanish, either, but his eyes gleamed when he saw the shining new weapons. If each of his warriors could be equipped with such weapons, he could eliminate the Cherokee and the white settlers all the way to the far blue mountains.

"You will find, my friend," de Rojas said, noting with satisfaction Oklawahpa's interest in the weapons, "that the gracious king of Spain and his governor in the New World are generous."

"Only two boom-sticks," Oklawahpa grunted.

"In New Orleans there are boom-sticks as numerous as the leaves on the trees," de Rojas assured him.

De Rojas had discovered a problem upon his arrival at Oklawahpa's winter quarters. The messenger who had been sent months earlier with a copy of the treaty of Pensacola had never arrived. However, de Rojas had another copy of the treaty, and his first task was to get Oklawahpa's agreement and his mark on the parchment. The loss of the messenger concerned de Rojas, but there were dozens of ways the man could have perished in the wilderness. Of greater concern than the treaty was the secret order meant for Oklawahpa's eyes only, which had been concealed in the hilt of a stiletto. But de Rojas was certain that the stiletto was rusting and being gradually buried by detritus somewhere in the forests, or was in the possession of some savage who would probably never discover the secret compartment in the hilt or be able to read the message if he did discover it.

"You bring boom-sticks for all my warriors," Oklawahpa ordered.

De Rojas smiled expansively. "That is our desire.

Your wise men have sworn friendship with Spain at Pensacola. You and I know, however, that the great war leader of the western Chickasaw must be in friendship with his Spanish brothers, or the treaty means nothing. It is the wish of the great Spanish chief in New Orleans to work with his Chickasaw brothers to make these lands, and more, Chickasaw forever. With the Spanish as allies, the Chickasaw will have muskets, sugar, fine knives, and beautiful things for their women. And, together, the Spanish and Chickasaw brothers will rid the land once and for all of the Cherokee and their white allies."

"White man, be he Spanish, French, or English, is hungry for land," Oklawahpa observed.

"We already have plenty of land," de Rojas denied. "We have Florida and Louisiana. We have the vast lands of New Spain in the west. We want only to trade in friendship with the Chickasaw, to give the Chickasaw muskets and other valuable gifts in exchange for nothing more than the furs of this plentiful land."

De Rojas knew that if Oklawahpa were given weapons, he would clear the area to the east and north of Cherokee and the whites. Then it would be an easy matter for the Spanish to enslave the Chickasaw and Choctaw, putting them to good use, while claiming the Indian land for Spain.

"You say you will fight at our side," Oklawahpa said. "But I see only two men."

"More men are coming," de Rojas promised. "A squadron of lancers on horses. Cannon."

"Horses no good for fighting here," Oklawahpa said. "Trees."

"The lancers can fight in open areas from horse-back," de Rojas said. "And in the forest they will dismount. Our muskets and cannon will drive away the Cherokee like leaves before the storm wind. Great things await only the agreement of Oklawahpa."

"My young men want boom-sticks."

"Two wagon loads," de Rojas said. "And a wagon load of powder and ball."

Oklawahpa grunted.

It was a ceremony of two days' duration to sign the treaty. One of the provisions was Chickasaw permission for the Spanish to establish strongholds at various points on both banks of the Mississippi all the way from the far south to the northernmost extent of Chickasaw lands. It was from these forts that the Spanish planned to seize the territory from the Chickasaw and secure it forever.

Guy de Rojas and Ramón de Vega had been assigned to sleep in the same lodge. On the second night of the ceremony, after Oklawahpa had made his mark, as the village began to quiet slowly, de Rojas stood in the center of the lodge, the smoke from the open fire making him squint his eyes. "So it begins, Ramón," he said.

De Vega, at first disappointed to find no gold in this part of America, had begun to see the great possibilities of the agreement between de Rojas and Oklawahpa. There *was* gold in the virgin forests— but in the form of pelts, the hides of beaver, fox, mink, and bear. Perhaps he would be able to return to Spain in victory after all, with a fortune to reclaim the lands that his family had lost.

"Oklawahpa is ready to fight," de Rojas said. "While his attention is on fighting the Cherokee, we must establish ourselves securely here, on the river. Later, when the time is right, we will be able to crush him."

"He will attack the Cherokee and whites as soon as our cavalry arrives?"

"No. He has had no scouting party in Cherokee lands during the winter. First he will send out a large group, and I will go with them, to acquaint myself with the lie of the land. You will stay here. When the cavalry arrives, you will set the soldiers to building a fort immediately."

"You handled the red devil well, señor," de Vega said.

De Rojas waved a hand. "It is simply a matter of understanding the workings of the Indian mind."

For days, Renno's scouting party had moved only a few miles a day. The slow progress was necessitated by the living habits of the Chickasaw, their passion for privacy. On its way to the Mississippi River, the group was moving through the heart of Chickasaw territory now, and each clump of forest, each small stream, each clearing might well prove to be the dwelling of a small family group.

Thus it was that the straight march west was turned into an unpredictable zigzag course, for it was vital to reach the river without encountering any Chickasaw who could spread the word that a raiding party was on the loose. The last thing Renno wanted—although his blood cried out for action—was a head-to-head battle with a much larger Chickasaw force.

The night camps were fireless and silent. Sentries were posted at all points. At first Roy Johnson had insisted on taking his turn at sentry duty, but Renno had told him bluntly that it was best to have Cherokee or Seneca posted in the forest surrounding the camp.

On the whole, Colonel Johnson had adjusted well, even though he was grateful for the slower pace through the more populated areas. He was hard of body and fit of spirit. He too was tired of inaction, and when the lead scout came slipping silently through the trees in front of the main party to warn of the presence of a Chickasaw hunting party, Johnson felt his blood rise.

Renno directed his men to skirt to the north of the Chickasaw hunting party, and in the soft, cool spring rain, the men moved as silently as ghosts, yet swiftly to avoid the three Chickasaw warriors, who had stalked and killed a yearling buck. An unexpected change in the direction of march of the Chickasaw brought a crisis, for the three enemies were now moving directly toward Renno's main body. The white Indian ordered concealment, fearing that swift flight might cause noise or leave sign for the enemy. As if by magic, twenty-one men disappeared into the forest, all grouped closely, weapons ready. The young Cherokee Se-quo-i stood next to Renno.

The Chickasaw, feeling secure because they were in the heart of their own lands, laughed and talked in admiration of the buck they had killed. Their voices faded as they passed down the trail, totally unaware that they had walked within a pace of death. Renno held his own position for long minutes, instinct telling him to remain motionless. Not a sound came from the others. Renno saw Se-quo-i looking at him questioningly. From a position to the front, El-i-chi, as scout, sent forth a questioning call, the soft cooing of a dove. Renno did not answer, and El-i-chi, trusting his brother's leadership implicitly, was then silent.

It was long minutes before it became apparent that Renno's stir of doubt, his hunch, had not been groundless. Yet another Chickasaw warrior, bow in hand, trotted silently down the trail toward Renno's concealed position. This Chickasaw was a straggler from the hunting party. Alone, he was more alert than the others. He ran lightly, with his eyes darting from side to side, taking in everything, aware of the slightest sound. It seemed as if he would pass without incident, but about twenty feet down the trail from the point where Renno and Se-quo-i were motionless and invisible in a clump of undergrowth, the warrior suddenly stopped, looked hard at the ground, and then tensed, quickly stringing an arrow to his bow.

From his distance, Renno could not see any sign to alert the Chickasaw, but the warrior was definitely suspicious. He walked in a crouch, arrow ready to be drawn, checking the undergrowth on each side of the trail. He stopped again and examined the ground, and now Renno could see that leaves had been disturbed in the direction opposite to the sign left by the Chickasaw hunting party. Moving a fraction of an inch at a time, Renno lifted his bow and drew back, unsettled in his knowledge that the Chickasaw would probably be able to cry out and warn his friends before he died. Renno felt a feathery touch on his arm and glanced out of the corner of his eye to see Se-quo-i with his blowgun in place. Se-quo-i's eyes questioned. Renno nodded.

The huff of Se-quo-i's breath came seemingly at the same instant of a dull, smacking sound as the sharp, thin dart from the blowgun penetrated the left eye of the Chickasaw warrior and buried itself inches deep, driving into the enemy's brain. The Chickasaw crumpled in total silence.

Renno leaped from concealment. He ordered two men to heft the dead man's body, and then he led the party at a run in a direction away from the Chickasaw hunting party. When he felt that they had traveled far enough, he told his men to bury the Chickasaw and conceal all signs of fresh earth.

"One moment, please, Renno," Se-quo-i said respectfully, leaping forward, knife in hand, to scalp the fallen enemy. He held the scalp high and did a little dance of pride. A warrior dipped two fingers into the blood of the dead man and drew parallel marks on Se-quo-i's chest.

"So," Renno said to Se-quo-i, "your boy's weapon has proved its worth." That was as close to praise as he would go, but he saw Se-quo-i's chest swell. "Now you will dig the hole to bury him," Renno ordered.

Renno pushed the men hard. A full moon rose with the sunset, giving enough light for travel, and it was well after midnight before Renno called a halt, choosing a camp set well back in a glade of trees. As they approached the river, there were more and more open areas of grassland. Renno fell asleep immediately after the sentries were posted, and was awakened by the repeated hootings of an owl. He sat up swiftly, reaching for his bow. The sound was coming from behind them. The hooting continued at intervals. Renno slipped into the shadows of the woods, finding his way by the light of the moon, now far down in the west, until he was standing at the side of the sentry posted to the east of the camp.

"Seneca," the sentry motioned to Renno in sign language. Renno was of the same opinion, but all his men were accounted for. He signed the sentry to keep his position and eased forward, all senses alert for the smallest movement, the softest sound. He located the man who had been making the owl calls by his breathing—it sounded as if he had run far. Renno approached from the rear and found the man standing beside a large tree, ears cocked for a reply as he made one more owl hoot. Renno's strong arm went around the man's throat, his hand over the man's mouth. The man was young and strong, but as his feet were lifted from the ground and pressure was applied to his windpipe, he was helpless in Renno's grasp.

"I am Renno. Make no sound," Renno whispered, removing his hand from the man's mouth.

"Nondaga," gasped the young warrior.

Renno, recognizing the name, released his hold and turned Nondaga to face him.

"A message," Nondaga managed to get out, rubbing his throat.

"Come." Renno led the way back to camp. He was concerned. True, Nondaga was a Seneca, but if a Seneca could follow and find his camp, perhaps an enemy could also find it.

The entire force had been alerted. They gathered round as Renno led Nondaga into the clearing, weapons at the ready.

"A message," Nondaga repeated.

"First," Renno said, "you have performed a miracle to find us. How did you do it?"

"I had great difficulty," Nondaga admitted. "Had I not known that a large body of men was moving, I would never have seen the sign you left."

Renno nodded, somewhat reassured. It was true that a man who knew what he was looking for was more likely to find it.

"I smelled the sweat of many warriors," Nondaga continued. "I was far to the south, and the scent came on the wind."

Renno nodded. He had used the same technique himself to locate both friend and enemy. He would see to it that all the men washed thoroughly in the next stream they came to.

"Your message . . ." Renno said.

"It is of great sadness," Nondaga began.

Roy Johnson moaned low in his throat when Nondaga reached the crucial part, telling Renno that Emily had drowned in a flood-swollen river. The words seem to wash over Renno's head. He heard them, but they seemed to have no impact. He turned away and looked up at the early-morning sky. She could not be dead, he told himself. If she were dead, there would have been some sign, some message to him from the manitous. He felt no emptiness in him, no feeling of despair as he would have felt if Emily were dead.

His first impulse was to strike out toward the east, to run until he had reached the point of his wife's disappearance. But he had his duty. He estimated that they were within two days' march of the river now. His desperate need to go and find his wife had to wait until his duty had been done.

"We will not give up hope," Roy Johnson said to him when they were alone, the rest of the group either sleeping or trying to sleep. "She wouldn't drown. I taught her to swim when she was four years old."

"Wake the men," Renno said, unable to speak of it, even to the father of his wife, a good friend. "We will have an early start."

An hour after dawn, the party was moving single file through a dense wood. The dew of morning glistened on every twig, every sprig of grass, and every leaf. A jay scolded them harshly from the safety of a low limb. A fox had left sign in the dewy grass, and a late-ranging raccoon, surprised by the silent approach of the lead scout, ran up a tree and peered out in masked curiosity from behind the bole.

Renno set a fast pace. The country had been changing rapidly. They had to seek concealment in scattered copses or in the beds of streams, for the land was flat, and in places, one could see for a mile or more across grassy expanses. Renno had wanted to reach the big river at a site well to the north of Chickasaw Bluffs, for no Cherokee or Seneca had penetrated so deeply into enemy territory, and he knew that there would be a concentration of Chickasaw around the bluffs. The riverside thickets gave Renno's party concealment, and then he was seeing for the first time the Father of Waters, the Mississippi. It was in flood and extended from the high ground on the eastern side into the distance, having pushed muddy brown water over the flatlands on the far side. Renno was glad that it would not be necessary to cross it.

They rested in the security of the river thickets. Once a Chickasaw warrior was seen paddling down the river in a dugout canoe. El-i-chi, his blood heated by the peril of being so far from home, so deep within the lands of the Chickasaw, suggested that the man in the canoe be captured for questioning. Renno merely shook his head. But as it turned out, a prisoner was taken. When two Cherokee warriors came up from the bank of the river half dragging a ragged apparition in tattered buckskins in the clear style of the Chickasaw, Renno was displeased; the man should have been killed and hidden quickly. The white Indian soon saw, however, why Rusog's warriors had not killed the man: he was maddened by the spirits. The prisoner's clothing, ripped to the waist, showed ribs. He was undernourished and gaunt. The Chickasaw's hair was a long matted mass, with mud and burrs tangled into it. As he was dragged to be thrown to the ground at Renno's feet, he laughed wildly.

"He was digging in the mud and eating shellfish," one of the Cherokee said. He pointed to his forehead and shook his head.

"Stand up," Renno told the ragged Indian, who, laughing, looking around, totally unaware of his danger, stood, and reached out a dirty finger to touch Renno's musket.

"Pretty," the simpleton said.

"You are Chickasaw?" Renno asked.

The simpleton drew himself up, squared his shoulders. "I am the great chief," he said sincerely.

"Greetings, Great Chief," Renno said. "We are friends."

"All are my friends," the simpleton said with a bubbling laugh.

"You live there?" Renno asked, pointing downriver toward the bluffs.

"I live in chief's house."

"Do you have many warriors?"

"As many as the raindrops."

"Are you hungry?"

The simpleton laughed and looked around. El-i-chi, on cue, handed him a hunk of pemmican. The simpleton tore into the food with blackened and broken teeth, laughing all the while.

"Are there white men there?" Renno asked.

The simpleton stopped chewing, narrowed his eyes cunningly. "Many paleskins. Many boom-sticks, big, blow fire, and whole world trembles."

Roy Johnson's eyes narrowed. "Cannon?" he whispered to Renno.

"With this one, who knows?" Renno said. "How big boom-sticks?"

"As big as man's thigh," the simpleton responded. "And they walk on round legs."

"Fieldpieces," Johnson said, shaking his head.

"How many boom-sticks?" Renno asked.

"Many and many."

"Show me," Renno said, holding up his fingers.

The simpleton held up a hand and began to concentrate with a serious, almost pained expression. "Will you give me more food?"

"When you have talked."

"This many," the simpleton said, holding up four, then five fingers.

"How many paleskins?" Roy Johnson asked.

The simpleton looked at Johnson. "Many and many, with huge four-legged beasts sprouting from their bottoms. They carry big, sharp sticks. Go stick, stick." The simpleton lunged, pushing an imaginary lance toward Renno. "Monsters breathe fire on cold mornings. Fire and smoke. They go fast, like wind. With me as great chief, they will kill all the world."

"Can we believe him?" Johnson asked after Renno had sent the simpleton away with two warriors.

"He's talking about mounted lancers and cannon," Renno said.

"And fieldpieces. Probably horse-drawn," the colonel said.

"I will see for myself," Renno said, turning away to prevent any discussion.

The simpleton had been thrust down onto the ground by two disgusted Cherokee warriors, who were now sorry they had captured him. No Indian would kill a man who had been maddened by the spirits, so the simpleton was quite safe, but he was also a problem—he would babble what he had seen to anyone he encountered, so he would have to be kept prisoner until Renno's band was well on the way back to Cherokee lands. Those who had captured him at the river's bank had been given the man as their responsibility. Both men were surprised when Renno strode up, razor-keen stiletto in hand, looking as if he had all intentions of scalping the simpleton alive. Instead, he cut off the simpleton's long, filthy hair as near to the scalp as he could place the blade; then he ordered the simpleton to take off his tattered, dirty buckskins.

Renno himself donned the ragged clothing and put the wet, muddy, bedraggled Chickasaw moccasins on his feet. The lank and filthy hair of the simpleton was tied and braided onto his own hair, but Renno still did not look like a simpleton until he slumped his shoulders, let his arms dangle, and laughed the simpleton's demented laugh. Johnson alternately chuckled and grimaced in revulsion at the effect.

It was late in the afternoon when Renno started walking south toward Chickasaw Bluffs. He made his way openly, stooped, occasionally stopping to stare and laugh at some particular flower or weed, his eyes always seeking ahead for possible danger. He had left behind all his weapons save the stiletto, which was concealed under the ragged buckskin shirt. At the end of an hour's rambling walk he could see the lodge houses of the Chickasaw on the high bluff and, behind them, directly on the bluff, a partially built log stockade. As he neared a small grouping of lodges, a few young boys, naked in the spring warmth, began to trail him, now and then throwing mud balls and pebbles and laughing as the madman danced and howled in frustration when he was hit. A plump Chickasaw matron came to the door of her lodge and spoke sharply to the tormenting boys, who, with hoots and insults, ran away, leaving Renno to amble, arms hanging loosely, through the scattered lodges until he had an unobstructed view of a cleared field and the uncompleted stockade across it.

There were no adult Chickasaw men visible. He saw, in the near distance, a large lodge, large enough and fine enough to be the home of a chief. He avoided the big lodge and made his way closer to the stockade, where swarthy white men were hoisting a huge log into place. Through a gap in the unfinished outer ring of the stockade, he saw a smart-looking group of horsemen drilling in a square. At the four corners of the square sat small but deadly looking field cannon.

The horsemen, wearing a type of chest armor and helmet that Renno had never seen before, carried long lances, large swords, and pistols. They were quite impressive as they wheeled their animals in formation on the parade ground to the barked orders of a brightly uniformed officer.

Renno had seen enough. He had amassed more information than there appeared on the surface. He felt, for example, that the absence of adult warriors near the bluffs could mean one of two things: the

Chickasaw warriors were either hunting or were marching as a war party. He doubted that there had been time to prepare for a full-scale war, but the thought of a large Chickasaw war party roaming in the western areas of the Cherokee lands made him uneasy. He began to make his shambling way out of the area but was halted by the sharp voice of the same plump matron who had rescued him from the teasing of the small boys.

"Here, dummy," the woman called.

Renno looked her way and laughed.

"You, come here," the woman ordered.

Renno looked around. There was no warrior visible anywhere, only a couple of younger adolescents practicing with tomahawks, and not too skillfully. He considered ignoring the woman but chose to obey her summons.

When he was a few feet from the doorway of the woman's lodge, she threw a section of deer ribs toward him. Renno let the bones fall into the dust.

"Well, you'll just have to eat them dirt and all," the woman said. "Because that's all you're getting from me." She stood, watching expectantly. Renno had no choice but to stoop, laughing wildly, and pick up the well-gnawed bones out of the dirt. There were some small pieces of meat clinging to the ribs, and under the watchful eye of the woman, he pretended to tear at them with his teeth, laughing all the while, and then he turned to run, as if he feared that the woman would change her mind and demand her meat back. When he was out of sight, he tossed the bones aside with disgust and quickened his pace.

"Everything the simpleton said is true," he reported to Roy Johnson when he returned to their hiding place. "I saw fifty-four lancers and four field guns." He described the armor and weapons of the lancers.

The colonel let out a low whistle. "They're Spanish, all right," he said.

"And they mean to stay," Renno told him. "The fort they're building, defended by the cannon, could hold off almost any attack, including one from the Chickasaw themselves. The warriors are in the field. I saw not one in the village."

"I guess you got what we came for," Johnson said.

Renno's job was done. Now his heart was elsewhere. He wanted to leave the scouting party in El-i-chi's command and find Emily. He almost said as much, but he remained silent. Somewhere, most probably between his men and the boundaries of Cherokee lands, was a large body of Chickasaw warriors, so he had to stay with his men until they were back on Cherokee land. He could not yet follow his heart. He had to continue to rely on his faith that Emily was not dead, that if so important a part of his life had ceased to be, he would somehow have known.

"At darkness," he said, "we will begin our journey home."

Chapter V

The Cherokee and Seneca scouting party was able to move at a swift pace as they put their faces toward the morning sun after a short sleep. The location of Chickasaw dwellings was known, so the only danger of discovery would come from hunting parties or some lone Chickasaw exercising his need to stretch his legs and enjoy the freedom of movement in the thickly populated area.

The Chickasaw simpleton was at first a problem—he had no concept of danger and therefore saw no need to be silent. Silence was far from his nature. The flight of a bird, the sudden appearance of a wild-flower, a cool breeze on his face, everything was cause for bubbling laughter.

"Maybe we should all be simple," Roy Johnson said. "At least we'd have no worries and be as happy as Crazy Fox."

The simpleton, each time he had been asked his name, had insisted that he was the great war chief Oklawahpa. The name that eventually stuck, Crazy Fox, had been applied by Johnson, who, seeing the skill with which the simpleton coaxed food out of the men, had said, "He's crazy, but when it comes to begging food, he's crazy like a fox."

"His laughter will bring down the Chickasaw on us," El-i-chi had complained.

Still, it was bad medicine to harm or kill a man who had been demented by the spirits. If they left Crazy Fox behind, he would probably begin describing his new friends to the first Chickasaw he encountered, so the only choice was to take him along. The problem of keeping him silent was ultimately solved by Renno. He selected a smooth, colorful pebble about the size of the ball of his thumb from the bed of a stream and showed it to Crazy Fox, pretending to be in awe of the pebble.

"This is the sacred stone of the manitous," he told Crazy Fox, his face serious. "It must be guarded with love and great care. It must be kept warm and wet, and so we carry this sacred stone here." He popped the pebble into his mouth. "The sacred stone can be removed only to eat or drink," he said, "otherwise bad, bad medicine."

Crazy Fox was fascinated. He was allowed to handle the pebble, and he turned it over and over in his hand, his eyes wide in awe.

"Since you are brave, Great Chief," Renno continued, "we have selected you for the honor of guarding the stone."

Crazy Fox's eyes were still wide when Renno carefully inserted the pebble into his mouth with stern instructions that Crazy Fox's mouth must not be opened until the party halted for food and rest. Crazy Fox, of course, had a couple of accidents, laughing once at the flight of a rabbit, and another time, for no apparent reason, spewing the pebble out of his mouth. This prompted Renno, who had been running behind Crazy Fox, to lay the flat of his tomahawk strongly against the madman's skinny rump and to warn him that if he forgot once more, the manitous would flay the living skin from his bones and eat it. As a positive reinforcement, Renno took a musket from one of the younger warriors, unloaded it, and allowed Crazy Fox to carry it. Thus, entrusted with guarding the sacred stone of the manitous and looking, in his imagination, very much the warrior, Crazy Fox ran with them silently.

Once away from the most dense areas of Chickasaw population, Renno put Se-quo-i to work hunting small game with his blowgun, and, in the depths of a small wooded glen, allowed fires. For the first time in many days, they enjoyed the taste of cooked rabbit and squirrel meat.

Renno's excellent memory for landscape features and sign told him that they were nearing the area where they would have to skirt a Chickasaw village. They were traveling twice as fast as they had on their way to the Father of Waters, and within three days they would be at the unmarked boundaries of Cherokee land.

El-i-chi was acting as one of the scouts when the party started the day's travel that would take them past the last concentration of Chickasaw lodgings. Renno had told El-i-chi to veer toward the scattered village to check for the presence of warriors. He was still concerned by the fact that there had been no warriors present at Chickasaw Bluffs.

As it happened, El-i-chi and one of the Cherokee, who had been scouting ahead, arrived at an appointed rendezvous point at almost the same time, each with reports that ruined Renno's plan to leave the party under El-i-chi's leadership that very day and run ahead.

"Many warriors," the Cherokee said, waving his hand toward the west. "They have traveled far and are resting."

"Have they come from the east?" Renno asked.

"Yes. Those I could see carried no scalps."

"Twenty warriors marched into the village as I watched," El-i-chi said. "They were greeted happily by the women and children."

"The warriors ahead of us," Renno asked the Cherokee, "how far to the north must we travel to avoid them?"

"Far. Very far. I saw two hunting parties move toward the north," the Cherokee said. "There was sign of more hunting parties to the south."

Renno mused. He had come too far and the information he carried was too important to risk discovery and an uneven battle.

"There are no more than a hundred," the Cherokee added. "If we take them by surprise at the fall of darkness, we can count much coup."

El-i-chi silently raised his tomahawk, agreeing with the Cherokee warrior. All the men had obeyed orders well, but there had been times, Renno knew, when their blood had run hot with the desire to fight instead of run to avoid the Chickasaw.

It was not in Renno's nature to avoid an enemy, but he was the war chief. The decision was his responsibility. True, his men could kill more than their own numbers, and those who died would have honorable deaths, and their bravery would be sung around the fires for a long, long time. But there was more at stake than one battle; there was more at stake than honor. Both he and Roy Johnson were sorely concerned about the Spanish presence on the Mississippi River, and both understood that the entire Cherokee nation and the fledgling state of Franklin were at peril.

And yet, Renno considered, perhaps there was a way to be a Seneca, a man, to have honor, without losing all the brave young warriors in a hopelessly outnumbered battle. Renno's eyes flashed. He drew himself up to his full height.

"It is my thinking," he mused, with El-i-chi and the Cherokee warrior listening intently, alerted by the change of Renno's stance, "that we must give the enemy a demonstration that he is planning war against a great people, and not against hapless hoe farmers."

El-i-chi opened his mouth in a silent whoop of delight and did a little war dance. Then, at his brother's request, he called all the men together.

"We will accomplish two purposes," Renno said to the gathering. "First, we will show that the intended victim of the Spanish-Chickasaw conspiracy has teeth. Second we will pull the large force of warriors that lies across our path together, into one group, so we may travel around them."

Once the decision was made, only a minimum of coordination and planning was needed. The Cherokee and Seneca warriors were more than ready and would fight with all their weapons and provisions with them, so that a night march could begin immediately after they had struck.

The village selected for the raid was a typical Chickasaw settlement. That ever-present Chickasaw urge for privacy had prompted those Indians to build their twenty-plus lodges along the east bank of a small stream, and the buildings were strung out over a distance of more than half a mile. Renno's men spent the late afternoon getting into position, moving with great care, slipping by pairs into concealment in a half-circle around the widely spaced Chickasaw village.

A celebration was going on in the village square in front of a large lodge, obviously the council house. The population of the entire village seemed to be there. Warriors—either just returned from some sort of expedition with the large band of Chickasaw camped to the east or preparing to rejoin the main group—were the center of adoration by the village's women and children. Drums pounded as darkness became total. The proud Chickasaw warriors displayed their weapons and might in a war dance around a huge fire.

According to Renno's instructions, his force began to consolidate their positions with the advent of darkness, drawing in the flanks. The Chickasaw, Renno noted, felt so secure, that they had not put out guards. Now several fires in the compound were flaring high, and the flames cast bizarre flickering shadows across the clearing. Silently he motioned to El-i-chi, who took ten of the warriors and moved to the south, to attack from the left.

Renno was pleased to see that the Chickasaw warriors were drinking heavily from pots of what obviously was corn beer. He was sure that he and his warriors could best the Chickasaw, drunk or sober, but sheer numbers gave the advantage to the Chickasaw. Renno's wish was to deal destruction while losing no one from his own force, and drunkenness on the part of the Chickasaw warriors would contribute to that goal.

He waited. There were no sounds from his well-disciplined force behind him, but he could feel their eagerness, their impatience. The simpleton was still silent, guarding the sacred stone in his mouth, and Renno had appointed a warrior to watch over him and keep him out of the battle.

When, after a tense wait of over an hour, Renno gave a soft owl hoot and turned to see his half of the force ready, arrows strung, he moved forward.

Deadly arrows shot out of the blackness of the night without warning to the Chickasaw. The Chickasaw warriors who died instantly, arrows in their hearts, never realized that they were under attack. The others, having survived the attack's first wave, seized weapons in deadly silence as the Seneca and Cherokee forces broke into the village compound from the north and south.

Chickasaw women and children fled in different directions, a few of them screaming as Renno led his men in the charge. His tomahawk flashed in the firelight, and the first Chickasaw warrior died without a sound. The remaining Chickasaw warriors screamed war whoops. Their numbers already severely diminished, they met the attack bravely, with knife and tomahawk, only to be cut down by the oncoming Cherokee and Seneca.

Renno caught a glimpse of Rusog, his face grim and terrible as he lashed out with a backhand blow to slash the throat of a charging Chickasaw, even as Rusog's first victim was falling with a crushed skull. He heard a shrill whoop from El-i-chi, warning him—a Chickasaw warrior was leaping toward him, tomahawk raised, and Renno let the Spanish stiletto fly, saw it sink to the hilt in the Chickasaw's throat. Then he turned, leaped, and slashed with his bloody tomahawk at yet another warrior.

It took only minutes.

There was a great silence. At his side a Seneca stood poised on the balls of his feet, looking for other opposition, tomahawk ready. Some of the men were already scalping the fallen enemy. A woman's weeping came from the darkness beyond the glow of the fire. As he quickly retrieved the stiletto, Renno reflected that it was time to finish the job and depart, but he would not deprive the men of their rights. He allowed a time for the victors to claim their spoils in the form of Chickasaw scalps.

"El-i-chi, Rusog," he said, motioning with his hand that it was time for them to set fire to the lodges.

He heard splashing in the nearby stream. The women and children were fleeing, running west across the creek. Rusog called out to his men, who began to light torches from the blazing fires and run toward the Chickasaw dwellings, making tails of flames in the night as they moved. First one lodge and then another smoked, flared, and began to blaze. Renno knew that the flame-lighted sky would surely be noticed by the large Chickasaw body and would draw them here.

El-i-chi, leading his assigned group to fire the lodges to the east, ran swiftly to the last lodge, leaving the others to be burned by his men. When he reached the lodge, he approached the doorway carefully. He stood for a moment in silence and heard the sobbing of a small child.

"Come out," he ordered, "and go with the others."

He waited for a moment. There was still a muffled sound of sobbing from inside. He put his head into the darkness. The glow of a fire had been reduced to a few embers, so the interior of the lodge was in shadow. He saw a dark mass on a sleep shelf and moved toward it quickly, his left hand extended and right hand ready with his tomahawk. His hand encountered the arm of a small child.

"You will not be hurt," he said gently. "Come, run to join the others. They are across the stream."

His concern for the child almost cost him his life. From out of the darkness there flashed a tomahawk that he sensed rather than saw, so he instinctively ducked and felt the sharp blade brush his scalp lock. He struck out with his tomahawk, and the blade became embedded in a wooden pole in the lodge's wall, wrenching itself from his hand. He reached for his knife, falling back, just as a dark form launched forward toward him from the darkness. El-i-chi caught the arm swinging the tomahawk and twisted. Their bodies collided and fell to the floor, El-i-chi grappling with the attacker who had come so close to killing him.

The attacker was small but wiry, possessed of the strength of desperation. They rolled, and El-i-chi heard a gasp of pain as they tumbled across the smoldering fire, the attacker's buckskin-clad back crushed down into the embers, and then they were clear, rolling toward the doorway as El-i-chi used all his strength to wrest the tomahawk from the attacker's hand.

As he reached for his knife, the attacker broke free and plunged out the doorway, with El-i-chi leaping in pursuit. The attacker pivoted, and El-i-chi saw the gleam of a knife blade. He charged to the attack, slashing upward toward the enemy's belly, but his blow was countered, metal clinking against metal. El-i-chi's greater strength prevailed, and the enemy's knife was knocked away. The attacker, now unarmed, turned to run, and El-i-chi had to extend himself to catch him, throwing his weight on the enemy's shoulders so that they both smashed to the ground. After a short trial of strength, El-i-chi sat astride the Chickasaw, his knife raised. From a few yards away the glow of light from a burning lodge showed him a sight that halted the downward plunge of his knife. The buckskin shirt of the attacker had been torn open during the struggle to reveal a pair of perfect breasts. Then he saw the girl's face, a thing of wonder, of great beauty, made even more impressive by the hatred that contorted it, by her flashing black eyes.

"I do not make war on women," El-i-chi said, disengaging himself, rising. The girl leaped to her feet, poised for flight. "Go," he said, sheathing his knife. "Take the child with you."

Instead of moving to the door of the lodge to get the child, the girl leaped toward El-i-chi, and her onslaught bore him to the ground, where he was quickly punished by flying fingernails that left red grooves on his face, and by a set of strong white teeth that clamped onto his forearm and brought blood gushing.

"*Aiiiieee,*" he groaned as the pain of the bite hit him. The girl seemed intent on tearing off a section of flesh, so he slammed his fist into her forehead. Pain shot through his hand and arm. It seemed that he had broken his hand, but the girl slumped loosely atop him, her teeth giving up their hold on the flesh of his arm.

He left her lying there and went inside to thrust

the weeping small child from the lodge, then picked up his guttering torch, fired the walls of the lodge, and stood, torch in hand, over the unconscious girl. Her firm, perfect breasts were exposed. Her lithe, long legs were sprawled. Her face, in relaxation, caused a hard drive of sheer desire in El-i-chi's loins. For a long time now he had been feeling the urgings of nature. Indeed, he had been examining the nubile girls of both the Cherokee and Seneca villages with heated interest, but never had he felt as he felt now, standing over the Chickasaw girl and, in the light of the burning lodges, examining those exposed and beautiful breasts, the classic face, the strength and symmetry of her legs.

He heard Renno hooting the signal to move. He licked his lips in momentary indecision. Then, with a nod to himself, he bent, used a rawhide thong from his belt to lash the girl's hands and feet, lifted her with a grunt, and threw her over his shoulder.

For hours, until well past midnight, Renno set a fast pace. His warriors had tasted blood, had counted coup, had collected scalps, and now it was time to return home to their own village. His scout caught up with the main body to confirm that Renno's plan had worked, that the large Chickasaw force was rushing toward the burning village. The way home for the Seneca and Cherokee had been cleared of enemy.

Even though Renno was not running from an enemy, he felt the urge to give the Chickasaw force his face, and not his back. He was running toward something far more important than killing a few Chickasaw— to plan for the war that quite obviously loomed and to give Roy Johnson time to get the news to the white settlers and seek help from the United States, if that were possible. And it was time for Renno to leave the band in El-i-chi's charge and run ahead at top speed to confirm his gut feeling that his wife was still alive.

After midnight, with many miles put between his men and any possible pursuit—the Chickasaw would be unable to track the group with any speed in darkness—Renno slowed the pace and called Roy Johnson forward to explain his intention to find Emily.

He had not yet had time to check if his group had sustained casualties, so he made his way back down the still-moving line of men, counting and calling names. All were there. Three men, two Cherokee and one Seneca, had taken wounds of honor, but none serious enough to slow them on the journey home. All were accounted for, except El-i-chi, but Renno waited on the dark trail. At last he heard his brother's breathing as he approached. It occurred to Renno that El-i-chi was breathing very hard and feared for a moment that he had been severely wounded. When he saw the bulk at El-i-chi's shoulders, he signaled his presence with a soft hoot, then stepped out of the darkness.

"Who is this?" Renno asked, gesturing at the body, knowing that he had counted all the men present in line ahead of El-i-chi.

"A woman," El-i-chi said.

Renno was silenced with sheer disbelief. Soon a hundred Chickasaw warriors would be on their trail, and his brother was acting as if he had been on an ordinary raid with time to take prisoners.

"I want her," El-i-chi said flatly. "She fought me as fiercely as any warrior would have fought."

"We make no war on women," Renno said, "but if they fight as warriors, they must die as warriors." He reached out, jerked the woman from El-i-chi's shoulders, and tumbled her to the ground. "I will do it," he said, pulling his stiletto.

"I want her, brother," El-i-chi said defiantly, putting a staying hand on Renno's arm.

A late moon gave enough light for Renno to see that the girl's eyes were open.

"There is only one other possibility," Renno went on, ignoring what his brother had said. "Release her. Let her take back a message from the Cherokee and Seneca, that the Chickasaw will be attacking a force that is completely ready should they decide to make war on us."

"I want her," El-i-chi repeated.

"Chickasaw women make poor slaves," Renno said.

"She will not slow me, Brother," El-i-chi said, a note of pleading in his voice. "Never before have I seen a woman that I wanted."

"I need you to run ahead. You will be in charge."

"I will set the pace," El-i-chi said.

"Not if you have to carry this one."

El-i-chi lifted the girl to her feet, helped her to balance on her hobbled feet. "You have heard my war chief," he said. "I give you a choice. I will kill you now, or you will run with us, keep up with us, and not try to escape."

"Kill me, then," the girl countered, looking at them defiantly.

Renno lifted his stiletto.

"Wait!" El-i-chi said. "Leave her to me."

"Then you have decided to forfeit the lead," Renno said. "You will obey Rusog's orders."

"So be it," El-i-chi replied with a sinking heart. For the girl, he had given up his chance to lead a war party, and for a moment, as he leaned to cut the lashing at her feet, he hated her. He jerked her arms roughly as he untied them and retied them tightly in front of her. He secured a leash around her waist. "You will run ahead of me," he said. "I do not think you want to die. If you are slow, I will encourage you, thus." He stabbed his knife into the girl's buttock, not quite deeply enough to penetrate the buckskin of her skirt.

"At my first opportunity I will kill you in your sleep," the girl retorted.

"Brother," Renno said with some sadness, not for the girl, but for El-i-chi, "I must leave you now. But think about this. You should not try to bring this girl with you. Kill her and conceal her body so that its presence will not help the Chickasaw to track us. That I am ordering you to do, as your war chief."

"I hear," El-i-chi said.

Renno left his musket, bow, and arrows with his father-in-law. Armed only with tomahawk and stiletto, thus lightening his burden, he quickly gave Rusog instructions to push the men hard, avoid battle, and not to slow the pace until they were well

within Cherokee territory, where other Cherokee
warriors were organized to guard the areas behind
them against Chickasaw incursion.

Renno's heart leaped as he set out. He had far to
go, and long, long days had gone by since Emily's
disappearance. There was much at stake, and yet, as
he ran lightly through the moonlit forests, across
meadows where the morning dew was already forming, he knew hope. The manitous would have put
sadness in his heart if Emily were truly dead.

He did not slow his speed at dawn. He felt a
certain exhilaration. His lungs pumped the cool morning air, and his legs worked smoothly. A red vixen
fox broke from cover and for a minute longer, ran
ahead of him, tail trailing gracefully, and he put on a
burst of speed as if to catch her before she flicked off
the trail and disappeared into the trees.

He ate on the run. His provisions were low, but
he felt no need to ration himself. Instead, he finished
the remainder of the pemmican and corn, paused in
his flight only to drink deeply from a stream, and ran
on.

Superbly conditioned, Renno was affected by the
pace only as the heat of the midday sun came down
on him. The day was warm for spring, and he lost
fluid rapidly through perspiration, but he pressed
on. He knew that a few miles ahead there was a
stream, and he concentrated his thoughts on the
coolness of the water. He would splash into it, cool
himself, and then he would drink as a thirsty horse
drinks before running on.

But his legs seemed to gain weight with each

stride. His thudding heart seemed intent on pounding itself out of his chest cavity. His lungs were fire. Then there was the stream, deep and cool, and he plunged in, surfaced, gasped, and swam to stand neck-deep as he drank, then swam to the other side. There he was tempted to rest. He threw himself down, leaned back against a tree, and filled his lungs with the mild air.

There was no dream, no vision—only a sudden awareness. His head jerked around, but he saw no intruder. The trees, the silent, deep stream, a squirrel chirring territorial claims from a tree on the far bank were all that he saw; yet Renno felt that he was not alone. He envisioned himself running, covering the ground in that long-strided pace, and then the mental image changed appearance slightly, and he sat bolt upright, for the image seemed to be chiding him.

Once, long ago, another Renno, his great-grandfather, had felt as he now felt, spent, exhausted, body aching so much that to run another step seemed impossible, and yet the great Renno had run and run, for days on end, sleeping only briefly, going without food and water for long periods, and he had not fallen, had not quit. The first Renno had endured, had done the impossible, to carry news of great import to the fledgling new nation of America.

Now Renno leaped to his feet. He seemed to have new strength. He ran only for himself, and for the mother of his son, but around him in the very air there seemed to be spirits, the shadows of his ancestors, giving him strength, expanding his lungs, lengthening his legs.

Doubt came to him when he neared the stream where Emily had disappeared. Weeks had passed. The storms and rains of the spring would have washed away any sign. Why did he still feel hope? What could he possibly expect to find that the others had not found?

Near the stream, he took time to feast on freshly ripe wild strawberries and then filled himself with the cool, clear water. He decided to test the stream himself, to ascertain the force of the current, to be able to make an estimate as to where Emily would have been carried after she fell in. The stream was no longer in flood stage, however, so the current was less swift. He had no difficulty in steering his way through the rapids as he let the stream carry him, but he did not chance the falls. He left the stream before it entered the narrow rocky gorge, and stood atop the falls, looking down into the clear, deep pool, hearing the thunder of the cataract as Emily would have heard it if she was swept over it. The fall of water was not more than thirty feet. It would have been quite possible for her to survive such a plunge, for there were no rocks below to be smashed against. The danger would be in having the breath knocked out of her by contact with the water below. But Emily was a sturdy woman—she would have kept her wits about her, and she would have survived a mere fall over the cataract.

He took time to pull a lethargic opossum from a hollow tree, having tracked the animal there, and to roast the greasy meat over the fire. It was the first hot food he had had in a long, long time, and it was good and gave him strength. Usually he scorned the opossum as food, but without musket or bow, he did not want to take time to snare or stalk game.

From Nondaga's descriptions and account of the search, he knew that his people had combed the banks of the stream for several miles. He set off downstream, and as the river widened and slowed, he soon saw that traveling along the bank would be difficult because of dense underbrush and an occasional canebrake. He used his tomahawk to cut the branches from a fallen tree, pushed the log into the water, and clung to it, following the same path that Emily would have followed had she not left the water. He reasoned that she had not been able, for some reason, to get out of the water, because if she had, the skilled trackers among the Seneca and the Cherokee would have seen sign. No. For some reason she had not left the river until she had drifted beyond the point where the search for her was given up.

The river was carrying him toward the southwest, and he knew that it joined a much larger river to the south. Then the big river flowed into Choctaw lands, where the white Indian agent from Virginia had wanted to build a fort. Renno had little intention of following the river that far, knowing that all his hopes were pinned on Emily's having drifted far from the point of her fall, into an uninhabited area. There was also the chance that she had made her way out of the river, to be helped by some friendly Cherokee family living far from the main settlements.

He slept on the shore and the next morning was

walking the riverbank when he saw something that gave him a feeling of emptiness: a sodden, shredded remnant of doeskin was exposed as it waved in the breeze from a dead snag sticking up out of the water near the bank. At the spring flood stage, he estimated, the snag and the doeskin would have been underwater, and the search parties would therefore have missed seeing it.

He waded into chest-deep water and lifted the doeskin from the snag. His heart leaped, and then he knew deep sorrow, for he recognized the beadwork; his mother had taught Emily how to make that particular pattern, a family trademark, so he knew without doubt that he had found a piece of Emily's doeskin dress. But he still did not feel the emptiness he was sure he would know if she were dead.

Renno surveyed the area. The river was friendly now, its banks low. Even with waning strength, Emily would have been able to climb out of the water. He searched the surrounding countryside and found it to be still, empty, and beautiful. He estimated that he was not more than two days' travel from that undefined area that separated Cherokee and Chickasaw lands. He searched every woodland, every little glen, taking time to kill and eat small game, spending the evenings in persistent and patient prayer to the manitous. And yet there was no answer, no vision, no dream to encourage him.

Under happier circumstances he would have enjoyed his search, for he traveled across new lands, felt the peace and wonder of the wilderness, saw the conflux of the stream into which Emily had fallen and the big river that ran southward into Chocktaw lands.

The days went by, and his sense of duty began to intrude onto his own desperate desire to continue the search. With no sign, no vision, it was as if the manitous were telling him that the answer was too simple to need reinforcement from them: Emily was dead. He admitted that at the end of yet another day's search, and alone, with no fire, he sat motionless, his face smeared with black mud, and began a fast of mourning. In that time, as he sat without moving, as he prayed for a vision, he made his last good-byes to the good and lovely woman who had been his wife and the mother of his beloved son.

Try as he might, El-i-chi could not bring himself to kill the Chickasaw girl. True to her word, she tried to escape twice, and once she came close to smashing out his brains with a strong fallen tree limb. Once he lashed her rear end with a leather strap. She made no sound of pain or protest, merely staring at him with hatred from her beautiful dark eyes.

Rusog, himself not too long removed from the impetuosity of youth, understood El-i-chi's obsession with the Chickasaw maiden and made no attempt to prevent him from keeping the girl. Rusog reasoned that the Seneca women would beat the rebelliousness out of her once she had been turned over to them.

At first the girl refused to eat.

"How can you kill men if you starve yourself to

death?" El-i-chi chided. With a baleful look, she seized a piece of meat and gnawed it with a fierceness that merely increased El-i-chi's admiration for her. Never had he seen a woman with such courage and fire, except, perhaps, his sister, Ena. That was it, he realized. This girl reminded him of his sister, who fought as a warrior, just as this Chickasaw had fought him. That was it! His sister had set such an example, that beside her all the conventional Cherokee and Seneca maidens paled. Now he had finally found a girl like Ena, and he was determined to keep her.

"I will kill any woman who tries to make me a slave," she told him one evening when the party was not far from home and it was safe to kill game and cook over the open fires.

"You have shown your courage and your loyalty to your tribe," El-i-chi said. "It is now time for you to face facts. I have taken you. True, I can make you a slave, but if you cooperate, that will not be necessary."

"What you propose sickens me, to lie with the killer of my brothers and my people," she hissed.

"It is also time to know your name," he said. "Or shall I give you a name?"

"I have a name," she said.

"Give it to me, then, or I will call you Wildcat."

"My name is Holani."

"I like that name. What does it mean?"

"Since the great Seneca warrior thinks he knows all else, let him guess."

"I will say that it means 'beautiful,' " El-i-chi said. The raiding party reached home without further incident, with Holani's spirit intact. The victorious warriors were welcomed with joy. Crazy Fox was greeted with understanding and assured that he would receive food and shelter and have a place in the tribe.

Roy Johnson immediately saddled his horse to make the trip to Knoxville. But first he held his motherless grandson in his arms until, with agitated squirms, Little Hawk made it known that he would prefer to be crawling on the blankets.

Holani was turned over to the younger women and was to be housed, under guard by the women, in the young women's house. El-i-chi warned Ena to have a close watch put on the girl and to allow her no weapons.

There was an incident immediately as the wildcat attacked four young Seneca women and gave a good account of herself until reinforcements arrived to bear her to the ground. At that point Ah-wen-ga herself became involved. By the sick-calf look on her grandson's face, she had realized that this Chickasaw maiden was not intended by El-i-chi to be a mere slave. She went to the women's house, where Holani was lying on a sleep shelf, her face bruised, her pride intact.

"I am Ah-wen-ga."

Holani realized immediately that she was in the presence of a great woman. She sat up and gazed at Ah-wen-ga with a look that was not totally disrespectful.

"We will have no more of this foolishness," Ah-wen-ga said flatly. "If you persist in attacking and harming my people, I personally will lash you to the post, light a fire at your feet, and watch you roast very, very slowly while the women flay you. Do you understand?"

"I understand," Holàni said quietly.

"I am going to be very frank with you, Chickasaw," Ah-wen-ga continued. "You have been brought to our village at a bad time, when our men must prepare for war because of the actions of your people in alliance with the Spanish. I am growing old, and my patience is short. I am saddened by the loss of one grandson's wife and am not happy with the idea of my other grandson taking a Chickasaw as his wife. Yet I will not interfere with El-i-chi's desires if you can summon your senses. You have an opportunity that makes you the envy of every marriageable maiden in this village and many more in the Cherokee nation, for El-i-chi is a fine young man and strong warrior with the blood of greatness in him. If you do not have sense enough to see this, then we will not keep you alive, for we need no slaves. It has been a long time since our women have been treated to a full festival of death. Will you consider your alternatives—a good life, I suspect, with a man destined to be a great chief and a great warrior, or the object of the ingenuity of the women for giving pain. That is the last I will say. The rest is up to you."

Holani was silent, but she was obviously impressed.

Chapter VI

Roy Johnson had refused to allow El-i-chi and Rusog to send warriors to accompany him to Knoxville. He rode fast and hard, a man with a purpose, and he experienced terrible feelings of dread and doubt. He had to tell his wife about Emily's disappearance, and he was also very concerned about the information gleaned from the scouting expedition. Spain was an old and still-powerful nation in spite of her reverses at the hands of the English. She held vast territories in Florida, Louisiana, and the Southwest. If she could indeed hold together an alliance of the most populous tribes in the Southeast, Spain had the resources to occupy as much territory along the Mississippi River as her greed dictated.

Back in Knoxville, Johnson found his wife to be in much better health. He was grateful for her renewed strength, for it was up to him to break the news to her that Emily was missing. They took comfort in the knowledge that Renno was searching for her, certain that she had not drowned. Nora and Roy Johnson decided to follow their son-in-law's lead by remaining hopeful, not grieving unless they had proof positive that their daughter was dead.

The next morning, to the colonel's surprise and pleasure, he found that the tinker who had translated the treaty from Spanish to English had made a return trip to Knoxville, the man having become enamored of a well-to-do widow on his last visit. Johnson's fears for the future were fed new fuel as he listened to the tinker read the paper that Renno had found in the hilt of the stiletto.

"Colonel," the tinker said, "it's a private message from Baron de Carondelet, the Spanish governor, to Oklawahpa. The governor spells out what he'll do for Oklawahpa and the Chickasaw if they'll fight with a soldier named Guy de Rojas and follow his orders. The governor promises Oklawahpa many muskets, fine weapons of steel, and beautiful gifts for his men and women. He says that the Spanish will send men on horseback and many cannon. And he promises that once the Cherokee and the white intruders have been driven from the land west of the Smoky Mountains, that land will be Chickasaw forever, as long as grass grows and water flows."

The stiletto paper was a specific spelling-out of Spanish intent, and Roy Johnson was worried. He largely dismissed a section at the bottom of the brief message as being ridiculous, for Baron de Carondelet said that fourteen thousand Choctaw warriors were now allied with Spain and would come to the aid of the Chickasaw if needed. Perhaps the Spanish governor was purposely exaggerating the number of Choctaw warriors available to Oklawahpa—a thinly veiled threat that if the Chickasaw did not sign and abide by the treaty, the Spanish would send overwhelming numbers of Choctaw into the disputed area to keep Oklawahpa in line. Johnson knew that the Choctaw could field no more than five thousand warriors in an all-out effort.

Johnson was actually less concerned about a threat from the Choctaw than the immediate and real threat of the Chickasaw, who were among the finest fighting men in America, with a long tradition of warfare. And he knew, too, that only one fighting force stood between the white settlements just west of the mountains and Oklawahpa's eager warriors: the Seneca and Cherokee were the only allies from whom the settlers could expect any help.

Johnson had no doubt that Renno and Rusog would fight to defend their homes and their hunting grounds. But how many white men would leave home to help defend Cherokee and Seneca land was a question. He would have to handle the situation carefully, making certain that everyone understood that the

Spanish-Chickasaw-Choctaw-Creek alliance was con-
ceived to swallow not just Indian land but also the
entire area west of the mountains.

He had much to do. Governor John Sevier of
Franklin had been keeping a close eye on the situation and sent for Johnson, to learn what had been
discovered on the scouting trip to the Mississippi
River. Sevier quickly agreed that the situation was
desperate and that time was running out. Letters
were immediately dispatched to the proper authorities in Virginia, North Carolina, and Georgia, enclosing copies of the stiletto paper and begging that
those states quickly send help to fight the invasion
force. Both Johnson and Sevier agreed that there was
little hope of any troops being sent by the established states, which were plagued by their own problems. The citizens of Franklin and the frontier and
their Indian friends were on their own.

Sevier also authorized Colonel Johnson to recruit
temporary members of the Frontier Regiment and to
ready it for action. Johnson sprang into action, and
the regiment was already drilling when he left once
again, bound for Renno's village. The regiment would
be ready to follow him in a matter of days.

Renno, having experienced his sorrow in private
mourning in the wilderness, had returned. Outwardly
he was the same; only he knew the weight of the
grief in his breast, the terrible feeling of emptiness
that had continued to grow from that first moment
when he had admitted to himself that Emily was
dead.

In council with the Seneca and Cherokee leaders, he suggested that messengers be sent to the outlying Cherokee settlements to warn of the threat from the Chickasaw. In that way, all warriors would be prepared for the call to gather into one unified force.

Renno had been back in the village for a full day and was having the evening meal in his mother's house, his little son lying at his side, when he first learned that El-i-chi had disobeyed his order and had brought the Chickasaw maiden alive to the village. When he heard this news, he stopped eating and leaped to his feet in quick anger.

"My son," Toshabe said gently, "he is young, and he has been stricken by love."

Renno's anger faded. "She has not succeeded in killing him, then?"

Toshabe smiled. "Let me say only that it is an odd courtship."

Renno had been expecting Roy Johnson when he arrived, his horse lathered, his clothing dusty. Renno was forced to admit that his search for Emily had been futile and that he had accepted her death. The color drained from Roy Johnson's face, and he cleared his throat as he searched in his pocket for his pipe.

"I don't know what I'll tell Nora," he said sadly, his voice strained. "Thank God we still have a piece of Emily in Little Hawk."

Renno nodded sadly and took his father-in-law's arm. A meeting had been called in the council house, and they were needed there, in spite of their personal sorrow.

Johnson waited to speak only until the ceremonial smoking of the pipes had been completed.

"My friends," he began, "we are all aware that the Spanish have moved to the north, made an alliance with the Chickasaw, and have designs on the lands of both our peoples. I have heard talk from many warriors, saying that the war will be a brief one and that the end result will be the taking of many Spanish and Chickasaw scalps. I beg you, my friends, not to underestimate this threat."

After a moment of silence Loramas spoke. "Our warriors and our Seneca brothers are brave and mighty, true, and yet you speak wisdom, Colonel Johnson. Listen to him, all of you."

"That you will fight for your homes and hunting grounds is beyond doubt," Johnson said. "We, too, will fight, side by side with our Indian brothers."

An approving murmur rose from the senior warriors and leaders.

"I would like to familiarize you with the history of the Spanish here in America," Johnson said. He waited for a moment in silence. "They have built their empire on slavery. In the islands first settled by the Spanish, the native Indian population, helpless against the armor, steel, and guns of the Spanish, was enslaved. Entire nations of Indians perished in Spanish mines on the Caribbean islands. It has been the same wherever the Spanish gain power. Indians, accustomed to living a healthy life in the open air, free to hunt and travel, have been forced to work endless hours in holes in the ground to mine the gold and silver so prized by the Spanish. Great nations far to the southwest, who built huge cities of stone, fared no better against the Spanish than the peaceful Indians of the islands. The great Aztec nation was totally destroyed in a very few short years. It is not that the Spanish are so powerful; it is just that they are greedy and persistent. They feel—and I say this without any intent of blasphemy to the God that I worship, or insult to you, my friends—that God is on their side and that any man who does not agree with their particular brand of religion is a savage and deserves no consideration, that he is, indeed, fit only to be a chattel to them.

"So, my friends, you will be fighting for more than home and hunting ground. The plan of the Spanish is to use other tribes to exterminate all Cherokee warriors and to enslave the women and children. If you doubt this, ask Renno, for as we journeyed to the great river, he saw Spanish slavery in action."

Renno stood. "What he says is true," he affirmed. "The Spanish have cannon on wheels, designed to be pulled by horses. But the cannon were being pulled instead by Indian slaves, seized from some of the less powerful tribes."

"To use a man in the manner of a beast . . ." Wegowa said, with so much feeling, he could not finish.

"If the Chickasaw make an all-out effort, our forces will be outnumbered," Johnson warned.

"That is no matter," said a young and fiery warrior, newly elevated to his position, with a sneering look of contempt for all Chickasaw.

"And," Johnson continued, "the Chickasaw will be

fighting side by side with a squadron of Spanish lancers on horseback. They will have cannon."

"This I fear," Loramas said, "for cannon can reach out and kill before a warrior has a chance to strike."

Johnson bowed toward Loramas. "Exactly, Grand Sachem. Thus, we cannot plan to meet the enemy head-on at a time and place of his choosing. The war chief of the Seneca has discussed certain strategies with me."

Renno looked around. His heart, still heavy with sorrow for the loss of Emily, was filled with concern for his friends' safety. He knew that at his orders they would charge into the guns and lances of the enemy, and he felt that great responsibility. "We have fought against superior numbers before," he said, his voice low. "We have always been victorious. But victory in battle does not come from bravery alone. We will be as cunning as the raven, as sly as the fox, as brave as the wolverine, as far-seeing as the hawk. We will not stand toe-to-toe with our enemy. We will strike swiftly, then disappear."

Around him, some of the younger warriors were beginning to use their flattened palms on the hard earth floor to make the sound of war drums.

"Already the Chickasaw has penetrated the lands of our brothers, the Cherokee," Rusog said.

A low growl came from the younger warriors.

Renno nodded. "My brother is right. Our scouts have been trailing a force of one hundred Chickasaw invaders. So far there has been no attack. The Chickasaw's purpose apparently is to scout the land in preparation for their great attack." Renno paused and looked around, a grim half smile coming to his lips.

"But we already know the land," he said, his voice rising. "We will not wait for our enemy to position his cannon or ready his mounted lancers. *We will strike first!*"

A whoop of joy came from the warriors.

Rusog's eyes glittered with a dangerous light. "Brothers," he said, arms upraised and fists clenched, "my grandfather, Loramas, Grand Sachem of the Cherokee, and my father, Wegowa, speak for the Cherokee. I speak only for myself. And I say we will strike! We will strike with the force of the fire from the sky!"

Hands drummed the war song. Warriors cried out in deep voices.

Rusog drew himself up straight and continued, "In the time of our ancestors this entire land was ours. The great tribes roamed wherever they would, and game was so plentiful that there was enough for all. Then the white man came. He came in small numbers at first, so our forefathers could not know that beyond the great waters the white man was more numerous than the birds of the sky."

Roy Johnson glanced uneasily at Renno. Rusog had once been falsely accused of murder by the white settlers, and before his innocence had been proven, war had almost broken out between the Cherokee and the whites. Johnson was wondering if Rusog still harbored hatred for the settlers and was about to say something that could be damaging to the needed alliance between the settlers and Cherokee.

"What has happened has happened," Rusog said, "and we cannot change it. The white man is here to stay, and he grows more powerful and numerous with each passing season. We have fought him; we have been friends with him. If the spirits will it, we will fight him again. But now we have common ground with our friends of Franklin. We have been at peace with them and now will fight side by side with them. When this fight is over and Franklin has become a part of the United States, our best interests will lie with the United States. I speak so because, as you know, I was wronged by the whites. But I have forgotten and hereby declare my friendship for our white allies."

"My brother speaks well," Renno said, pleased. "We will hear now from the great wise chiefs Loramas, Wegowa, and Casno."

Loramas and Wegowa motioned to Casno to speak first. Casno was growing old and his shoulders were stooped, but he was still a great force among the men of his community. He stood and gazed at the gathered company. "Far from our ancestral home we Seneca have found brotherhood and a new home of sweet fruits and rich lands. We will fight for this. Not one living Seneca will see the track of a Chickasaw moccasin or a Spanish boot in the dust of this village. This I pledge to all."

Low, deep voices chanted, *War, war.*

"I have only one more thing to say," Casno said. "At the untimely death of our great and beloved chief, Ghonkaba, when Renno was still young, I was appointed regent, to serve as sachem until Renno was old enough to lead his people. That time has come. I hereby declare myself medicine man, once regent, and I pledge my loyalty to our new sachem, Renno."

Renno sat quietly, his head bowed, accepting Casno's tribute with a glow of pride. Beside him El-i-chi grunted approval and clapped his brother on the back.

Loramas, Grand Sachem of the Cherokee, now stood. "Yes, Casno, we grow old," he said. "It is the time of young men. The spirits have blessed us with them, including my grandson, Rusog. I have spoken at great length about this with my son, Wegowa. We know that the young men will bear the burden of war, because I am too old and Wegowa remains weakened by last winter's fever. We have decided that along with the burden of war should go the glory and the honor. The mantle of authority must pass now to Rusog, who will surely prove to be as worthy a warrior as his father was." Loramas let his eyes move from Rusog to Wegowa. His eyes crinkled in humor. "I can only hope, my son, that Rusog will remember that wisdom sometimes comes with age and experience and that he and Renno will occasionally consult those who can no longer take the warpath."

Wegowa, still very gaunt and weak, for he had not recovered well from the winter sickness, stood and looked in admiration at his son, Rusog, and then at the others. "The manitous have decided that I will not be with you, my brothers," he said. "This is a great sadness in me, but we can give thanks that we are blessed with young men like my son and Renno, who take the place of those who grow old and weak."

Rusog stood tall and proud. "I promise to seek guidance in all things," he said, "out of respect for my grandfather and father."

Casno stood to face the gathering. "We will have the ceremony to celebrate the handing down of the leadership of the Cherokee and the Seneca, but not now. Now is the time for war. When our warriors return victorious, we will celebrate. For now, we must consider who will lead the war party, for a snake with two heads cuts a crooked path. There is one among us who, although but a young man, has the benefit of experience, who is a great warrior and a wise leader."

Loramas nodded. "You are right; a war party must have only one leader." He turned to face Renno. "Will Renno the Seneca accept this honor?"

"I do accept," Renno said.

Rusog went to his brother-in-law and clasped his forearm. "There will be no jealousy, no dispute from me or my Cherokee warriors about your leadership, for you are the logical choice to serve as our great war leader."

Renno looked Rusog in the eye. "I thank you, my brother." He turned to the men around him. "Now we will put on the war paint. We will hone our weapons and restring our bows and look to our powder, for our fate is in our own hands."

Captain Guy de Rojas sat on a rock, adding landmark features to a map he had been compiling since leaving the Chickasaw settlement on the river. Around him the Chickasaw had made a silent camp, for they were within the boundaries of Cherokee land. De Rojas was pleased with the way things were going: the squadron of lancers would make the long trek north without suffering the loss of man or horse, the cannon were ready, and his Chickasaw allies were eager for the fight. The lands over which he had marched were rich. There were beaver to be taken, and fox and bear. He, Guy de Rojas, would benefit from an active fur trade and would indeed become a wealthy and powerful man.

De Rojas much preferred this land to the steamy, hot, watery country of the far south. Here a man could breathe. Here the air was not always laden with a burden of water vapor. The Chickasaw women were far more attractive than the women of the Choctaw, and even though the Chickasaw were protective of their women—de Rojas had been womanless since his arrival—soon there would be a wide choice of Cherokee girls. Indeed, he had been much tempted to make a raid on a Cherokee village for that very purpose. The Chickasaw would have been glad to fight. In fact, they grumbled for the lack of fighting.

But de Rojas was a man with a mission, and the mission was not to waste time and men in small skirmishes. With one big push, he would wipe out all Cherokee resistance, and then it would be over and he could begin to establish his own empire, for he had limitless ambition. New Orleans was a long way downriver; the Spanish governor would be powerless to prevent him from doing as he pleased along the mid-Mississippi, and de Rojas was envisioning a vast territory ruled by him and him alone. He had only to keep the Chickasaw on his side, and he would have the finest army in America. He could use the stockade the Spanish soldiers were building to fend off any attack the governor might decide to mount against him.

Finished with his map additions, planning out the invasion route in his mind, he ate his evening meal and leaned back against a tree. The camp was settling down, with Chickasaw warriors talking quietly among themselves or preparing for sleep. Guards were posted. De Rojas left such details to the young war chief, Talihini, who had been handpicked for the scouting party by Oklawahpa. Talihini was taller than most Chickasaw and fiercely proud of his strength. He, de Rojas had found, was also a man of ambition and was a ready listener whenever de Rojas described the riches and glory that would come to Talihini as a friend of the Spanish.

De Rojas had given Talihini many gifts, including a vest of Spanish armor, which the young war chief wore with great pride, in spite of the heat and the weight of the steel.

As if aware that de Rojas was thinking of him, Talihini approached and squatted beside de Rojas.

"We will make an early start tomorrow," the Spaniard said.

Talihini nodded.

"Soon, my friend, we will not sneak around," de Rojas added. "Soon. Soon."

Talihini smiled. "Soon my brother will give Talihini

many riches. We will have many women, many slaves."

"Soon," de Rojas agreed, sighing. He was tired. He lay down, and Talihini rose. At that moment there was a flurry of movement from the other side of the encampment. Talihini moved quickly to see what was happening, while de Rojas sat up in interest. Talihini was back in a few minutes.

"It is nothing," the Indian said. "The guards have captured two Cherokee females."

De Rojas felt a quick stir in his groin. "I will see these females," he said.

"One is a child," Talihini said, making a face. "The other is scrawny and ugly."

"Nevertheless, I will see them," de Rojas said firmly, leaping to his feet. A fire burned in him; he had been long without a woman.

It was as Talihini had said, however. One was a small and frightened child, her buckskin dress in shreds, her hair tangled. The other, squatting beside the fire, was gaunt and filthy.

"Stand, wench," de Rojas ordered in Choctaw. The woman did not look up. He had learned a bit of Cherokee. "Stand and speak," he said. The woman rose wearily. She slumped. She was dressed in a garment fashioned of grass and leaves. The garment showed thin legs, a hint of breast, but she was so caked with filth and dirt that she was, to de Rojas, totally repulsive.

"What is your village?" de Rojas asked.

"I have no village," she muttered.

"Then where do you live?"

She spread her arms to indicate the forest, the wilderness.

"Have you no man, no people?"

"Only this," the woman answered, putting her arm around the small girl who had stood at her side.

"What are you called?" de Rojas asked.

The woman looked puzzled. Her lank hair fell around her face, hiding most of it, showing only a dirt-stained cheek and one reddened, swollen eye.

"Your name," de Rojas demanded.

The woman shrugged. "I have none."

Beside him, Talihini said in a low voice, "She has been maddened by the spirits."

"Where do you come from?" de Rojas asked.

She shrugged, and again a sweep of her arms indicated the wilderness. De Rojas looked down at the small, frightened girl. "You," he said harshly. "Are you mad too?"

The little girl said nothing, merely clung to the skinny legs of the woman.

"Can't you speak?" de Rojas demanded of the wide-eyed little girl. She shook her head negatively.

Suddenly de Rojas lashed out with his open palm. The woman, struck forcefully on the cheek, fell. De Rojas stood over her. "*You* will talk," he demanded.

"Yes," the woman said meekly.

"Talk then. Tell me your village, your name, where you are from. How many warriors in your village?"

The woman pulled herself into a sitting position, adjusted the leaf-and-grass skirt. "Always I have lived here," she said. "We eat the fruit and the berries and the nuts. We have no village. We know no one. I have no name."

De Rojas seized the small girl by the hair. He slapped her viciously first on one cheek, and then the other. "Do you have a name?" The little girl wailed but could not speak for fear. Twice again de Rojas slapped her, whipping her head back and forth. Then, in disgust, he shoved her into the arms of the woman, who seized her and watched de Rojas walk away, a fire smoldering in her eyes.

"Shall we kill them now?" Talihini asked as he walked by de Rojas's side.

De Rojas started to say yes, and then he looked back. She was skinny and filthy, but she was a woman. "I want to question them further," he said. "Keep them alive."

At the midpoint of the next day's march, de Rojas found himself standing on the banks of a good-sized stream. He had been thinking about the woman all day. He ordered her to be brought to him, and when she arrived, shuddering as she saw de Rojas, she looked more repulsive than she had looked by firelight. In disgust, de Rojas seized her and flung her into the water.

"Wash yourself," he ordered when the woman surfaced, gasping and coughing. She seemed to panic for a moment before she found footing in chest-deep water. She looked up at de Rojas. "Wash yourself," he repeated, and she made half-serious motions of rubbing her arms. "Take off that filthy garment," he ordered, and when she stood motionless, he gestured to a Chickasaw warrior, who leaped into the water and quickly stripped the woman. She hid her breasts under the water.

On a motion from de Rojas, the warrior dragged the woman from the water. She covered her breasts with one arm and covered her pubic area with one hand. Her ribs protruded, and she seemed to be all bone. Still, she was a woman, and de Rojas realized with a shock that she was a white woman.

"Come to me," he ordered, and the warrior shoved the woman toward him. There she cowered, and her dazed mind, shocked into activity by the quick surprise immersion in the cold water, began to function. It did not really seem to matter, on the surface, what the bearded white man did to her, and yet, deep down, underneath the confusion in her mind, something told her she was in danger of . . . something, something that she had to avoid. She forced herself to uncover herself and began to fling her hands and arms around wildly, forcing out a harsh, demented laugh.

De Rojas frowned. "Get her something to wear," he ordered. "Give her food."

For three more days the Chickasaw force continued to travel within Cherokee territory. At the end of the third day, Talihini told de Rojas, "Unless you want to fight now, we will go no farther. For days now we have been under observation of Cherokee scouts."

"I wondered if you had noticed," de Rojas said, for he had seen the signs and felt enemy eyes on him.

Talihini snorted at the mere thought that a white man could have noticed something he had not seen.

"Do not underestimate me, my friend," de Rojas said in a soft, deadly voice. "For I have killed more men than you have fingers and toes, and I was living in this wilderness when you were still sucking your mother's teat."

"The white chief is a great warrior," Talihini said between his teeth.

"As is my friend Talihini," de Rojas said, smiling without humor. "And should not warriors return with scalps?"

Talihini's eyes gleamed.

"Yes," de Rojas said, "as we prepare to return to Chickasaw Bluffs, we will leave the Cherokee something to remember us by. There is a village a half-day's march, there."

Talihini did not show his surprise, but he had not allowed his scouts to report directly to de Rojas and knew not how the white man had become aware of the Cherokee village.

"The Cherokee left *us* a message," de Rojas said. "We can do no less."

With a whoop, Talihini leaped into the air.

"We will strike at dawn," de Rojas said.

There was no time now to think of the woman, but there would be plenty of time on the trip back to the river. He marched close to the head of the column and directed the placement of the attacking forces on two small rises on either side of the small Cherokee village nestled below along a clear creek. When all was in readiness, he called Talihini to him.

"No prisoners, my friend," he said.

"My men have traveled far, and they have long wanted to fight. The taking of women is their right."

"Listen, Talihini," de Rojas said, "we are going into a war of extermination. The Chickasaw are great warriors, and you will have me and my men and my cannon at your side. But the Cherokee will not run or lie down to be killed. We must strike hatred and anger and terror into the hearts of the Cherokee, so they will fight recklessly, inflamed by emotions. No. Leave not one living thing."

"When the Cherokee struck our village, they did not kill women and children," Talihini pointed out.

"And that softness will cause them to lose the war," de Rojas said. "Is not Talihini fierce enough to show his determination?"

"It will be as you say," the war chief growled.

De Rojas watched from the top of a rise as the Chickasaw swept down on the village. It was a small village, fewer than twenty lodges, and the slaughter was over quickly.

Behind him, under the guard of a disgruntled warrior who was displeased at being left out of the fun, the white woman watched with impassive eyes as the few men of the village put up a disorganized and futile fight. She watched as women and children were dragged from their lodges to be slaughtered. The village square ran with blood, and the Chickasaw warriors returned in triumph, scalps dripping blood hanging from their belts, and the village in flames behind them.

Something in the woman's mind told her that she was in two kinds of danger, first from de Rojas's lust and second from the Chickasaw appetite for killing. She had been given a buckskin dress to wear, which fell to just above her knees. There was enough cunning in her to soil herself with dirt at the first opportunity, to roll in the detritus of the forest so that the dress became soiled and her hair tangled with dirt and twigs. And when she sensed anyone looking at her, she made hazy, meaningless motions in the air with her hands while laughing wildly. As she was forced to march with the Chickasaw, she sensed that it was de Rojas's intent to feed her well, so that her body would fill out. As a result, when she had opportunity, she threw her food away, preferring the familiar pangs of hunger to the unknown threat from de Rojas.

De Rojas could not understand why the woman was always so filthy, and why, in spite of the good food he ordered to be given to her, she remained emaciated.

The woman had begun to have headaches after having been flung into the water by de Rojas, and with the headaches came dreams—dreams of falling into a swiftly flowing river, nightmares of pain and hunger and suffering. She kept the little girl with her at all times and often tried to talk to her, but shock, fear, hunger, and time had rendered the little girl mute. She had not spoken a word, the woman remembered, since that dim and dazed time when it seemed that they had been born, bruised, in the midst of the forest.

There were times, when they were moving at warrior's pace, the woman had to carry the little girl.

She was very tired and had to eat to have the strength
to keep up the pace and to help the girl. The soles of
her feet had hardened, so she walked with confidence. There were times when she seemed to hear a
distant voice in her mind, urging her to flee, to run
toward the east, but she did not know why and was
too dazed to act on the impulse.

Once they were back in Chickasaw territory, de
Rojas slowed the pace. He prided himself on his
ability to outdo any Indian, but he was not a masoch-
ist, so he chose a comfortable walk and fairly early
camp. His mind was once again on the woman. He
put his sleep gear at a distance from the others and
ordered the woman to be brought to him. She stood
before him with her head down, her eyes hidden
behind her unkempt hair.

"Come closer," de Rojas said. She moved to stand
before him as he sat on his blankets. He put both
hands on her legs and moved them upward. Her
thighs were stringy and skinny, but her flesh was
warm. When his hand sought and found a very private area, the woman jerked away and turned to run.
He managed to catch her ankle, and she fell heavily,
her forehead striking a rock. She lay without moving.

Angered as much at himself as at her—for he was a
man accustomed to the best of women, both in New
Orleans and among the Choctaw—he let her lie. If
she lived, fine. If not, her scalp would adorn the belt
of a Chickasaw brave.

Gradually, after a flash of white light and a period
of blackness, consciousness began to return to the

woman. Her first thought was: *Renno, Renno, please come for me.*

And then there rushed into her aching head a flood of memory, of a wild river and her fall and of little Wynema, who had fallen into the river after her.

She stirred. She looked at the big man with the beard. He was sleeping. She knew, then, the full extent of her danger. "Oh, Renno!" she whispered, knowing she would choose death rather than dishonor herself and the man she loved by submitting to the Spaniard's lust.

She crawled away, found the little girl, and clung to her. She decided to continue her charade of madness, for the Indians respected those bedazed by the spirits. Perhaps, if she kept her wits about her, she would live and escape, to run toward the east, as her unconscious mind had been urging her to do.

When de Rojas saw the woman the next morning, she was filthier than ever. She had smeared grease from the evening meal over her face and neck, and dirt was sticking to it. At first he thought to throw her into the water again, and then he chided himself. Why had he not let the Chickasaw kill her?

The time had come. The Cherokee scouts had reported the brutal destruction of a defenseless Cherokee village and said they had trailed the invaders back into Chickasaw lands, where the enemy had slowed his pace and was heading west leisurely, drying the scalps of his victims as he went. Now the warriors of the Cherokee nation were on the move, committed to catching up with the invaders who had massacred the Cherokee village. At their head was Renno, surrounded by his Seneca. With the dawn, there would be an attack. The forces were about equal in number, for Roy Johnson's Frontier Regiment was not yet in position, and the main body of the Cherokee forces was far to the rear.

On the eve before the battle, Renno could not sleep. He knew that he should sleep, to gain strength for the day ahead, but sleep would not come. Memories of his wife tortured him, so as he lay awake, he prayed for his men and for the favor of the manitous.

What finally came to him was not true sleep but a state of half wakefulness. He was aware of the men sleeping nearby, the small night sounds, and of the feel of the cool night. He felt only an eerie heaviness, as if his body were being pressed against the earth by a great weight. Suddenly there was an unnatural rustling in the air, the sound of many whispering voices. When the voices began to be individually distinguishable, Renno's spirits soared, for all his illustrious ancestors were there, reaching out to him, speaking words of hope and encouragement. All of them were looking on him with kindness from eerie eyes, which were one moment human and next animal and then mere wisps.

In his state of semiconsciousness he knew great joy, for there was a promise of victory on the morrow. And more, there was the great Renno, for whom he was named, dressed in bleached white buckskin, a light shining around him, the white Indian. He was smiling and beckoning, so that Renno rose quietly

and followed the light, which became dim until he
had left the encampment, moving toward the south
and a stream where his men had watered. The light
went ahead of him, and he was not sure whether he
was waking or sleeping, but the feel of the earth
under his feet was real, and the sounds of the night
were real.

The light showed him the strong, handsome form
of his ancestor halted beside a crooked tree on the
bank of the stream. Renno drew near and halted a
few paces away, awed by the event. And then something occurred that would become legend, something that he could not understand.

The spirit of his ancestor pointed upward, and
Renno's eyes followed the motion to see a star sepa-
rate itself from its brothers in the sky and arc toward
him across the starry blackness until it seemed that it
was coming directly at him. He heard a whoosh of
sound and a violent splash in the water near the
half-submerged roots of the crooked tree.

At first he was awed into motionlessness, ponder-
ing the meaning of this great sign, and then he saw
his ancestor pointing to the water. Renno walked
forward and felt the cool of the water on his feet and
ankles. There was a glow coming from the shallow
water. His hand closed on warmth, and he lifted the
glowing object.

It was a stone. It had been polished by its journey
through the night sky. It gleamed metallically in the
moonlight, and its shape was that of a very large ax
head, a great stone ax head, but there was a heft and
feel to tell him that this was no mere stone. This was

a stone of steel. In complete awe, feeling the heat of the stone in his palm, he turned.

The spirit of his great-grandfather spoke. "Use it well, my son. When you have vanquished your enemies, return the stone to its place among the stream-washed roots of the crooked tree."

The spirit vanished.

By moonlight, Renno cut a sturdy limb from the crooked tree, debarked it, notched it, placed the ax head in the notch, and lashed it securely with rawhide. He hefted the ax. Its weight was impressive. Only a strong warrior would be able to wield it.

Renno returned to the camp by the first light of false dawn. The men were stirring. No one spoke, for they were in Chickasaw territory and not far from the enemy encampment—and his guards had hungry ears. Renno called his men into a group, then had each warrior walk past him, one by one, and place his hand on the wondrous ax head to feel its heat, a heat that would not fade.

Once every man had felt the heat of the medicine ax, Renno spoke in a quiet voice. "This is strong medicine. This great ax has been sent to me from the stars by my ancestors themselves. It is an omen of victory."

To demonstrate the power of the ax, Renno smashed a stone the size of his head, bending to deliver the blow. The stone crumbled, to a low grunt of approval and awe from the men nearest Renno.

Now it was time to strike at the enemy. Renno started to lift the ax, and to his surprise, it seemed to weigh as much as the earth itself. Try as he might, he could not lift it. Puzzled, he looked around at the questioning faces of the men. The great medicine ax had been given to him by his ancestors, and he had described it as an omen promising victory; to go into the battle without it would put doubt not only into his own mind, but also into his men's minds.

"A sign," he said, and would have added more had not a scout run silently into the clearing.

"Sachem," the scout panted, having run hard, "the Chickasaw were just joined by more than one hundred new warriors from the west."

A moan of awe went up from some of the warriors. The ax had truly given their leader a sign—to have attacked without knowledge of the new force would have meant disaster.

Renno bent, picked up the medicine ax easily now, and stuck the stout handle into his belt. "Watch the enemy closely," he told the scout. "Rusog, come with me. We must consider this new development."

Further information from the scout told them that the enemy now outnumbered them two to one and that the entire force had begun to move west, even though the newcomers who had just arrived from the west were protesting.

"There is dissension in the camp," the scout reported. "Those who have just arrived want to travel east, into Cherokee lands, to be blooded and to take scalps, but the orders are being given by a white man."

"This disagreement will work in our favor," Renno said. "We will move, but slowly. We will observe them during the day, and when they begin to lie down for sleep, perhaps still quarreling among themselves, we will strike with all our might."

Ramón de Vega had been left behind in Chickasaw Bluffs to oversee the construction of the fort and await the arrival of weapons and men from the south. He too was finding the climate of the mid-Mississippi to be to his liking and was making friends among the Chickasaw by avoiding the directness that was de Rojas's trademark. De Vega had gained advantages from his strategy: his lodge was warmed not only by fire but also by the charms of a plump and pretty Chickasaw widow whose husband had been drowned while fishing in the river.

De Vega had a suspicion that his commander had plans that went beyond the wishes of the Spanish governor in New Orleans, and he was using de Rojas's absence to make decisions about his own future. He wondered if he should be loyal to the Spanish governor and risk coming out of his New World adventure with nothing more than he had, or if he should declare his loyalty to de Rojas and perhaps become rich and powerful in a new country ruled by de Rojas.

De Vega, like de Rojas, had dreams of returning to Spain in triumph, but all in all, it was not bad where he was. He had never known a more loving woman than his Chickasaw widow. The simple food was good, and he, like most who were exposed to the wilderness, had come to love it. He spent time hunting with the younger warriors and could not get enough of traveling into places where a white man had never set foot. It was true that the Mississippi had been explored by Frenchmen from its origin to its mouth, but those early expeditions had covered only a tiny area on shore, and there were times when de Vega dreamed of outfitting an expedition and crossing the river to penetrate those vast and unknown areas to the west.

Furthermore, the river itself fascinated him: it was the unknown; it ran southward for hundreds of miles through treacherous shoals and sandbars and snags; it was too big, too swift, too powerful for upstream navigation. If men and supplies could be brought from New Orleans by water, life would be much simplified, he knew, but for now the only connection with Spanish territory was by a long, arduous land trek.

He was pleased when the last contingent of lancers arrived, bringing wagon loads of weapons for the Chickasaw. He was eager for the plan to get under way, so he went to Oklawahpa's lodge and told the chief that Guy de Rojas should be notified that the lancers were all at Chickasaw Bluffs and that the weapons had been sent as promised. De Vega had no real concept of the wild emptiness into which de Rojas had disappeared with his war party, but after Oklawahpa had assigned him four warriors as an escort and they had traveled days into virgin wilderness, he began to doubt that it was possible to find even a large group of men in that expanse. The warriors, however, were confident and set a pace that made de Vega very glad that he was in good condition.

Chapter VII

A noisy thunderstorm at day's end gave Renno just the right opportunity to move his forces into the proper attack positions, for the Chickasaw war party abandoned the march early and busied themselves in making bough shelters. The Chickasaw gave every indication of feeling safe, and Renno smiled grimly. The enemy would be taught a lesson. In war, one's guard should never be let down. In war against a courageous and resourceful enemy, there was no security anywhere.

* * *

Captain Guy de Rojas did not like rain. Of all the hardships of wilderness life, being cold and wet at the same time was, for him, the most onerous. The last hour of marching in the rain had dropped him into deep despair. He thought of the sunny, arid plains of his home, of Spain. He tortured himself with thoughts of the dark hair, olive skin, and flashing white teeth of beautiful Spanish girls who had scorned him. He cursed his fate at being born of a poor tradesman instead of being a son of the nobility, for he felt that he was as worthy as any man alive, and he had never got over his resentment. When he had exiled himself from his native country and found himself mired hip-deep in the swampy quagmires of an alien land, he had promised himself that one day he would return to Spain with riches beyond the wildest dreams of those petty noblemen who had treated him like a peasant.

And now he was walking through a thunderstorm, soaked by torrential rains, and making camp in a soggy woodland with everything wet—clothing, food, bedding. Not even when the rain stopped, with the coming of sunset, and he was able to coax weak flames from a reluctant fire, did he feel better. The only way he had ever been able to assuage these rages was by killing someone weak, someone vulnerable. Only then could he be truly assured of his power. Now there was only the woman on whom to vent his ire. He sought her out. She cackled madly at him and made insane gestures in the air with her grimy hands, and that infuriated him. He seized her by the arm and half dragged her to the stream by which the Chickasaw had made camp. Her struggles were useless as he ripped the buckskin dress from her body and exposed her long legs, which no longer seemed quite so stringy.

"Get in the water!" he ordered. The woman shrieked and danced. He slapped her, hard, with all his rage-given strength, and she fell into the shallows. He was wet already, so he rushed in and grabbed her arm, hauling her to her feet. He took a handful of sand and began to scour her skin roughly as she squirmed, whined, and cackled helplessly.

Emily, since all memory had returned to her, had been eating well in order to build up her strength for her escape. She knew that this was the time to act. Even as she feigned madness, her hand frantically searched the sand of the stream for a large stone. They were alone; one well-aimed blow, and she would leave de Rojas to drown, find Wynema, and sneak out of the camp to travel all night back toward home.

De Rojas continued to scour her with sand. It was painful, and he was so powerful that her struggles merely caused him to redouble his efforts.

When she was very, very clean, and her skin red from the scouring, he dragged her from the water and pushed her toward the encampment. She started to run, but de Rojas caught her in a few steps and slapped her hard.

"No more!" he hissed angrily. "No more will I be put off." He was half dragging, half carrying her away from the main Chickasaw camp, through the woods. When he found a clearing some fifty yards from the campfires, he threw her roughly to the

ground and, telling her that he would kill her if she
moved, began to build a new fire. He found dry
tinder in a fallen hollow log and soon had a respect-
able fire going.

"Now," he said, "let's find out what kind of woman
you are." He threw himself down, putting his weight
on her and seeking her lips. She tossed her head
from side to side and cackled, slobbering in a desperate effort to disgust him, but he was too far gone in
his lust. She felt his hands seek her breasts, and she
was screaming silently in her mind.

Renno, oh, please, Renno.

As if in answer to her silent prayer, the night
exploded. A great roar of musketry, flashes of muz-
zles, yells of surprise and pain, and Chickasaw war
whoops came to her through the trees that separated
them from the Chickasaw camp. It was as if de Rojas
did not hear, for he continued to grope her body, to
thrust his hands toward her most intimate parts,
parts of her body that had been known only by the
man she loved, her husband.

"No!" she screamed aloud. "Are you mad? Can't
you hear what's happening?"

"So," de Rojas said, "the madwoman is not so mad
after all." He straddled her and began to fumble with
the fastenings of his clothing.

Renno, his lips set in silence, had his men strike
from two angles. Even when the directed fire of
Cherokee and Seneca muskets reduced the odds of
battle with not a single loss to Renno's force, he said
not a word. His war party came like spirits of the

night, striking a terrible blow to the Chickasaw in an area where they had felt arrogantly safe, and that initial surprise demoralized those who lived through the first roar of musket fire. There was no organization among the Chickasaw, although, brave fighting men that they were, they seized weapons and, whooping their defiance, met the silent rush before falling victim to the deadly arrows.

The two brothers, Renno and El-i-chi, fought side by side, into the area with the thickest concentration of Chickasaw. And where the brothers moved, death came with them, in the form of quick and deadly blows from El-i-chi's tomahawk and instant oblivion as Renno's great ax from the stars smashed and mutilated and left a carpet of dead behind him.

Only then, as the fighting became hand-to-hand, did the Cherokee war cry ring out, and for the first time the Chickasaw heard the bloodcurdling death sound of the Seneca war cries. From the left the Cherokee were led by Rusog. From the right, the Seneca were led by Renno, whose weapon never lost its supernatural heat, a warmth that bathed itself in Chickasaw blood again and again.

Talihini, the war chief in charge of the Chickasaw force, had been peacefully enjoying his evening meal when the muskets roared, and he escaped the first onslaught to leap to his weapons and cry out orders designed to organize resistance to the attack. His voice went unheard in the chaos of battle, and he found himself fighting for his life against warriors dressed as he had never seen warriors dressed—men who did not look like Cherokee, men who fought like enraged bears. And yet he held his own and left a pile of enemy dead at his feet as he stood his ground and rallied a few men around him. His heart was filled with despair when he saw how swiftly his men were falling. Soon he knew that all was lost, and with a raging war cry he prepared to forfeit his life only at great cost to the enemy.

The surprise was so complete, the initial musket fire so terrifying, that the Cherokee were able to surge up from the left quickly, closing to form a solid line of attackers with the Seneca, who were meeting with the most resistance, having attacked from the side nearest the stream, where there was a greater concentration of Chickasaw. But there, too, surprise and resolve were creating swift and sure victory. Only one fighting knot of Chickasaw warriors remained, and the man who stood at the head of that group was, Renno saw, a man of strength and bravery, taller than most, powerful in shoulder and arm, with an expression of grim determination on his face. Renno fought toward the tall man, his great ax spreading fear and death. And then they were face-to-face.

For a moment Renno paused.

"I salute you," Talihini said, looking into the cold eyes of death without flinching.

"You have fought bravely," Renno answered. He made no offer for the tall warrior to surrender. Talihini's tomahawk was bloody. Dead Seneca lay at his feet. His breathing was ragged, his powerful chest rising and falling.

"May you have a good journey to the resting place of your ancestors," Renno said, lifting his ax.

"With you by my side," Talihini retorted, launching himself forward with a powerful thrust of legs and a deadly, curving attack with the tomahawk. The weapon rang upon contact with Renno's ax. Three surviving Chickasaw yelled out their song of death and followed Talihini in his attack. One was swiftly dispatched by El-i-chi, the other two engaged in single combat with Rusog and another Cherokee, and the action swirled away from Renno and Talihini, leaving the two of them in an island of death, each intent on killing, each young, strong, and in the prime of life.

Talihini was an expert with tomahawk and knife, and time and time again killing blows had to be parried by Renno's ax, and each time sparks flew and a jar of force ran down Renno's arm. Out of the corner of his eye he saw that the other Chickasaw had been killed, and that a silent circle of his friends surrounded him and his foe. This diversion of his concentration was almost fatal, for he narrowly ducked a blow that would have split open his skull. Filled with admiration for his opponent, Renno decided that it was time to end the contest.

He yelled a Seneca war cry, pivoted, feinted, swept under a blow of Talihini's tomahawk, and brought the great medicine ax swinging upward to take the Chickasaw under the chin. He heard the dry, brittle snap of bones, saw the tall, powerful body jerked backward by the force of the blow, and with his superb speed, finished it with a blow to the side of Talihini's head as he fell.

Renno stood panting, his eyes roving over the

scene of battle. The dead were stacked two and three deep. The clearing was now carpeted in red. The battle was over.

With joyous whoops of victory, the warriors fell to the taking of spoils. Renno, oddly reluctant to begin to collect his own scalps, stood, ax in hand, looking down at the fallen Chickasaw chief. A voice broke into his musings and he turned to see a Cherokee running toward him, a little girl in rags in his arms.

"Renno!" the warrior cried. "It is Wynema, who disappeared with Emily!"

Wynema had just witnessed a fierce slaughter, and she was shaking with shock and terror.

Renno's heart leaped. The girl who had disappeared with Emily, alive?

"Child," he whispered, starting to touch her, but realizing that his right hand dripped with blood that had run down the ax handle, he moved back. "Emily. Where is Emily?"

Wynema had recognized the warrior who had discovered her cringing under a blanket at the edge of the clearing. She was aware enough to know that she was among her own people again. She tried to speak. Her mouth worked, and her neck tendons stood out with the effort, but nothing came out.

"Is Emily alive?" Renno whispered, holding his breath for the girl's answer. When Wynema nodded, he felt a flood of joy.

"Where is she?"

"The Spaniard," Wynema managed, her little voice sounding harsh and strained. "There." She pointed toward the stream, toward which she had seen de

Rojas drag Emily just before the attack. Renno left on the run, saw quickly where there had been a struggle beside the stream, and followed the tracks of a man dragging a reluctant, barefoot woman into the woods.

Through his lust, Guy de Rojas heard the cries, the screams of dying agony, and realized that something terrible was happening. He had been on the verge of getting the woman positioned for his thrust, and he paused in indecision for a moment before he leaped up, quickly arranged his clothing, and dragging Emily behind him, got close enough to the Chickasaw camp to see that all was lost, in so few minutes. He cursed himself for underestimating his enemy, but then he told himself that this was but one minor skirmish, which would, after all, serve a purpose: the slaughter of the Chickasaw war party would inflame the rest of the nation to do his bidding. He had only to get back to Chickasaw Bluffs and tell his story, and Oklawahpa and his people would be so enraged that they would sweep in a bloody tide all the way to the far mountains.

Only for a moment did de Rojas concern himself about the horde of enemy warriors. He knew that they would spend a good portion of the night taking spoils and then celebrating their victory, and by that time he would be far to the west. He considered killing the woman. He would be able to travel faster without her, but he looked at her and saw the look of defiance in her eyes, and swift anger overcame his common sense. She had tricked him. Her act of

madness had been nothing more than a ruse to stay
alive and to keep herself safe from his desires. He
would use her well, and then he would kill her.

He dragged Emily to the stream, retrieved her
dress and threw it at her, then forced her to enter
the shallow water with him. All Indians were good
trackers. He would leave no trail for them to follow.
They waded through the stream for miles, until the
muscles of his legs burned and the woman was gasping and had to be supported. Then and only then did
he emerge onto dry ground and set a direct course
overland toward the river. They traveled all night,
paused only to pluck a quick breakfast of ripe and
half-ripe strawberries, and then he pushed on, driving the exhausted woman ahead of him. When she
faltered, he gave her a quick rap with the flat of his
sword.

With the aid of a torch Renno tracked the man and
the barefoot woman to a clearing where a fire was
dying. He saw signs of a struggle on the ground, and
rage roared up in him as he imagined Emily in the
power of the Spaniard. But she was alive, and that
was the most important thing.

The difficulty of tracking at night cost him precious
minutes until, by the light of a torch, he found the
point where de Rojas had entered the stream. The
man, Renno felt, was not inexperienced in wilderness wiles and might very well follow the stream for
miles before coming out onto dry land. In the darkness the chances of missing that point were great, for
if the man knew enough to try to hide his trail, he

would probably be wise enough to brush away any sign of his leaving the stream. Renno's only choice was to wait for morning. He was at a disadvantage in two ways: first, he could not hope to find the trail in the dark, and second, a fleeing man could travel faster than the tracker, who had to take time to look for signs.

He went back to the scene of the battle and spent a sleepless night sitting beside a smoldering fire, willing the dawn to come. The initial joy at the news that Emily had survived had given way to a worry and fear more severe than he had felt originally when the news came to him of Emily's disappearance. He cleaned the blood from the great ax, noted that the use of the ax in the battle had not left a mark on the stone, cupped the stone in his hands to feel the warmth that still emanated from it, as if seeking reassurance from its power, which was somehow linked to his ancestors.

At first light, having given instructions to Rusog and El-i-chi to send out far-ranging scouts and to hold their positions until the main Cherokee force had arrived, he set out along the banks of the stream. It did not lead directly west. He did not concentrate on the area at the edge of the stream, thinking that any overt sign would have been brushed away. Instead, he examined the brush at a distance, looking for a bent twig, an overturned leaf, grass crushed by the weight of a man.

The sun was almost at the zenith when his persistence paid off. He had backtracked twice, having covered a distance of miles from the site of the battle, and it was on that second trip that he found what he was looking for: the Spaniard had carefully used a bough to brush away all evidence of footprints in the soft mud along the stream and for a hundred feet into the brushy area leading toward a dense stand of hardwood. But the burrow of a mole had been disturbed, crushed in at one point, and brushed unnaturally. Renno picked up the trail in the detritus of the forest and could, for hours, travel at a swinging lope. But now the man had a long head start.

At day's end Renno had to halt. He knew, of course, that the man who held Emily captive was headed for the river, but by traveling swiftly, Renno could put himself between them and the river and, perhaps, intercept them before they reached the first sizable Chickasaw village. But to do so would be to leave Emily at the Spaniard's mercy for days.

Emily was not nearly as exhausted as she pretended to be. Tired, yes. De Rojas was setting quite a fast pace. She pretended to be spent, in an effort to slow his flight, for in her heart she knew that the force that had destroyed the Chickasaw had been led by Renno. He was, she felt, somewhere behind them. She could almost feel his presence. She feared what would happen to her when de Rojas stopped for the night, but his caution sent him walking down another stream for a half-mile before he forced Emily to climb a huge cottonwood tree, where the two of them perched rather uncomfortably, Emily getting very little sleep.

At first light on the second day of de Rojas's flight,

they forced their way through dense brush near the creek. Briars tore at Emily, and with sudden inspiration she broke off a long, stiff thorn and, when de Rojas was not looking, pushed the thorn into the ball of her index finger. By squeezing the finger with her thumb she could bring forth a small drop of blood. At intervals, when she had the chance, she would press her finger against the leaf of a tree, or on the stem of a small bush. By midday her fingers were sore and aching, for she had to keep making new punctures to keep the blood available, but she was leaving a trail that, to a man like Renno, would be as sure as signposts.

The meeting of two small parties—de Rojas and Emily, and de Vega and his four warriors—in the midst of hundreds of square miles of wilderness was not entirely by chance. Hunting trails crossed all of Chickasaw land, and the warriors accompanying Ramón de Vega knew that any Chickasaw returning from the river would follow a certain route. Guy de Rojas had the routes noted well and, in fact, had his map, so he was following the most direct and long-established route toward the river when he was suddenly faced by two painted Chickasaw warriors. The Chickasaw materialized from the trees in silence, and in a moment de Rojas was reaching for his weapons, knowing that not all Chickasaw were aware that he was an ally.

"Hold, Captain Chief," said one of the warriors, and de Rojas breathed easy. He was surprised and pleased when Ramón de Vega came trotting down the trail with two more Chickasaw.

"Ramón," de Rojas called out, "well met! What force have you?"

"You see my force," de Vega said, taking de Rojas's outstretched hand. "I have good news."

"And I, too," de Rojas said. "The Cherokee and an allied tribe attacked us. As you said, what force I have, you see."

De Vega paled to think of so many dead, and he was shocked to hear de Rojas call it good news.

"I will explain later," de Rojas said, laughing at the expression on de Vega's face. "At the moment I think it's best that we put a few more miles between us and the enemy."

As they marched, de Vega told de Rojas of the cavalry's arrival with the weapons, and de Rojas explained his reasoning for not regretting the massacre of his Chickasaw war party. De Vega was disgusted by his superior's coldness but had to admit that the disaster would inflame Oklawahpa. If the war chief had not been totally committed to de Rojas's plan, he would be now.

Both de Rojas and Emily ate hungrily of the food carried by de Vega's party, and de Rojas allowed an early camp. He had left, he thought, a very confused trail, and now he felt secure, with the four Chickasaw posted around the clearing. He was so confident that he allowed a fire and roasted a turkey taken by one of the warriors. He tore into the meat with enthusiasm and looked at the woman, who sat silently across the fire from him. When he finished eating, he wiped his hands on his trousers and rose.

"Ramón," he said, "I have some business with this

woman. Perhaps you wouldn't mind making your bed at some distance."

De Vega had been studying Emily's face by firelight. She was thin and gaunt, and her blond hair was snarled and dirty, but there was about her a look of quality. That she was white was a surprise and a question to him.

"You have no idea who she is, why she was wandering in the wilderness?" he asked.

"She chooses to be coy," de Rojas said. "It is of no matter."

With some misgivings, de Vega moved his blanket into the trees. He could not see the clearing, only a glow from the fire. He was well acquainted with his commanding officer's attraction to the ladies, and although it bothered him that the woman was white, he reasoned that she must be one of those unfortunate wilderness women who had been taken as a child by the Indians. He shrugged, then rolled into his blanket. He dozed almost immediately and was awakened by the sound of a struggle.

Emily had been watching de Rojas carefully as he had spoken to de Vega. She understood from his gestures and furtive glances in her direction that he had plans for her. Now she was looking for a chance to run, but de Rojas did not give it to her. He watched her unblinkingly as the other Spaniard left them, and then he came around the fire and jerked her to her feet.

"We can accomplish my purpose in one of two ways, my little madwoman," de Rojas said in Cherokee. "With or without your cooperation. I assure you it will be less painful if you cooperate."

Emily, feeling that Renno was somewhere near—oh, God, he had to be—had been thinking. It was time, she felt, to drop the charade. "Do you speak English?" she asked.

De Rojas raised an eyebrow. "Of course," he said.

"I am the daughter of Colonel Roy Johnson, commander of the Frontier Regiment of the state of Franklin. My husband, war chief of the Seneca, led the battle that destroyed your men. I assure you that if you go on with this, one of them will kill you."

De Rojas began to consider the possibilities. The woman, he felt, was stupid to give him such valuable information. She would—in case he was overconfident and was caught before he reached the protection of Chickasaw-populated areas—be a valuable bargaining card.

Taking de Rojas's silence for intimidation, Emily said, "He is very near, my husband. He is following you. Release me, and I will speak for you. Perhaps he will not kill you."

That threat was too much for de Rojas. With a snarl, he ripped the lacings of Emily's buckskin garment, and her white breasts and stomach were exposed. She tried to pull the garment back together, but he was on her like an animal, ripping the buckskin away. She gasped and struggled, and then she was falling, his weight atop her. She tried to bring her knee up into his crotch, but he blocked it with his thigh and slapped her hard. She cried out, and it was that sound that awoke Ramón de Vega.

De Vega crept to the tree line of the clearing. He saw de Rojas atop the woman, tugging at his own clothing even as he pinned her down. She was sobbing, fighting, and her sobs touched de Vega. She was, after all, a white woman.

De Vega walked into the clearing, into the light of the flickering fire. "Captain?" he ventured. De Rojas seemed not to hear. He had the woman's legs spread, and his manhood was more than evident. She was jerking her body in an attempt to avoid his thrust.

"Captain," de Vega said louder, putting his hand on de Rojas's shoulder. "The lady objects."

De Rojas leaped to his feet and, with a back-handed swing of his powerful arm, sent de Vega reeling. Emily seized that opportunity to scuttle away. He grabbed her by the foot and pulled her to him, striking her brutally, leaving her stunned, as he seized a burning limb from the fire and, in one quick motion, sent de Vega to the ground with a heavy blow.

It was going to happen. She was dazed, helpless. Her struggles were weak, her moans a sadness in her as he forced her to open for him and lowered himself.

The roar that came to de Rojas's ears was that of an enraged bear. He jerked his head up and saw an avenging demon, tall, bronzed, with a deadly huge ax raised high. He scrambled off Emily and, tugging his trousers into place with one hand, grabbed a long knife with the other.

She was alive. That knowledge was a fire of joy in Renno's heart. And the man who had struck her, while he had killed the last of the four Chickasaw guards with a razor-edged stiletto, was squatting beside her. All of Renno's blood cried out for vengeance. He could feel the medicine ax glowing with warmth and could visualize it crushing the Spaniard's skull like an egg. But that would be too quick, too merciful. The Spaniard was armed with a knife. Renno put the ax in his belt and took out the stiletto.

"Renno, thank God," Emily sobbed.

Brought to his senses by Emily's voice, de Rojas seized her by the hair, jerked her to her feet, and placed his knife so tightly at her throat that the sharp blade grazed her skin, sending a trickle of blood down her neck.

"If you want her alive," de Rojas said in a low voice, "throw down your weapons."

For only a second Renno was indecisive. Alternatives raced through his mind. If the man were allowed to leave with Emily, he would, without doubt, kill her quickly lest she slow him in his flight. Renno could not allow the Spaniard even a moment alone with Emily.

De Rojas was taller than Emily; the top of her head came up to his shoulder. Bent as he was, holding the knife at her throat, only his eyes and forehead showed. Renno slowly withdrew the great ax from his belt, as if he were going to toss it to the ground. When the ax was securely in his hand, with a roar that was both prayer and rage, he threw the weapon with all his strength. If he missed, Emily would die. The ax whistled as it turned end over end, seeming to move in slow motion. The handle headed straight toward Emily's face, until, with the last of its revolution, the heavy stone ax head glanced off de Rojas's forehead.

Renno had moved with the ax, leaping forward, his eyes on the knife at Emily's throat. Even a dying reflex action by the Spaniard could be fatal for her. There was a *thunk* like the fall of a ripe melon on stone, and even as Renno was a step away, de Rojas's arm relaxed, the knife falling from his hand, and Emily was jerking free, to throw herself into Renno's arms.

The fallen enemy was forgotten. Renno had his wife in his arms. She was alive.

"I knew you'd come," Emily cried through her happy tears.

Renno ran his hands over her shoulders. She was so thin. "We will have to feed you much," he said.

She laughed through her tears. "Yes," she said. She clung to him, and all was right. She resisted when she felt him trying to push her away, and then remembered de Rojas. She had seen and known her share of death, being a frontier girl, and did not consider herself to be bloodthirsty or vindictive. Yet she wanted de Rojas dead—not for what he had done to her, for all he had done was bruise her, but for the times he had struck Wynema. Thinking of the little girl, she asked, "Wynema?"

"She is safe," Renno said, pushing her away. He immediately tensed and reached for a weapon, for the fallen Spaniard was gone. He leaped toward the tree line but caught movement out of the corner of his eye. The other one was moving, sitting up with a groan. He leaped to Ramón de Vega's side and raised his stiletto.

"No! Wait," Emily said. "He tried to help me."

Renno wanted, more than anything in the world, to go after de Rojas, but he could not leave Emily alone with the other Spaniard.

"You want him to live?" he asked.

"He tried to stop de Rojas."

Renno nodded. He squatted in front of the dazed man. "Your name, Spaniard."

"I am Ramón de Vega."

"There are four dead Chickasaw in the trees. Are there more behind you?"

De Vega looked into cold, deadly blue eyes and knew that he would have to choose his words with care. "I'm sorry, it would not be honorable for me to give you information."

Renno thrust the sharp point of the stiletto into the hollow of de Vega's throat. "Are there others behind you?" he asked in a soft, chilling voice.

"I will die, since obviously you are a savage. But I will die with my honor intact."

"You speak of honor?" Emily asked shrilly. "What honor was there when your superior officer beat a small child?"

"De Rojas is de Rojas. I am Ramón de Vega."

Renno increased pressure on the knife, remembering the trickle of blood that had run down Emily's neck under de Rojas's knife blade, but as the point pierced the skin and de Vega's eyes widened, Renno pulled the knife away and leaped to his feet. He had reached two conclusions: first a white man alone in the wilderness could be tracked down quickly, so de Rojas would die. Second having this Spaniard alive would prove to authorities in the United States that there was a Spanish presence in Cherokee land and that the threat of a Spanish takeover was real. Perhaps the white men back in Knoxville could coax some information out of de Vega. He tied de Vega's hands securely.

"Are you able to walk?" he asked Emily.

"With you I could walk all the way to the Atlantic Ocean," she said, coming to his side to cling to his arm.

He led her into the trees, out of sight of the Spaniard, held her in his arms, and kissed her. "You must have been starved, you're so thin."

"No, I'm fine." She put her lips close to his. "I pretended madness, Renno. I kept myself thin and filthy, and I drooled when he looked at me. He didn't . . . he didn't . . ."

Somehow he had not questioned the fact that she was still his and his alone. Somehow, he knew. He hushed her by placing his hand over her mouth. "I know," he said. "Now we must rejoin the others. When you are safe with them, I will go after de Rojas."

When soft hoots of an owl in the darkness through which they had been traveling for most of the night answered Renno's whippoorwill call, Emily knew they had reached the Seneca camp. She was happy, but also tired. Soon she was lying snug beside the campfire, listening to everything anyone could tell her about her son and eating a great chunk of roasted venison. She slept in her husband's arms.

El-i-chi promised Renno, in the morning's light, that if he were given a few minutes alone with the Spaniard, the man would talk, would beg to be allowed to talk. Renno shook his head. "He will be sent back to Knoxville. Send three men. Tell them to meet the Frontier Regiment and turn this man over to Colonel Johnson."

"You are going out again?" El-i-chi asked, seeing Renno's preparation.

Renno grunted in the affirmative. "For the other Spaniard."

"I will go with you."

"You and Se-quo-i," Renno said.

"Se-quo-i?"

"Is there a better tracker than he?"

El-i-chi laughed. "After you and me and Ena, no."

The three warriors moved fast, faster than the traditional warrior's trot, and the clearing where Renno had found Emily was reached quickly. At first it was easy to follow the trail left by de Rojas, for he was fleeing in panic. Soon, however, it became more difficult, and the sharp eyes of Se-quo-i, who had shown amazing tracking ability during the journey to the big river, were quite often the ones that picked up a sign.

Nevertheless, it was slow, and to Renno's amazement de Rojas had well survived the blow of the medicine ax, for he was moving strongly and swiftly. For hour after hour they followed the trail, lost it once after a thunderstorm, and had to make wide sweeps to pick it up again. As they penetrated more deeply into Chickasaw lands, they began to see evidence of much activity. Small parties, of two to ten men each, had left careless tracks as they moved toward the west from the various Chickasaw village groupings.

"They gather more swiftly than the Cherokee," El-i-chi said.

Renno made no comment, for El-i-chi's statement was a condemnation of the customs of the tribe with which the Seneca were allied. Renno knew that El-i-chi was still young enough to lose bouts with impatience, although he himself had reached the point at which his own impatience could be hidden behind a stoic mask. But custom was custom, even in perilous times, and the process of bringing all the Cherokee together for a major war had been going on for some long time.

First, runners had gone out with the call to war from Loramas, Grand Sachem of the entire tribe. That itself had taken time. The Cherokee lived in villages of not more than forty households, each an independent entity within the overall structure of the tribe. Each village had its elders, the "beloved" men, old and wise. Usually all men over the age of fifty-five formed the council of elders, and in some villages, the deliberating council was large, making for prolonged discussion, even though the outcome—obedience to the call from the Grand Sachem—was foreordained.

After deliberation by the elders, the war organization went into effect. A red standard was raised over

the village. Four of the elders assumed war roles
based on their knowledge and experience. The village war chief was elected by the warriors, and often
the other three war leaders—the war priest, the
speaker for war, and the surgeon—were also elected,
another procedure that called for long speeches and
much deliberation. Then the four war leaders appointed four junior officers—a flag bearer, a stand-in
for the war priest, and two other war leaders. Even
the selection of scouts required discussion, for being
a scout was a position of honor.

Once the organization was in place, it was time to
fast. A war dance lasted through the night. As the warriors danced, the deeds of heroes of the past were
recounted to induce young warriors to emulate them.
At dawn, after the all-night war dance, the warriors
went to the nearest stream and plunged in seven
times. The war speaker made his last exhortation,
and then and only then did the war party leave the
village, carrying its own standard.

It was all time-consuming. Once on the trail, the
village war parties had to hunt for their food, for a
man does not fight well after marching on nothing
more than, for example, parched corn. It was a time-
honored and inflexible code of behavior, and the
result of it was that Renno faced an indeterminate
period of waiting before all the Cherokee were gathered. Yet a leader could not defy ancient custom. A
warrior deserved to prepare himself for death in
battle in the same way his ancestors had prepared
themselves. He would fight the better for knowing
that all was right in his preparations.

Perhaps, Renno thought, the Chickasaw were more eager for war, for they were answering Oklawahpa's call quickly and in great numbers. If so many men could be gathered in the eastern areas, where the population was less dense than in the west, he knew that the Chickasaw warriors in the west would be gathering like flies to an old kill.

For fear of blundering into one of the Chickasaw war parties, the pace was slowed. Renno wanted his hands around de Rojas's throat so badly that he could almost feel the man's flesh giving under his fingers, but when the booted tracks of the Spaniard joined those of a party of over twenty Chickasaw, the white Indian began to realize that his vengeance would have to wait.

Far-ranging Seneca and Cherokee scouts were out, looking for concentrations of the enemy. El-i-chi, Se-quo-i, and Renno continued westward until El-i-chi, who was in the lead, sent back a soft coo of warning. Renno motioned Se-quo-i into concealment and told him to wait; then he crept forward. El-i-chi was waiting for his brother, hidden at the crest of a brushy hill. Renno crawled to his side, moving like a snake, scarcely causing the grass and weeds to wave around him.

The Chickasaw warriors of the eastern areas were congregated in a wide glade between stands of forest, along a stream. For a mile downstream and out of sight around a bend as the trees thickened, their fires sent light smoke into the air. Renno quickly estimated that the Chickasaw in his view numbered at least seven hundred. Smoke from fires farther down the creek added more to his estimate. And this, he knew, was not even the main force; led by Oklawahpa, the main force would march from the west. El-i-chi was right, he thought. The Chickasaw had been more efficient than the Cherokee in gathering men. Renno had at his disposal not more than five hundred warriors, which came mainly from the areas close to the village of Loramas, with, of course, all of the Seneca warriors. The bulk of the Cherokee fighting men were still at least two days behind. Once the two forces united, the entire might of the Cherokee nation, joined by the Seneca, would number only slightly more than this one section of Oklawahpa's army.

Renno had never been cowed by superior numbers, and if he had been as sure of the fighting abilities of all the Cherokee as he was of that portion of the nation that had been trained and led by Wegowa, and of his own Seneca, he would not have spent five minutes lying in the weeds and grass studying the Chickasaw encampment. Both he and Roy Johnson had doubted the Spanish estimate that Oklawahpa could outfit and put five thousand warriors in the field, but now Renno was not so sure. And when the Chickasaw forces were united, there would be cannon and mounted Spanish lancers whose armor would turn an arrow.

Whispering into his ear, El-i-chi said, "They are careless. There are no guards posted. We can go down there"—he pointed to a bushy ravine leading down to the stream—"and kill a few without anyone knowing we are here."

Renno shook his head, then began to inch back away from the brow of the hill. Only when they had put distance between the large encampment and themselves did he say, "They are both careless and confident, brother, and we want them to stay that way." As they made their way back toward the east and El-i-chi's sharp ears caught the approach of a small group of men, however, Renno saw no reason why the odds should not be reduced by some small fraction.

Five Chickasaw warriors, two of them carrying freshly slain deer, were moving at a leisurely pace toward the west. Renno led El-i-chi and Se-quo-i to a point along the trail ahead of the slow-moving enemy and said, as he tested the heft of his bow, "Our war begins now. No gunshots."

Se-quo-i was toying with his blowgun. "Use the bow," Renno told him. "Yours are the two carrying the deer." He looked at El-i-chi, whose face showed that fierce desire and fire of a warrior about to go into battle. "Yours is the one farthest to the left."

"Two for the young one, two for you, and only one for me?" El-i-chi complained.

Renno let his lips curl in a smile, but he remained silent. He placed Se-quo-i in the center; he himself was on the right. They were concealed in the trees at the edge of a small glade. The Chickasaw would emerge not twenty yards away. When Renno heard their voices conversing in a normal tone, he said, "Such overconfidence insults me. We will show them the faces of those who are about to kill them."

The five enemy warriors came up the trail two

abreast, the two who were carrying the deer carcasses at the rear, a tall, strong warrior leading the
other four. As they cleared the trees, Renno, bow
and arrow ready, stepped forth, El-i-chi and Se-quo-i
at his side. The leading Chickasaw gave a startled
whoop and began to fumble for his bow, but his
glimpse of the faces of his death was to be brief, for
three arrows sang out as one, Renno's piercing the
breast of the leader, the other two finding equally
fatal marks. Then Renno's arrow was followed by the
whooshing song of his great medicine ax. Only a
fraction of a second behind the ax came El-i-chi's
tomahawk. The ax did its deadly work on the skull of
the Chickasaw who had his own tomahawk drawn
back for a throw, and El-i-chi's blade buried itself in
the stomach of the warrior as he fell. The last man
had tossed aside the carcass on his shoulders and was
turning to flee when Se-quo-i's second arrow entered
his exposed side and penetrated to the heart. Within
a few minutes the scalps were taken, the two deer
carcasses hoisted onto the shoulders of Renno and
El-i-chi, and with Se-quo-i leading, the victors moved
on at a swift pace. The meat was fresh, too good to
leave behind. There was, of course, much game, but
the problems of feeding a large concentration of men
in a small area quickly depleted, or frightened away,
the available meat animals.

Within an hour of their arrival at the camp the
venison was roasted and almost ready for eating, the
aromas of its cooking wafting to Renno as he sat in
conference with Rusog.

"A thousand men, and that is not the entire might

of the enemy," Renno said, "but we have faced such odds before."

"If there are two Chickasaw for each of us, there will be much chance to gain honor," Rusog said with satisfaction.

"What news from the main body of your people, and from the Frontier Regiment?"

Rusog gazed at the sky for a moment. "We have news."

Renno waited.

"It came from one who had run hard, with two warriors."

Renno knew that Rusog would get to the point at his own time. He was patient.

"Now there are two women in our camp," Rusog finished.

Renno knew immediately who the other woman was. "Good," he said. "Ena can help to take Emily and Wynema back to the village."

"Ena is determined to fight at our side," Rusog said.

"And I would have her at my side in preference to most warriors," Renno admitted. "I will speak with her. First, what of the others?"

"By moving fast, a day," Rusog said. "But the Frontier Regiment waits for the last of its men, and they are two days' fast march behind us."

"Summon to us six of your strongest and fastest men," Renno said to his brother-in-law.

Rusog beckoned, and one of the subchiefs came to him, listened, nodded, and ran off, to return within minutes with six young, lithe warriors.

"You will find the camp of the Chickasaw in that direction," Renno told them, pointing. "You will go around the camp in groups of three. Go three miles past, select vantage points. Watch to the west. Under no circumstances, no matter what you hear from your rear, are you to leave your posts. When you have arrived at your vantage points, build a pile of dead brush so big that should the main force of the Chickasaw approach from the west, you will set fire to the brush and we will see your smoke."

Rusog looked at Renno quickly but waited until the six warriors had departed before speaking. "We will not wait for the arrival of the other Cherokee and Colonel Johnson's regiment?" he asked.

"The Chickasaw are playing at war," Renno answered, a wolf's smile on his face. "They eat and laugh along the banks of the stream. They think they will come against us in all their might, in all their thousands, at a time of their choosing. That is not to be."

Rusog nodded, a light coming into his dark eyes. "I like the way my brother thinks. I will pass the word."

"I will not ask that Ena come to me," Renno said with a grin, "for she would know my reasons and, perhaps, hide herself."

"She is there," Rusog said, pointing at his wife.

Renno found his sister seated on a doeskin blanket polishing a wicked-looking knife. When she saw him she started to smile, and then looked away guiltily. Renno sat down beside her. She remained silent, and Renno waited long moments before he spoke.

"In the tribe of your chosen husband, the women keep the fires of home," he said.

"I am Seneca."

"Even the women of the Seneca do not fight at the side of the warriors."

"Once I led," she reminded him, her green eyes flashing. "Once I was a scout, the closest one to the enemy."

Renno nodded. "Would my sister bring shame to her husband by acting the man?"

She shook her head in irritation. "It is not my husband but my brother who urges me to go home to a safe place and tend the fire."

Renno laughed. The blood of the white Indian did indeed run in his sister's veins.

"My wife does not share the warrior's skill," he said. "She and the child Wynema must be escorted back to our village. I ask you to do this."

"It can be done by some of those young warriors just into their teens, and by old men," Ena said, looking at him, but not begging.

"I know that Ena is a match for two, three common warriors," Renno said, "and yet my heart still would not be easy. I would think of my sister coming against four Chickasaw, perhaps, and of her hair decorating the lodgepole in a Chickasaw dwelling, and I would forget my fierceness."

"I must stay, Renno. I must."

He shook his head sadly. He had hoped that she would listen to reason, that he would not have to exercise his authority. "Then I must order you to go. We march before the morning mists. At that time you, with a proper escort of the young ones and the old ones you mentioned, will march to the east. That is the way it will be." He rose and, without looking back, walked away. Ena's knife zipped past his ear and embedded itself deeply in a tree trunk. He still did not turn.

He found the venison to be delicious. From somewhere, Emily had come up with herbs to season it. She sat close to him as they ate. She herself ate a huge quantity of the stew, finished, wiped her mouth, and smiled at him.

"You must not cook so well," Renno said, answering her smile. "Such goodness tempts a man to do nothing but stay around the lodge to treat his belly."

"I would like that," she teased, but she quickly put her hand on his arm and said, "No, I would not change you, Renno."

"Little Hawk will be happy to see you."

"Oh, yes," she said, then frowned as she placed one hand on her shrunken breast. "I have no more milk for him."

"By now my mother and grandmother are feeding him spring squash, new peas, and chewed meat," Renno reassured her.

But Emily made a face. She had seen the way Indian mothers fed their infants, by chewing food and then placing it into the baby's mouth.

"He will be strong and will not need your milk," Renno said.

"I will tell him of his father," she said. "How strong and brave *he* is."

Renno nodded, not with ego, for it was only fitting

that a boy-child be told of the deeds of his father. He himself had sat with awe and great attention as a child to hear of the deeds of his ancestors.

"Ena will accompany you," Renno said. "Sleep now, for we move in the darkness after midnight."

"So soon?" she asked, clinging to him. "Let me stay, Renno. Let me be here to greet you after your victory."

"Perhaps you will encounter your father on the way," he said. "If you do, tell him to be on the lookout for small bands of Chickasaw gathering toward the west, and tell him we march to the west after the battle tomorrow."

"You will not consider letting me stay?"

He looked into her eyes. "Would you, like Ena, have my mind distracted with worry for your safety?"

"No," she whispered. She was pressed tightly against his side. "I am not sleepy."

A surge of desire sprang up in him. He had had no opportunity to be alone with her, and he had put the thought of making love out of his mind because she was so thin, so tired looking. "Nor am I," he said.

"The forest is deep, and we could find privacy," she whispered.

They gathered grasses to make a soft bed. From far away came the lonely call of a whippoorwill. For a long time, they held each other tightly, thinking how close they had come to losing each other. Renno gently stroked his wife's back.

"I searched for you, Emily, and although I tried to face the probability of your death, in my heart I knew you were still alive." He felt her warm, soft breath in his ear, and he tightened his grip. "It will be good to be a family again, to see you and our son together in our lodge."

The thought was reassuring, and as he sought her lips with his own, he found peace, at last having her back in his arms.

Their love reaffirmed, they went back to the camp. Few of the warriors were sleeping. Many honed knives and tomahawks. Others retied bows, checked the straightness of arrows, looked to the priming of their muskets. As Renno and Emily walked through the area, the warriors saluted him gravely, spoke his name. None questioned. None approached. Each man was communing with himself and with the manitous, and Renno was pleased, for he recognized the readiness to fight, the tension, the anticipation that comes to a man only when he faces war and the choice— made by his own strength and his good right arm—of honor or death.

The fire had burned low. Renno replenished it with dry branches and sat watching Emily replait her yellow hair. Se-quo-i came to the fire, nodded, and extended a hand in which he held a bowl.

"What is this?" Renno asked.

"All the comforts and pleasures of home," Se-quo-i responded, grinning.

Renno put his fingers into the bowl to find a paste of flour, honey, and ground nuts. It was one of the more delicious Cherokee desserts. "Did someone else bring his woman?" he asked.

Se-quo-i laughed. "Honey Bear, from the village

of the two hills, does not travel without his sweets. He asked that I bring some to you and your wife."

"My thanks to Honey Bear," Renno said, extending the bowl to Emily. She scooped some of the sticky, sweet paste.

"*Ummm,*" she said as she licked and swallowed.

"Great Chief," Se-quo-i said, "you have ordered that I fight at the far rear."

Renno merely nodded.

"I would be at your side," Se-quo-i said.

Renno thought for a moment. "You have proved yourself to be a fine scout and a danger with the blowgun and bow and arrows. Because of your abilities, I will give you permission to go where your heart urges."

"Thank you," Se-quo-i said, then withdrew.

"All the comforts of home," Emily said, smiling, after Se-quo-i had walked away, his back stiff in pride.

"It will put meat back on your bones. When you are at home, eat meat, honey, and corn. When I return you will be fat and pretty."

She made a face. "Not too fat."

"No, not too fat," he said, placing his hand on her shoulder and falling silent.

"When you return we will feast together," she said. "I will crisp Jerusalem artichokes in cold spring water and salt them and feed them to you myself. Bring me a great fish as you come, and I will bake it with fried green tomatoes and baked squash in honey—"

"Then *I* will be fat," he said, laughing. He pushed

her away and rose, then lifted her to her feet. "It is time," he said. "Come, we will find Ena."

Ena sat, legs crossed, face impassive, in front of a fire. Rusog was with his men, perhaps lest he be involved in the decision of forcing Ena to leave the scene of the coming battle. A man can be as brave as a mountain lion and still not want to make his wife unhappy.

"It is time," Renno said.

Ena rose gracefully, walked to put her arms around Emily. "My sister," she said, "forgive me for not coming to you sooner. I rejoiced at the news that you were well, but I knew you would want to spend this little time with this one"—she nodded at Renno—"even though he is a stubborn and heartless man."

"Be kind to him, Ena," Emily urged. "He thinks only of you."

"I can think of myself," Ena said.

"Rusog will choose men to accompany you," Renno said in a stern voice. "Travel fast throughout the remainder of the night. Rest only after you have crossed the rocky river and are within our own lands."

"Since you will not allow me to take my proper place with my husband," Ena said, "I have arranged for another to fight in my stead."

Renno showed no expression, but he was puzzled. Ena snapped her fingers, and with a cackling chuckle, the Chickasaw simpleton, Crazy Fox, pranced into the light of the fire.

Crazy Fox had painted his face with garish red and highlighted it with black and white. His huge nose was a red berry protruding from a field of white, and his eyes were at the core of concentric circles. He wore the buckskin costume of the Cherokee, and at his sash were two knives, one with a broken blade. A stone tomahawk that would not have cut mud was in his hand. A bow with one side flat—the wooden fibers having been broken down by long use—hung on his shoulder.

"Who brought this one here?" Renno demanded angrily.

"When I left our village," Ena replied, "he must have followed me at a distance. By the time I detected his presence, it was too late to take him back."

"I Cherokee now," Crazy Fox said. "I protect you, Great Chief."

"He goes back with you," Renno said in a tone that allowed no challenge.

"Why, brother," Ena said mildly, "I felt sure that you would welcome this addition to your forces, since you insist that I not be a part of them. He bears great respect for you and still possesses the sacred stone you gave him."

Emily watched unhappily as Crazy Fox posed, lifting his stone tomahawk high and laughing happily as he danced around Renno.

Rusog chose that time to appear, with six warriors, four very young and two old, and little Wynema.

"Husband," Ena said, "I have given our brother a warrior to fight in my stead, but he is not pleased."

Rusog's face went grim. He had never seen or even heard of a woman whom he would prefer to this strong, willful Seneca woman, but there were times when a man had to control his own.

"Enough," Rusog said gruffly. "It is time to go."

"The simpleton goes," Renno ordered.

"Of course," Rusog replied.

Renno had said his good-bye to Emily in the forest. He gave her a sign of blessing with his hand and watched as the small group disappeared into the darkness.

There was no need for words between Rusog and Renno. A look, a clasp of arms, and the two separated, each going to his own fire to await the passage of midnight.

Chapter VIII

Renno's hopes for surprise were still alive at dawn, as the force of Cherokee and Seneca moved smoothly forward, increasing their pace with the light.

Two factors contributed to Renno's being able to position his men on three sides of the Chickasaw camp without detection: first, since the Chickasaw were traditionally makers of war, it was difficult for their war leaders to imagine being attacked; second the Chickasaw were of such number that the sheer size of the encampment gave them a sense of false security.

Renno had found a solution to his reluctance to have so young a warrior as Se-quo-i in the forefront of the battle at his side. As they marched through the late night hours, he had to keep in touch with Rusog, so he utilized Se-quo-i as a runner. By noon, with the sun high and hot in the sky, Se-quo-i, having covered twice as much ground as the others, and at a dead run, was tiring rapidly. Rusog was on the far left, to the south. Renno was on the right, to the north. He lay on his belly atop the same rise where he and El-i-chi had first scouted the encampment, and now Se-quo-i was just behind him. The Chickasaw were, if anything, more numerous, but they were obviously waiting for something—most probably, Renno thought, the arrival of Oklawahpa and his main force from the west. Renno scanned the western sky and looked for the smoke that would signal the coming of that overwhelming force, but all he saw was clear blue, with gathering thunderheads in the southwest.

Renno had not told Se-quo-i the signal for the attack. It was quite a simple signal: the Seneca would charge head-on, howling the Seneca war cries. Then the Cherokee warriors, positioned in a semicircle to the south, would charge, and thus the attack would be a wave, breaking first at the north and then curling around. In that way, the Chickasaw's attention would be focused on the battle with the Seneca before Rusog struck from the south. The Chickasaw to the south, along the stream, would be moving north, thinking that was where the action was. Then the Chickasaw would be surprised by El-i-chi's warriors' attack from the rear.

"One more message," Renno whispered to Se-quo-i. "Go far back behind the ridge so that you may run quickly to Rusog. Tell him all is ready."

Se-quo-i, still panting from his last run, set off, and Renno gave him five minutes to be safe and well out of the fight before he looked to his left, saw El-i-chi on his flank, poised and ready, leaped to his feet, and threw his mouth open in the mighty cry of the Okwari, the Bear Clan of the Seneca.

From many throats the cry answered him, and he started down the slope and leaped the small creek, to meet the whooping, surprised reaction of the first Chickasaw seeing the danger, with thunderous swings of the great medicine ax. All around him the cry of the Bear Clan roared and echoed, and the unprepared enemy began to fall quickly.

So confident had the Chickasaw been that a few had been playing at the Chickasaw version of stickball. A player came whooping at Renno, armed with only his game stick, and fell, as three others had already fallen, to the heated blade of the great ax.

The war cries were Cherokee now, coming from Renno's left as the wave of warriors began to break farther down the creek, and all was bedlam—shrieks of anger, perhaps of fear, of pain, of death, and of war. Surprised as they were, the Chickasaw still fought, trying to rally by village groups to face the onslaught of Seneca—whom many felt to be the finest fighting men in the world.

Far from their traditional home, this group of Seneca was, in a way, exiled from their own people, but by their own choice had followed their great leaders to the south. Many had been a part of making a new nation, a nation of whites, the United States. They had fought Frenchmen, Englishmen, and Indians of many tribes, and now they fought for their chosen home, for their freedom, for honor, and to count coup—although that ceremonial activity was quickly forgotten as the battle became heated.

The first and only firing of Seneca and Cherokee muskets had launched the battle and had cut down on the odds. Then the battle was waged with flying arrows. But as the forces closed, the combat was hand-to-hand, with knife and tomahawk, and a great ax wielded by a pale-skinned warrior whose contorted face meant death to Chickasaw warrior after Chickasaw warrior.

Se-quo-i, running south a good distance behind the ridge from which Renno had attacked, heard the first war cries and wondered what had happened. Had the Chickasaw detected his people before the surprise could be launched? He halted and started to run back toward Renno's position so that he could be at the side of his leader, but then he turned reluctantly toward the south, because he had his orders. It was only when he heard the full bellowing of the Cherokee war cries that he suspected that Renno had deliberately put him out of danger with his order, so he turned and ran quickly and directly toward the battle. He arrived on the top of the ridge in time to see Rusog's end of the enfolding wave break from the tree line and strike those Chickasaw who were running to join the battle. Ahead of Se-quo-i, a hand-to-hand struggle was going on as Chickasaw met Cherokee at the creek. The waters of the creek were running red as Se-quo-i charged down the hill, no longer tired, nocking an arrow with which he made his first kill as he dropped to one knee and took aim. Then he was in the midst of it, working his way toward the north, where the fighting was most fierce.

To the west, there was another observer of the battle: Captain Guy de Rojas, a man who had learned his lesson well. He had tried to warn these local war leaders to be on guard, saying that they would not be fighting an ordinary enemy when they clashed with the Seneca and the Cherokee. Because he was not so well-known among the Chickasaw of the east, his warning had been ignored, indeed almost laughed at. So he had made his camp in a well-hidden place, alone. He would not be surprised again as he and his scouting expedition had been in the woods and in the dark. He heard the first Seneca whoop and saw, from his safe perch high among dense trees, that the attack was led by the same pale-skinned warrior who had almost killed him. His head still ached where a huge bump was healing.

"What manner of man are you?" he whispered while the strong pale-skinned warrior swung his terrible weapon with such power that a skull exploded in a red-and-gray mist—and even then the ax did not cease movement but swung to kill again on the backhand blow.

De Rojas knew that this loss—for he quickly saw

that an enemy victory was inevitable—could have been avoided. With planning and care, a picket line of men could have been posted on the ridge and in the woods, blunting the enemy charge and giving the main body time to position itself and ready its arms. But now there came a great charge of Cherokee from the south, sweeping up Chickasaw, leaving bodies strewn about, making the stream run red, and still those devils, that smaller force, pressed on, fighting as he had never seen men fight, moving through a sea of enemy bodies, and bellowing war cries.

When Chickasaw warriors, feeling that flight was now the better part of valor, began to run past his position and abandon the fight, de Rojas climbed down from his tree and began to trot toward the west. He joined a small group of Chickasaw and recognized one of the young war chiefs who had refused to heed his advice. The war chief could not meet de Rojas's eyes, but he was a sadder and a wiser man. When de Rojas spoke, this time the young war chief listened.

"Gather those who flee and form a line of pickets behind us," de Rojas said. "The enemy will not pursue us in force, but he will send out small groups to probe. Tell your men to strike and fall back. We will meet Oklawahpa within two days."

The Chickasaw war chief now obeyed with alacrity.

"They were as many as the blades of grass," complained one warrior who stayed behind, as he examined a small wound on his arm.

"They were fewer than you," de Rojas pointed out sharply.

The warrior bristled and lifted his tomahawk.

"Strike if you care to," de Rojas challenged, for he had a pistol cocked, the muzzle pointed at the Chickasaw's breast. "But a wise man will listen. They were fewer, and it was the fault of your leaders that you have been disgraced."

Many Chickasaw did not flee. They were men of honor, warriors of a great tribe, with a great tradition. They could not believe—not until they felt the piercing pain of arrow, knife, tomahawk, or the sudden oblivion brought by Renno's heated medicine ax—that the Chickasaw nation could taste defeat. They formed between the crushing jaws of the twin forces, and the jaws closed on them, blocking the escape to the west into the forest. They fought well—too well, in Renno's estimation, when, as it ended, and only scattered man-to-man battles continued, he looked around to see the creekside meadow reddened and covered with bodies. He had lost men, as had Rusog, although the Cherokee had accounted for twice their own numbers, with not half the losses.

Scalp-taking added to the carnage. Renno stalked the meadow, calling the roll of his men in his mind, ticking off names as he saw faces, heard victory whoops, and looked down sadly at the fallen, for the Seneca had not escaped the battle unscathed.

El-i-chi. Where was El-i-chi? The distinctive pale skin was not visible. There was Rusog, coming toward him holding aloft his tomahawk in victory. There, at Rusog's side, bloody scalps on his belt, was young Se-quo-i. Renno recognized and accounted for most of his men, but still there was no El-i-chi.

"We must pursue the stragglers," Rusog said, breathing hard. "We must destroy them to a man."

"My brother," Renno said, spreading his hands to indicate the bloody field, "we have struck our blow. In the forest they will rally, and although we would kill them, they would take their toll firing from shelter."

Rusog's chest heaved. "You speak wisdom," he said.

"Now we have lessened the odds against us once again," Renno said. "That is good. But now that they know they face a worthy foe, there will be no more easy victories, my Brother. We will need all our strength."

From deep within the forest Renno heard a rattle of musket shots. He turned to Se-quo-i. "Can you still run?"

"Yes, Great Chief. Where do you want me to go?"

"Not far, just within the forest. Call out my orders. Tell all to return here and not to pursue the enemy."

The taking of spoils had been completed and men were tending wounds and comparing stories when Se-quo-i returned, with El-i-chi at his side. Renno felt a great weight lifted from his heart at the sight of his brother. El-i-chi and Se-quo-i were followed by a dozen Cherokee and Seneca who had followed the fleeing enemy into the forest.

"The Chickasaw are there," El-i-chi said. "I went to see if they would have the courage to stand. They fire from concealment and fall back."

"They are brave," Renno said. "A worthy enemy."

He looked around the meadow. "We will move to the north, upstream, away from this place, and try to rest before we fight Oklawahpa's army."

When Emily had first fallen in love with Renno and had decided that in spite of their cultural differences, she would spend her life with him in his world, she had spent time with Renno's mother, Toshabe, and grandmother, Ah-wen-ga, to learn Seneca ways. During her early days with the tribe, she had both admired and been in awe of Renno's sister, Ena. She had also thought that Ena was one of the most beautiful women she had ever seen. Very slender, with the green eyes and brown hair of a white woman, Ena seemed to be able to do anything, even those things usually reserved for men, like scouting. Now, as a young but mature woman, Ena had a figure that was slightly more rounded and as close to feminine perfection as Emily had ever seen, and in marked contrast to Emily's own present emaciated state. Although Emily's muscles were hard and she felt strong, she fancied herself to look like a skeleton when compared to Ena.

Emily's time as a Seneca had cemented a relationship between the sisters-in-law. There had been times when, as a new wife, young, away from her home and her people, Emily had needed the companionship of someone her own age. Sometimes she had had questions that would have embarrassed her if she had taken them to either Ah-wen-ga or Toshabe. Ena, then, had become her confidante, her friend, and she was pleased to have Ena's company during the long trip back to the village.

Emily herself insisted on a fast pace, and the young warriors often took turns with Emily in carrying Wynema, so the child would not slow their progress. She had a burning desire to see her own child. With that reward in store, the night's journey was no hardship for her, and when Ena called a rest as the sun rose, she reluctantly sat down on a mossy fallen log and began to eat.

Unbeknownst to Emily, Ena had been smoldering with resentment during the night's march because Renno had ordered her home. She had now come to a decision. The two older men with the party were experienced, dependable warriors who themselves were disappointed at being deprived of the most exciting war in the history of the Cherokee. Ena knew that they would obey orders, and with the young men to furnish muscle and energy, Emily would be safe in their care until they reached the village.

"You will continue alone," Ena told Emily, finishing her food, standing, and gathering her weapons.

"Ena, you can't go back! Neither Rusog nor Renno want to have you at risk," Emily said.

"It is my desire and my duty," Ena explained.

"Your duty, dear sister, is to obey your chief and your husband," Emily said. She, too, had matured. Never before would she have dared to reprimand the willful, fiery Ena.

Ena's green eyes flashed with anger, but only for a moment. "I understand your concern," she said. "But

I must go." She joined the men, who were seated at a distance, chewing on *canutchie*, and gave them their orders. One of the older warriors questioned Ena's decision, but she merely glared at him, and then she was gone.

Emily could do nothing to stop Ena's going, but she approached the warriors and asked, "Should one of you go back to tell Renno that Ena is returning?"

The elder of the two senior warriors said, "We go with you, for the wife of Renno must have protection."

As Emily walked, guarded front and rear by the warriors, she looked over her shoulder. Far in the distance, as they crossed a ridge and could see back toward the west, she saw a column of smoke pouring into the clear morning sky. Below her, Ena had disappeared into the forest.

The column of smoke seen by Emily had already been noticed by the warriors in Renno's war camp. The scouts he had sent out, far to the rear of the Chickasaw force that he had just defeated, had done their work. Renno climbed to a point of vantage. First one and then two columns of smoke told the same story. The position of the smoke was right; it was the signal that Oklawahpa's western Chickasaw had gathered together for the ultimate battle. That meant that the Seneca and Cherokee would have little time to rest from their last battle and little time to prepare for the next one. To make matters worse, the total force of the Cherokee was not yet in one position. Several village-size war parties had joined during the night; others, in two main groups, would not arrive until during the day.

But Oklawahpa was on the move, coming with his main force. The destiny of the Cherokee nation and of the Seneca would be decided within the next few days.

Guy de Rojas almost lost his scalp when, having left his Chickasaw companions behind as scouts and pickets, he stumbled upon an advance party leading Oklawahpa's huge army. An arrow whistled past his ear before he yelled out in fury. He was seized roughly by several stalwart and eager young braves and bundled unceremoniously back to the spot where Oklawahpa stood—an angry, unbelieving Oklawahpa, for he was listening to an account of the slaughter on the creek. When he saw de Rojas, he abruptly motioned the warrior who was telling of the battle into silence and turned, arms crossed in fury, to glare at the Spaniard.

De Rojas was not an impressive sight. He had long since ceased wearing armor in the warmth of the spring days, and his recent problems and headlong flight had wrought havoc with his clothing.

"Twice now, Spaniard," Oklawahpa thundered, "you have led my men into ambush and defeat!"

De Rojas glared back at the war chief. His own thoughts were murderous. Twice now his life had been put in peril by the overconfidence of the Chickasaw. But de Rojas knew that he was in no position to express his opinion of Chickasaw leadership. He knew that each individual Chickasaw warrior was a match for any man and that the fighting spirit of the warriors was not in question. The problem was, he felt, that the leaders of the warlike nation had grown complacent. They had been living on the Chickasaw reputation for fierceness in war, whereas the enemy was not awed by what Chickasaw warriors had done in the past.

"It is true," de Rojas said in a reasonable voice, "that misfortune has struck twice. There is a reason for that, Great Chief."

Oklawahpa continued to glare at him, waiting for that reason.

"You know that in the past the Cherokee have fought well," de Rojas said.

"We have fought better," Oklawahpa retorted.

"But the Cherokee has traditionally been a worthy foe. Why else does Oklawahpa send his war parties to the north and the west instead of into Cherokee lands?"

Oklawahpa's face darkened, and de Rojas knew full well that he was angering the chief, but that was his intention.

"Is it not true that the Cherokee fights more bravely than, for example, the Quapaw or the Shawnee?"

Oklawahpa forced away the sudden urge to see de Rojas burning and being flayed by the women, because he had committed himself to a course of action that would be impossible without the arms and the supplies furnished by the white men from Spain. He had seen great wagons come from New Orleans, delivering the muskets now carried by his warriors. Behind him was a troop of Spanish cavalry on great horses, and he had seen the fiery belch of death delivered by the field cannon of the Spaniards.

Oklawahpa's face remained impassive, and he took a deep breath. "To say that for fear we avoid fighting the Cherokee is a lie, Spaniard. Are we not here? We will sweep the Cherokee before us as the winds of winter drive the fallen leaves. We will take his scalp and his women and burn his lodges, and his land will be ours."

"As you believe in four things," de Rojas said, using a ceremonial tone to give his statement weight, "the clouds, the sun, the clear streams, and the Beloved One who dwelleth in the blue sky, believe what I am about to say."

"Speak, then," Oklawahpa said.

"Hundreds of Chickasaw are dead, and the vultures now pick their bones because your war leaders speak a better battle than they fight."

Oklawahpa and one of his young chiefs took angry steps forward, hands going to their knives. But then Oklawahpa paused and waved his young chief back. "Go on, Spaniard."

"Your leaders must recognize one new fact," de Rojas said. "No longer does the Cherokee sit on his own lands, waiting for you to choose a time and a place to fight. Witness the blood of the creek. That is a Chickasaw creek, in Chickasaw lands, and yet your braves lie rotting there."

"The Cherokee have occasionally attacked us," Oklawahpa pointed out.

"A few hot-blooded young ones counting coup, striking and running," de Rojas said. "Like you, they have played at war. But now they are together, marching against you, and unless you realize that you're fighting a new kind of enemy, more Chickasaw blood will flow."

"I have given orders to form for an attack," Oklawahpa said. "The blood of our dead will be avenged quickly."

"Yes," de Rojas said, making his disgust more evident by spitting. "Try to do that. Go whooping and running into the jaws of death, and their pale-skinned chief, who is not Cherokee but of a tribe I know not, will close those jaws around you and crush you as he crushed a thousand men at the creek."

"We will destroy many with your cannon," Okla-wahpa vowed.

"Not if the guns are miles to the rear, as they apparently are now. Not if my gunners don't know where to fire for fear of killing Chickasaw instead of Cherokee. Great Chief, if we are to win, we must combine our methods. I have praise for the Chickasaw warrior—he is brave, a match for any man—but if he is put into hopeless positions by his leaders, he will only fight bravely to his death."

"This man who questions the leadership of the Chickasaw should answer by the test of the individual combat," challenged Oklawahpa's young chief.

"Silence!" Oklawahpa ordered.

"There were no guards posted at the creek," de Rojas continued. "The pale-skinned leader put his men into position not a hundred yards from men who were playing ball, and he did it without one Chickasaw seeing or hearing, because no one was looking or listening. Is this the wisdom of Oklawahpa's leaders?"

Oklawahpa's eyes widened in angry surprise. He turned to the warrior who had been telling him about the battle. "Is this true? Were there no scouts, no guards?"

"Great Chief," the warrior said uneasily, "we were many. We were in our own lands—"

"I pray to the Beloved One who dwelleth in the blue sky that all the war chiefs died bravely," Oklawahpa said. "If any lived, bring him to me now. He will join the slaves in pulling the Spaniards' cannon." He nodded to de Rojas. "Come. We will talk."

Oklawahpa led the way to a grassy knoll where his own camp had been set up. He motioned, and a young warrior poured two bowls of steaming herb tea and then departed. De Rojas sat on a skin and sipped the tea.

"A pale-skinned chief?" Oklawahpa asked.

"He is not a white man. He wears his hair not like a white man or a Cherokee, and he leads others who dress differently, in small ways, and are well-trained. This pale-skinned one led the attack at the creek. He fights with a great war ax." The Spanish captain did not mention his other encounter with the pale-skinned warrior's wife and with his great ax, but he glowered at the memory. "When we meet this man again, he is mine. I want him."

Oklawahpa nodded assent. "Now we will talk of the position of your cannon."

De Rojas experienced great self-satisfaction as he

pulled out the map he had drawn. It was battered and torn, but still legible. He spread it on the ground.

"The cannon should be mounted on high ground," de Rojas said, pointing, "with a field of fire as large and as free of trees as possible. The more open the terrain, the more effective the cannon and the horsemen."

"Perhaps, since the Cherokee are now led by this pale-skinned chief, they will not choose to fight on such ground."

"They will fight. Somehow they seem to know our intention to take everything that is theirs. Why else would they abandon their usual defensive tactics and invade Chickasaw lands?"

Actually, de Rojas now suspected that not only had the messenger from the Spanish governor to Okla-wahpa been intercepted by the Cherokee—only knowledge of the Treaty of Pensacola could account for the Cherokee success in offensive maneuvers—but also that the secret orders hidden in the hilt of the stiletto must have been found.

"We outnumber them," de Rojas continued, "but they will fight to the last man in defense of their lands and homes. We will not heedlessly charge into their carefully prepared positions. Instead we will taunt them, tempt them with small clashes, and lead them into the attack on our own ground, where the cannon will thin their ranks and where my lancers can decimate them from horseback. Ahead, about three hours' fast march, is the kind of position we can best utilize. Order your war chiefs to form their men along the tree line of a great meadow that

slopes eastward toward a line of cottonwood trees
and a small muddy stream. My lancers will be positioned in front of a small rise at the north end of the
meadow. The cannon will be mounted on the rise
and will be protected by the lancers and about one
hundred of your men." De Rojas was pointing to the
battle site on the map.

Oklawahpa was leaning forward, intensely inter-
ested. "The Cherokee will go around the meadow
and attack from the north and south."

"Yes," de Rojas agreed. "But then we will send a
large force of men directly across the meadow, in the
open. They will be protected by the cannon. The
Cherokee will have to meet the charge, I hope, in
the open meadow; otherwise, we'll have your men
split their forces, penetrate behind them, and attack
their rear. And when we draw them into the open,
the lancers will sweep them."

"Good," Oklawahpa said. "The Chickasaw is not
accustomed to defensive battle, but here we only
pretend to be on the defensive, is that not true?"

"That is true," de Rojas said. "We make them
think we are subdued by the previous defeats, and
we draw them into our trap."

"It is good."

"One thing more," de Rojas said. "We must know
the strength and location of the enemy. We must
send out many scouts."

"It will be done."

After the discussion, de Rojas first found himself
some food, then began to look for clothing more
suitable than his tattered uniform. Since most of the

Chickasaw warriors were stripping to their battle dress, consisting of nothing more than deerskin loincloths and moccasins, he was able to find a pair of buckskin trousers, a fringed doeskin shirt, and moccasins that had been taken from a dead man. He slept then, and when he awoke, he went forward to arrange for proper positioning of the cannon, to give instructions to the young officer in charge of the lancers, and to check on the disposition of Oklawahpa's men. He found that he had chosen his ground well. Scouts began to filter back with reports that large bodies of men had joined the enemy forces, but that they were not yet on the move.

Chapter IX

The coolness of spring had given way to a premature summer. The air was still and the sun hot, causing Cherokee and Seneca alike to shed their shirts and expose their torsos to be painted with the colors of war. Renno, Rusog, and their appointed war chiefs were gathered at a distance from the nearest body of men. From time to time a scout would come back to report. A picture of Chickasaw intentions was being painted by those reports as Oklawahpa began to place his men in their defensive positions facing a large grassy meadow and a shallow muddy creek.

Rusog, always fiery, suggested an immediate attack before all of the Chickasaw could be put into position. Renno and some of the older war chiefs advised caution, for the situation was still too fluid to commit the outnumbered army to what might well be the final and climactic battle.

Anticipation surged through the camp when Roy Johnson arrived, having ridden hard, to report that his Franklin Frontier Regiment would be with the allied Indian force by evening. The white fighting men would be few in number, no more than a hundred, but their presence denoted the friendship between Indian and white settler, and all of the Indian leaders respected the firepower and discipline of the regiment.

Renno, taking Johnson aside, immediately told him how Emily had been found, sharing in the older man's relief and rejoicing. Explaining that Emily had been given an escort home, Renno smiled as the colonel placed a firm hand on his son-in-law's shoulder and stared into the younger man's eyes in mute thanks.

Finding his voice at last, Johnson told Renno that his only remaining regret was that his reunion with Emily would have to wait until after the present campaign was over. He then went on immediately to report that the questioning of Ramón de Vega in Knoxville had revealed no new information, the Spaniard continuing to honor his loyalties with absolute silence. The man had been sent, under guard, into North Carolina in an effort to convince representatives of the United States that the Spanish threat to the mid-Mississippi was real. Nothing more had been heard of the Spaniard.

Now the primary concern was for Renno's war chiefs to gather together quickly, so his father-in-law could be briefed on the position of the enemy and possible strategy.

"It's not like the Chickasaw to choose a defensive position," Johnson said, lighting his pipe. "I think we should be prepared for a trick."

Renno nodded. "His defensive position is also an excellent place from which to launch an offense," he warned. "We must prevent this. We must engage him on two fronts, to the east and south. It appears that he will place his cannon here"—using a stick, he had sketched out a rough map in the dirt—"and to make things more dangerous for us, the cannon are accompanied by the lancers and a force of Chickasaw."

"Far range of fire?" Johnson asked.

Renno nodded, his expression serious. "He can decimate anything that moves in the meadow, and his fire can reach into the trees across and along the creek."

"My men should face the Spanish lancers," Johnson said.

"Does the colonel think that the Cherokee cannot fight the mounted Spaniards?" challenged a grizzled, stalwart senior warrior. That was Danega, who had fought with Ghonkaba, Renno's father. Beside Danega, already risen to the status of senior warrior and in charge of one section of the Seneca forces, was his son, Dawida, as tall as Renno and thicker in the chest, a man upon whom a leader could heap responsibility.

"The regiment can lay down a controlled volley of fire," Johnson explained mildly. "That will be more effective against a cavalry charge than Indian tactics."

"Our war chief has considered the problem of the lancers," Rusog said gruffly.

Johnson quickly saw that some Indians resented his efforts to impose his opinions. He knew that the winning of the battle and the safety of the entire territory depended upon the Indians and Renno's leadership.

"I am sure that the sachem's plans are well laid," he said, nodding toward Renno, hoping to defuse the resentment.

"You bring fewer than one hundred men," old Danega said gravely, looking into Johnson's eyes. "Where are the others? Where are the men of the United States?"

There was a long moment of silence.

Danega stood. "Not long past," he said, "the white men of the colonies begged for the aid of the Seneca in fighting the British, and we answered that call. Our young men fought, and many died. We were told that we were fighting for freedom for all, not just for the freedom of the thirteen white colonies. Because our decision to fight at the side of the colonists was against the treaties of our tribe, we who fought became homeless. We left the sacred hunting grounds of our ancestors because we were considered traitors to our tribe and to our alliance with the Iroquois League. Our brothers the Cherokee opened their arms and their hearts to us, and with them we have found a new home. True, this is not the home of our ancestors, and the ghosts of our fathers and our grandfathers walk the earth looking for us in vain, for we are far away. And now our home and the home of our brothers is threatened again—again by the white man—and where are our former friends? Where are the armies of the colonies, beside whom we fought and died to save *their* lands, and to gain *their* freedom?"

Johnson took a while to formulate his answer. He himself had been more than chagrined when his call to arms produced so small a force. In spite of all the evidence he had presented—the copy of the Treaty of Pensacola, the stiletto paper, the actual physical presence of Ramón de Vega, a Spanish prisoner—many of the white settlers considered the threat to have been blown out of proportion. No one seemed to care whether or not the Spanish established trading posts along the Mississippi. No one seemed to understand the terrible implications of such an action— their homes were not threatened; after all, many said, between their homes and the big river were the Cherokee. And many of the settlers saw no reason to leave their farms at a time when it was necessary to begin planting the year's crops, just to face what seemed to be an exaggerated threat.

"Danega's questions are questions that I myself have asked," Johnson confessed, shaking his head sadly. "I have no excuses or answers. I can only say to my brother that I myself am here, that the regiment will be here before the sunset, and that we will fight. As the sachem knows, we have made efforts to obtain aid from the established states. That none was forthcoming is a puzzle, but also a fact. We are in this together, my friends. We will fight together, and we will make the Chickasaw die for his threat to our lands."

It was obvious that Danega was not satisfied by Johnson's answer. He gazed thoughtfully toward the west before speaking.

"We, the Cherokee and the Seneca, are all that stand between the Chickasaw and their intention to sweep the earth of all Cherokee between the great river and the blue mountains. Yet the white man sees this as nothing more than just another war between tribes. Is that not true? The white man speaks of savages. And yet long before the white man came, the Indian knew the value of allies. The Iroquois League stood against all enemies for hundreds of years until we Seneca chose to stand beside the colonists in the war against the redcoats. The Iroquois League was great, and its planning was wise. I cannot read the white man's words, but I am told that the League's wisdom can be found in the Constitution of the United States." Danega paused, and his eyes shone darkly as he looked at Roy Johnson. "We had much land then. When the white man drove the Delaware from his land, we took him in. Then the Tuscarora moved up from the south and became the sixth tribe of the League. But we willingly abandoned everything to fight for the white man and his land. And now, when we are faced with an enemy in superior numbers, with cannon and mounted cavalry, we are alone!"

Rusog grunted agreement. Renno said nothing, keeping his face impassive. He had noted a growing dissatisfaction among some of his people. Most were well settled and content in their new homes, but some of the older ones, such as Danega, often spoke of what they still called home, of the traditional Seneca hunting grounds in the northeast.

"Danega speaks great wisdom," Roy Johnson said. "I can only pledge to put my body beside his in the battle, for I, at least, know that we fight not only for your land, but for ours. If Danega risks spilling his blood, I risk spilling mine. I can do no more."

"Well spoken," Renno said.

All made affirmative sounds. Danega had spoken his heart, but now was the time to turn to the fighting.

"Renno, have your scouts told you anything about the availability of ammunition for the cannon?" Colonel Johnson asked.

"They have a limited supply of round shot," Renno answered. "That concerns me less than grapeshot, of which they have at least three wagon loads. They also have a good supply of powder, so I expect to see the use of canister shot utilizing pebbles."

Johnson knew that the Cherokee had never faced cannon before. Some of the Seneca had seen the effects of artillery during the War of Independence. He waited for Renno to continue.

"The situation may change," Renno said, "but as of now the cannon are protected by the lancers and a force of about one hundred Chickasaw. It is my intention to draw the lancers into combat and eliminate them early in the fighting."

Johnson chuckled. The idea of needing to lure cavalry into a charge was a concept that only an Indian could have. He himself knew that the cavalry, eager to prove their worth, would not take much luring.

"Then, while the main force of the Cherokee is being engaged, El-i-chi will capture the cannon from the hundred warriors left as guards. Do you have men who know cannon and can turn the captured guns on the Chickasaw?"

This seemed to be overconfidence to Johnson, but he did not express his doubts. Renno had surprised him in the past and would doubtless continue to do so in the future. "We have a couple of Washington's veterans who were artillerymen."

"They will follow El-i-chi," Renno decided.

"And the rest of the regiment?" Johnson asked.

"Here," Renno said, stabbing at the map in the dirt to indicate a point on the far left, on the flank in the south. "From cover. Your musket fire will concentrate on the Chickasaw right as they charge."

"You mean *if* they charge."

"They will charge," Rusog said with a smile that did not reach his eyes.

"El-i-chi will begin his infiltration of the enemy positions as soon as the Chickasaw have settled in with intentions of staying put," Renno said. "Please have your artillerymen with him."

Johnson did not relish having to ask men to go

behind enemy lines with a small force of Seneca, but he was sure that his veterans would volunteer.

"I'll ride back to meet the regiment," he said. "I'll have the artillerymen report to El-i-chi as soon as they arrive."

Danega remained with Renno after the others left, stepped forward, and clasped arms with the young war leader. Danega was an impressive warrior, chest bared and painted. Age wrinkled the skin around his dark, piercing eyes, and his hair was cut in the traditional scalp lock.

"Renno, son of my beloved leader, we are a long way from home," Danega said.

"Has Danega not been contented here, in what is now our home?" Renno asked.

"Yes, but my heart lies in the snows of the North with the ghosts of my fathers," Danega said. "When this is over, Renno, I will go there. I will die there so that my ghost will not wander far fields and forests looking for the spirits of those who have gone before me."

"You could find *orenda* here, as well," Renno said. "But you are wise, and of the age of honor. If you must go, my heart will go with you."

Left alone, Renno reviewed all his plans and was pleased. Then, as he heard reports from the scouts that told him the Chickasaw were indeed massing to face the meadow and muddy creek, he let his mind wander. How different were things back in the traditional hunting grounds? He knew that there was a steady push toward the west by the white settlers, that the push was into lands of the Iroquois League.

How was it with the Seneca who had remained true to their treaty of friendship with the British? Had they suffered by having sided with the losers in the war? And how would it be with his people if, someday in the future, he or his son, Little Hawk, led the exiled Seneca home? It was a thought to be meditated on. When the war was over, he would fast and pray and seek wisdom from the manitous.

Ena had traveled fast and far. Twice, in spite of her skills and her care, she had had to identify herself with the distinctive Seneca dove call as Renno's rear guards detected her presence. Each time she had been recognized, for she was, after all, sister of the Seneca sachem and wife of Rusog, who, when Loramas and Wegowa died, would lead the Cherokee by his own judgments. She allowed no time for questions from the warriors she encountered and quickly left them, moving northward. She would not be able to join the fight too early, lest she be seen by Rusog or Renno and be ordered away again.

It was invigorating to be alone again, and in a place of peril. Once she had led, as scout—and there had even been a dispute between her and Rusog about her daring, for she had ranged far ahead. But now there was no one to prevent her from finding out for herself the disposition of the enemy forces, and this knowledge and skill would be of value. Thus, she formulated her plan and skirted the friendly forces to the north, moving like a shadow, exercising wilderness skills that were a match for any warrior.

Each day she expected to hear the distant roar of

the Spanish cannon, but she reached an area to the north of both forces without that sound and began to work her way ever so carefully to the south, knowing that she had to be behind Chickasaw lines now and likely to encounter enemy scouts or sentinels at any time.

The first sign of danger, however, came from her rear. She heard a slight sound, then another, this time from in front of her. This activity prompted warning caws of a crow. The quick, harsh sounding was taken up by other crows, and as she stayed motionless in the shadows of a virgin stand of hardwood, she saw a Chickasaw moving very carefully. So there was at least one warrior ahead of her, and at least one to her rear, for the sound of someone approaching carelessly was evident.

She melted into the shadow, as still as death itself. As she did so, she saw the Chickasaw to her front freeze also, then start to withdraw into the trees—for he, too, had heard the sounds of someone approaching from the east.

But before concealing himself completely, he turned and caught sight of Ena just as she disappeared behind a bush. He immediately started to nock an arrow.

The rest happened so quickly, Ena could hardly recall it accurately later. Crazy Fox, the maddened Indian, came bumbling into the open, shouting a warning to her. Distracted, the Chickasaw turned and, seeing Crazy Fox dressed as a Cherokee, loosed his arrow at the simpleton. The arrow buried itself in

Crazy Fox's heart. He fell with no outcry, only the thud of his body breaking the silence.

Ena did not wait. Before the Chickasaw could reach for another arrow, her own arrow struck him hard and swift, and the half-wit, who had died trying to save her, was avenged. She felt regret for Crazy Fox, but only for a moment. He had been foolish to follow her, foolish to betray his presence to the Chickasaw; but he had died well, and he would take his place among the bravest warriors in the land beyond the Great River.

With grim satisfaction, Ena took the Chickasaw scalp and moved on, claiming the dead man's arrows for her quiver.

Late in the day she began to hear an odd series of sounds from a great distance ahead. As she moved closer, she recognized the squeaking of axles, which told her that wagons were moving. She had to conceal herself from a pair of Chickasaw scouts, not wanting to kill them lest some sound escape to warn others who were obviously close by.

When the sounds of the moving wagons were quite near and she could hear the voices of men speaking in Spanish urging on horses, she climbed a tree, keeping its large bole between her and the sounds.

The Spanish artillery and its wagons were moving past the tree line on the fringe of a large grassland. Ahead was a knoll, which was the destination of the artillery train. Horses strained to pull heavily laden wagons, and sweating Indian slaves dragged the four Spanish fieldpieces. Now and again a Spaniard would send his lash curling over the bloody bare backs of the unfortunate slaves, and with the sharp crack would come a torrent of curses as the Spaniard urged the slaves on.

She stayed in the tree to watch the positioning of the cannon. The wagons containing powder and shot were parked behind the knoll, the horses hitched and ready to move at an instant's notice, and for a moment she considered doing something to stampede the horses, thus causing the wagons to overturn. Or she could, in the dark of night, sneak up and set fire to the powder wagon.

However, the site was well guarded by alert Chickasaw. And there were the lancers, the last group of them, a rear guard, coming jangling up the meadow to surround the knoll. It would be far too dangerous to sneak into that nest of enemy, she concluded, but she had memorized the position of the guns and the supply wagons, then counted the exact number of Chickasaw and of the cavalry.

Ena had seen the results of canister and grapeshot on troops and knew it would be a fearful slaughter if Renno sent men against the fortified knoll. It was her duty, she thought, to tell Renno the disposition of the artillery. She climbed down the tree slowly, taking great care not to expose so much as a hand, nor to make a sound. She dropped the last few feet to land silently, then started to move. The rustle of leather saved her life, as a Chickasaw warrior moved in concealment in the woods. She made a quick turn as an arrow hissed by, an arrow that would have impaled her if she had not moved so quickly, and her eyes caught the movement among the trees as the enemy nocked another arrow. She was then hidden in the woods, surrounded by an eerie silence. She was surprised that the warrior had not cried out an alarm. She heard the soft crackling of the detritus of the forest floor. She guessed that the warrior was young, intent on counting personal coup. That suited her well.

The enemy, knowing that she was alone and far behind his lines, would expect her to flee. She made an obvious trail toward the north, then backtracked quickly, leaving no sign, and concealed herself. Within minutes she heard the muted sounds of approach, and the warrior, young, strong, eyes gleaming in anticipation, came trotting down her trail. She let him pass her place of concealment and then stepped out behind him. She had been lucky once, with the first Chickasaw she had killed, in having him die silently. Now, with the large force of enemy so near, she could not afford to have one whisper of sound.

The enemy had reached the point where her trail disappeared. His eyes had been intently on the ground and to the front. Soon he would turn, cast around for the trail. She ran five quick, silent steps. She did not have the physical strength of a man, but she had quickness. She came upon the warrior before he heard anything. He was just starting to turn his head when she covered his mouth with one hand and made a quick slash with her knife across his throat with the other. His body bucked, and she was almost thrown to the ground as he struggled, but his life's blood was spurting from a severed jugular vein, and soon she lowered him gently to the ground. Well-blooded, two new scalps at her belt, she slipped into the forest and began to move back toward the east and south.

Twice she had encountered enemy scouts. A scout held a position of honor, and the position went to proven warriors, skilled men. Yet she had killed two of them. She therefore had little respect for the Chickasaw. They were strong fighters but not as skilled in wood lore as the Seneca.

Her knowledge that she was superior in skill to the Chickasaw, or at least to the two warriors whose scalps dangled at her belt, did not make her careless. She still moved from tree to tree, from concealment to concealment, as silent as the ghost of a departed soul. And yet death's silent wings brushed her, coming from nowhere, coming out of a silence without any prior warning to her. One split second she was examining the way ahead of her, planning her route, and the next, a strong hand had closed over her mouth and she felt the hardness and heat of a male body pressed against her. She knew that she had only an instant before the sharp blade slashed at her throat, and in that instant she wondered where she had failed. How had she failed to sense the presence of another enemy?

When the home village came into sight late in the afternoon, Emily, with Wynema in her arms, ran ahead of the escort, not pausing to return the startled greetings of women and children who were surprised to see her, having thought she was dead. But one of these women was Wynema's mother, who, after a moment's paralysis from shock, raced after Emily, who was running swiftly to Ah-wen-ga's lodge. It was there that Wynema was seized by her mother and held tightly, while others gathered around and exclaimed in joy at the young girl's return and apparent health.

Wynema's mother clasped Emily's hand and, with eyes luminous with tears, looked at the blond woman. "I cannot thank you enough, for you have obviously cared well for my child in times of hardship. I will come to you later when I am not so overwhelmed, to thank you properly."

Ah-wen-ga, having heard the exclamations, appeared in the doorway, with Little Hawk, fat and happy, in her arms. Emily halted and, breathing hard, let her eyes feast on her own child.

"*Aiii*," Ah-wen-ga said in surprise. And then, "Thanks be, you are alive!"

"Oh, my baby," Emily said, beginning to cry, and reached out to take her son.

She clutched the little boy to her breast, closed her eyes in grateful prayer, and did not heed the tears of happiness that ran down her cheeks. His happy sounds and his healthily plump little body against her made for a joy that filled her.

"Ah-wen-ga," she said gratefully, "he seems well."

"He is spoiled, arrogant, demanding, and he has the imp in him, but he is well," Ah-wen-ga said, smiling. "But come, my Daughter, you are tired."

"Yes," Emily said, "but so happy, Ah-wen-ga."

She followed Ah-wen-ga into the lodge. A cooking fire was glowing, a pot of stew sending off a savory aroma. Behind Emily a gasp told of the arrival of her mother-in-law, Toshabe. The two women warmly embraced, and then, holding the squirming, happy Little Hawk, Emily told her story from the beginning.

In the midst of her account, Ah-wen-ga spread a skin blanket and said, "Put the squirming one down here." Emily was reluctant, but the blanket was near her, and she was tired and hungry, so she put Little Hawk on the blanket and continued her account. During the last part of it she talked with her mouth full, as she ate some of the stew and watched proudly as Little Hawk moved strongly, making crawling motions.

"He will be moving as quickly as a lizard within days," Toshabe said as the boy pulled himself off the blanket and began happily to pat the hard dirt floor. Emily picked him up and put him back on the blanket.

During the climactic part of her story, her narrow escape from being raped by the bearded Spaniard, the attention of Ah-wen-ga and Toshabe was on her, and she, caught up in the memory of the unpleasant events, forgot to watch Little Hawk for a few moments. The baby, moving with surprising speed, reached out for the fire's glowing coals. Emily glanced toward Little Hawk, gasped, and moved quickly, but Ah-wen-ga was nearer to the baby, and faster, and she picked him up and held him with his face near hers.

"So," Ah-wen-ga said, "the fledgling is already strong enough to try his wings. And the fire is so pretty, is it not?"

"He is showing off for his mother," Toshabe said.

She nodded at Emily. "He has not crawled so strongly before, for he is very young for it."

"His father crawled as early," Ah-wen-ga observed.

"So it is time for the fire lesson," Toshabe said.

Ah-wen-ga nodded and kissed Little Hawk on his chubby cheek. He gurgled happily.

"All right, little one," Ah-wen-ga said, turning him to face the fire. "See the pretty fire? So pretty, eh?"

Ah-wen-ga extended Little Hawk closer to the fire, and he cooed and gurgled, reaching for it.

"We must show the little one that the fire is pretty, but painful, as well," Ah-wen-ga explained, positioning herself to hold Little Hawk on one arm while she seized his right hand and pushed it toward the fire.

Emily gasped as Ah-wen-ga thrust Little Hawk's hand so near the glowing embers that there seemed to be no distance between soft baby flesh and searing coal. Ah-wen-ga held the hand there firmly, although the boy began to squirm and get a distressed look on his face.

"Stop it!" Emily cried, just as Little Hawk gave out a wild, pained howl and began to fight in panic while his hand still was held close to the glowing embers.

Emily leaped toward Ah-wen-ga and dragged the howling baby from her arms.

"It might be that you will have to give him the lesson of fire once or twice more," Toshabe said calmly, "although, with his father, it had to be given only once."

"I cannot let you do that to my child!" Emily said in English. When she was very upset, she still tended to think and speak in her native language. Then, in Seneca, "I won't allow you to burn his hand deliberately to give him a lesson."

Toshabe looked at Ah-wen-ga in surprise.

Emily was examining Little Hawk's hand while he continued to shriek. The palm was red, but not blistered. Emily kissed it and hugged him close.

Ah-wen-ga's voice was sympathetic when she spoke. "I know our ways are sometimes difficult for you to accept, Emily. But this manner of teaching a child to avoid the fire has always worked well. I am sure you are tired from all that has happened to you. Perhaps you should go rest, and we will visit later. Leave Little Hawk with us, so you can sleep. Then we will talk about how to teach him the lesson of fire. I am sure you don't want him to teach himself—he would surely get badly burned."

"I will just make certain he doesn't get near the fire," Emily said testily. "I have always watched him—"

"Who watched him while you were away?" Ah-wen-ga demanded. "Who was watching him just now, when he almost put his hand among the coals?"

"I know," Emily said. "But I will watch him."

"In a few days, a few weeks, he will be moving with the swiftness of the green lizards of summer but with less intelligence," Ah-wen-ga warned. "And we live by the open fire. In the winter we heat with the open fire. In the summer we cook. Think, my Daughter, have you ever seen an Indian baby suffering from a burn?"

"No," Emily said doubtfully, as Little Hawk's sobbing began to diminish.

"It is because, when they first move, and first show interest in the pretty fire, we give them the lesson of fire. Enough to hurt, but not enough to maim or kill, as might happen if they are not taught to avoid it."

"I am sure our daughter understands now," Toshabe said kindly.

Emily did understand. She had accepted the ways of the Seneca because she loved Renno enough to give up her own culture and live within a code set down, some whites said, by savages. She had watched them dip her newborn infant into a creek from which the ice had to be broken. She had seen his hand held cruelly up to the fire. Yes, she understood. She understood that she and her son were caught in the culture of a people who did not think, or feel, as she thought and felt. For the first time since her marriage, she knew doubts.

"And it is time you stopped that noise," Ah-wen-ga said, meaning Little Hawk's diminishing sobs. "Indian babies do not cry."

"Oh, yes," Emily said sarcastically, her anger venting itself now. "Indian babies do not cry, for the sound of the baby's cries will lead the enemy to the hidden camp. I know, Ah-wen-ga, for you taught me well. That, however, is something for the past, when such cruelty as holding a hand over a crying baby's mouth until the child turned blue was necessary for the safety of the whole tribe." Emily's voice began to rise hysterically. "But this is not a hidden village.

There are no cruel enemies lurking in the trees down there just waiting for one baby's cry to expose the whereabouts of their victims. And Little Hawk, my son, is *not* an Indian baby."

Perhaps it was the relief in finding him well, of being home and safe, after long, long weeks in the wilderness, of being tired, hungry, and in danger. Whatever the reason, she was very angry. She herself would obey the customs and rules of her husband's people—she loved Renno too much to rebel against his wishes when she alone was concerned—but when they started hurting her baby . . .

Feeling guilty because she knew her behavior was childish, Emily stalked out and headed for her own dwelling, clutching Little Hawk to her breast. In her lodge things were in place, and it was clean, but there was no fire. There was no food. She set about making a fire, borrowing a bed of embers from a neighbor, and when it was blazing, she put Little Hawk on his blanket on the floor, watching him carefully. Fascinated by the fire, he cooed at it. He pulled himself along the floor, his hands and knees sliding from under him, but he did not once attempt to go near the fire.

Emily slept with Little Hawk in her arms. Before falling asleep, she whispered to him that his father was coming soon, that she loved him so much, that he was, indeed, the most beautiful little boy in the world. And under her breath, "I won't let them hurt you anymore, my little son. They say you are a Seneca, but you are a Johnson, as well. You are white, Little Hawk. Learn the skills of your father, if you will, but remember you are white, and that we, too, have customs, and a culture, and simply because Seneca have been doing certain things since the dawn of time doesn't make them right."

As it happened, perhaps because the lesson of the fire had been given by Ah-wen-ga so early, Little Hawk had to give himself the lesson, and it was infinitely more painful than Ah-wen-ga's. It happened within two days, while the entire village was waiting, hoping, praying for good news from the west. The fire had burned down to glowing embers, and Emily would soon bank it under ashes to preserve the coals for the morning, when she would cook again. She had turned her back for only a few seconds, but Little Hawk moved to the bed of glowing coals swiftly, reached down into the fire pit for the pretty red things, and seized a coal the size of an egg. He could not turn it loose. His howl of intense pain jerked Emily's head, and she leaped, picked him up, heard a sizzling sound, and smelled the scent of burning flesh.

"Now you have seen an Indian baby with a burn," said Ah-wen-ga to Toshabe when they saw the scabbed, painful burn the next day.

Toshabe shook her head sadly. "Perhaps not," she said. "Our daughter says that this one is not Indian, doesn't she?"

Ah-wen-ga's thoughts were far to the west, where by now, she felt, the decisive battle might already have been fought, but in whose favor she did not know. The white one had been doing so well, had indeed been the ideal Seneca wife. But now there was a weak point in her.

"The boy is Seneca," she said with firm conviction.

Chapter X

It was vital to put the Spanish cannon out of action, and El-i-chi, who was still quite young, knew that he was continually being tested because of his important role in the overall plan. The respect for Renno was so great that there was no open muttering against Renno's choice of El-i-chi as the man to stop the cannon, but both brothers knew that should El-i-chi fail, there would be those who would question—if any remained alive. If Renno's plan to turn the cannon against the Chickasaw worked, El-i-chi would be greatly respected, along with his brother.

El-i-chi consulted Renno during the selection of the strike force that would attack the cannon. Renno advised that the force be made up of more Cherokee than Seneca, since that was the proportion of their expedition. El-i-chi would have preferred an all-Seneca force, but he bowed to his brother's wisdom and chose seventy-five Cherokee and twenty-five Seneca. Somewhat against Renno's wishes, he included Se-quo-i among the Cherokee. He then moved his group away from the main body and held them at the ready.

El-i-chi had had little time to think of anything but his duty and the coming battle, but now and then, in quiet moments, his thoughts dwelled on the wild and willful girl he had carried home from the initial scouting raid against the Chickasaw. When he thought of Holani, he often knew mixed emotions. Always the image of her in his mind would kindle the fire in his blood—and often the fire in his temper—for in the brief time he had known her, the girl had been infuriating.

What he had done in kidnapping Holani from her tribe was a time-honored custom among almost all of the American Indian tribes. Not only was the taking of female captives done by most—with many of them being made favored wives, thus becoming full members of their husbands' tribes—but the casualties of war were often compensated for by the taking of young boys. Had not El-i-chi's own great-grandfather become Seneca in such a way?

In almost every case, a captured woman, offered the chance to become a favored wife, would accept with grace and often with gratitude and genuine love. Not so in Holani's case. She had been rebellious for the entire time El-i-chi had been near her, and when he had left to go to war, she had given him no fond words of farewell. She had said with a grim, false smile, "Perhaps you will find, Seneca, that my Chickasaw brothers fight more strongly than a woman."

Well, there would be time . . . if he lived. There were times when he could picture himself overcoming Holani's hatred with gentle words and soft touches. There were other times, as he remembered her spirit, that he promised himself that he would escort the wildcat to the boundaries of Chickasaw land, give her a swift kick in her shapely rump, and send her back to her own people. Such a thought, however, left him with an empty feeling.

On the night when action was imminent and he moved his force away from the main body of warriors, El-i-chi told himself strongly that it was time to put thoughts of the Chickasaw woman out of his mind. He withdrew and in solitude consulted his manitous. He received no dream, no vision, but he came back to the camp with a feeling of spiritual renewal and a determination to make the name El-i-chi stand out in Seneca and Cherokee lore.

The veteran Seneca warrior Danega had been given the assignment of luring the Spanish cavalry away from the cannon and into the meadow, thus easing the odds against El-i-chi's men. Danega accepted the assignment with stoic calmness, and El-i-chi was pleased to know that the action upon which his own success depended was in the hands of so dependable and brave a warrior. He was also pleased to know that Danega's son, Dawida, would fight beside his father.

Danega's part of the plan would have to be put into action first—and successfully—if El-i-chi were to have even a small chance of doing his own job.

Danega's men were in place. Now El-i-chi had to move his force, for he had to skirt to the north and come down upon the site of the cannon from the flank of the massed Chickasaw forces. He set a careful, silent pace, for there was time—Renno wanted all Chickasaw forces in place before beginning his attack.

Fortunately, the forest to the north offered good concealment, so it was possible to move a force of one hundred warriors. They used their own judgment, as if each man were alone in the wilderness, but keeping in touch with his fellow warriors around him. For a mile, then two, then three, nothing impeded the movement. And then, out in front of his men, El-i-chi froze, waiting in a silence so profound that a feeding squirrel came down to dig for the last of the buried winter acorns not five feet from where he stood.

The Chickasaw El-i-chi had spotted passed a few yards away, moving so quietly that only a swaying of brush betrayed his passage. El-i-chi, leaving his musket and bow behind for ease of movement, fell in behind and gradually began to close the distance. He almost betrayed himself when the enemy halted, melting into the shadows of a large oak. It would be great personal coup to kill this one in silence, El-i-chi told himself, for the enemy showed patience, waiting for long, long minutes before moving again.

El-i-chi resumed the deadly stalking and caught the Chickasaw in deep shadow, among huge virgin trees, leaping the last few feet, still without making a sound, to close his hand over the warrior's mouth and bring his razor-sharp knife to the enemy's throat.

It was El-i-chi's sharp nose that saved Ena's life and prevented El-i-chi from killing his own sister. One of the few items of the white man's life that had been insisted on by Emily, when she came to live with the Seneca, was soap, which reeked of lye and fat, and Emily had converted her sister-in-law, Ena, to its use. That distinctive smell lingered on Ena, even though days had passed since she had last used the soap. As El-i-chi's arm came swinging up, knife at the ready, his face was pressed closely to Ena's head, where the lingering aroma of the homemade soap was strongest.

Ena, in that split second, knowing that she was as good as dead, reacted, grasping her own knife from her belt, her mind telling her that it was too late even as her left hand came up in a vain effort to block the throat-slashing movement of her attacker's hand. Then, suddenly, she was pushed violently away, and as she went she whirled and slashed, her own blade whistling past El-i-chi's midsection.

Ena froze, knife arm ready for a back slash, saw El-i-chi's grim face, so handsome behind its war paint.

El-i-chi's bloodlust had his heart pounding, so that it was but an instant's transition to anger—raging red anger at this warrior maiden for placing herself in a position of nearly being murdered . . . and by her own sibling. He had had his belly full of fiery women. His left hand lashed out and made a sharp, clear sound as it struck Ena's cheek with such force that she was knocked to the forest floor.

"An odd greeting, brother," Ena said, her ears ringing with the force of the blow.

"You were ordered to go home," El-i-chi hissed, anger glittering in his eyes. "I almost had the blood of my own family on my hands."

"I bless the spirits that you do not," Ena said, rising, shaking her head to dispel the ringing of her ears. "I was coming to find someone to report—"

"Ena, our brother has given you an order," El-i-chi said. "He is our sachem. Now what am I to do with you?"

He knew that he could not send her back toward the main body, for there were a hundred warriors moving through the woods, each on the lookout for an enemy scout.

"I must reach Renno," Ena said, "for I know the exact positions of the Spanish cannon."

"You have seen them?"

"Yes."

El-i-chi formed his decision quickly. "You will stay with me."

"Renno must know," she insisted.

"We go to capture the cannon," El-i-chi said. "Come, tell me exactly what you have seen."

They squatted and cleared an area of ground on

which Ena drew the positions of the cannon, wagons, and lancers.

"There are only a few scouts to the north of the position," she said. "With care they can be silenced. Then we will have to take the lancers first."

"The lancers will be lured into the meadow," El-i-chi said.

"Good. The Chickasaw still show their usual overconfidence. Most of the Chickasaw guard force is camped behind the knoll. They can be taken quickly from the north and the west."

"Stay behind me," El-i-chi ordered. He had heard a soft cooing, indicating that his force was closing on them. It was time for him to scout the way ahead.

"But I know the way," she told him.

Warrior maidens, Eli-i-chi was thinking, in some disgust. "By my side, then."

Ena smiled at him and touched his shoulder. "I am pleased that it was a Seneca who surprised me," she said, "not only because I am still alive, but for other reasons. I feared that I was losing my skills to allow a Chickasaw to kill me."

El-i-chi grunted. He had noted the two fresh scalps at her belt. He felt pride in spite of himself. He motioned to her to follow, leading the way back to where he had left his bow and his musket. Then they set off in the direction of the enemy, traveling only yards apart.

Before they had gone twenty paces, Se-quo-i emerged from some underbrush and joined them. El-i-chi beckoned to the youth to fall in behind Ena.

*   *   *

When the firing broke out to the south of Renno at dawn, he feared that the battle had begun, that the Chickasaw had attacked in force. He ran quickly to a point of vantage. Where the meadow narrowed and the muddy creek ran into dense trees, he saw Chickasaw warriors running back toward the west and realized that the action had been nothing more than a probe from the enemy. Three Chickasaw dead lay at the edge of the trees. They were quickly scalped by Cherokee, and then, once again, all was quiet.

Renno ran back to the wide meadow, found Danega, and saw that his force of mixed Seneca and Cherokee was ready. But he also knew that Roy Johnson had not had enough time to get his regiment into position to the south, so he told Danega to wait until the sun was three hands high. It would be the Franklin Frontier Regiment's responsibility to pick off the enemy that Danega's group would lure into the meadow. As for El-i-chi, he had had all night to get into position. Renno did not doubt for one moment that El-i-chi had reached the goal, so the hours of daylight would be dangerous for El-i-chi and his men, exposed as they were, with Chickasaw between them and friendly forces. Yet it was a situation that could not be helped.

Captain Guy de Rojas, mounted on a splendid black gelding, left Oklawahpa's war tent and rode toward the north. He found the cannon to be in good positions. They were loaded with round shot, for the initial firings would be into the trees. There the

Cherokee attack would form, and there he would demoralize those Indians, who had never faced cannon. As a result, he knew that their attack would be disorganized. Once the Cherokee were in the open—if they were fools enough to charge across the meadow—they would be decimated by grapeshot, as long as it lasted, and then canister.

One of Oklawahpa's sons, Oklatumpa, was in charge of the Chickasaw party guarding the cannon. In de Rojas's eyes, the son was too young, too inexperienced. Oklatumpa stood proudly as de Rojas reined in his horse atop the knoll and swept his eyes over the meadow to the tree line across the creek. To the naked eye, it seemed as if the large Chickasaw force faced only the wilderness.

"What say your scouts to the north?" de Rojas asked Oklatumpa.

"There is nothing to report," Oklatumpa responded.

De Rojas nodded, and then a tendril of suspicion curled into his mind. "Do the scouts report nothing, or do you assume there is nothing because they have not reported?"

"If there had been anything to report, they would have come," Oklatumpa said, answering the question in a manner that made de Rojas's eyes shift quickly to the north. He had seen the pale-skinned leader of the Cherokee in action, and he knew the man was no fool. De Rojas felt his skin contract, as if it expected the impact of ball or arrow from the forest that crowded the knoll.

"Send out more scouts," the Spaniard ordered,

and his tone of voice made the proud son of the grand chief lift his shoulders. "A thousand warriors are food for the vultures because of such . . ." De Rojas started to say "stupidity," but he paused, not wanting to fight with this young warrior. "Because someone assumed that the Cherokee fought as he had always fought. Send men to the north."

Oklatumpa made the order in a harsh voice, and three warriors leaped to their feet and disappeared into the forest.

De Rojas dismounted, let his horse's reins trail. The animal began to crop the new grass. From the slope of the hill to the south, where the lancers waited, a young officer in brilliant uniform and torso armor came walking proudly.

"My captain," the young officer said, saluting and standing stiffly at attention, "we are ready. You have chosen an excellent field of battle."

De Rojas was silent for a moment. Yes, it would be a good field for cavalry action if the Indians were fools enough to charge across the wide, open meadow. But he doubted that they would.

"Your main mission is to guard the cannon, Cortez," de Rojas said. The officer in charge of the lancers bore a proud name, the name of the conqueror of Mexico, and de Rojas hoped that was a good omen.

"I understand, my captain," Cortez said. "Should the enemy charge, are we free to maneuver in the meadow?"

"As long as you avoid getting within musket range

of the Cherokee doubtless hiding in the trees on the other side of the meadow," de Rojas said.

De Rojas was nervous, and he told himself that he had no reason to be. He had been assured by the Chickasaw—and the best intelligence of the Spanish governor agreed—that the Cherokee would be hard pressed to put two thousand warriors in the field. He had at his disposal almost four thousand warriors, plus cannon and lancers. And yet he kept turning his eyes to the woods to the north.

"Cortez, I want you to move your force," he said. "I want them arrayed in a line abreast, facing the northern woods."

"Yes, Captain," Cortez barked, moving swiftly to put the order into effect.

De Rojas felt only marginally better when the lancers moved smartly into position. He warned Oklatumpa to be on his guard against an attack from the northern woods. The young warrior looked disdainful. "The enemy is there," he said, pointing to the woodlands across the muddy creek. "He slinks in fear among the trees, wanting us to come for him so that he can shoot in safety from the cover of the trees."

"But you will be on guard?" de Rojas asked disgustedly.

"We are always on guard," Oklatumpa said.

De Rojas had intended to be at Oklawahpa's side during the battle, the better to be able to give suggestions to counter the strokes of the enemy's pale-skinned commander, but he knew the importance of the cannon. He decided to stay with the lancers, at least for the moment.

Roy Johnson was also positioning his men. He knew that some of them were grumbling about white men being ordered around by an Indian. Not until he had reached the position assigned to him by Renno, on the bend of the creek as it turned westward, did anyone dare approach him openly to complain. He was not surprised to see that the complainers were burly twin brothers, Ned and Marcus Pierce. In the past the Pierce brothers had not been the best of friends to the Cherokee, but Johnson thought they had learned that the best course for the citizens of the would-be state of Franklin was to be solidly allied with the Cherokee.

Ned Pierce, the young owner of a small blacksmith shop in Knoxville, was the spokesman. "Colonel," he said, "we don't like this."

"I'm not tickled pink with it myself," Johnson replied. "I'd damned well rather be back in Knoxville with my wife."

"We don't mean the war itself," Marcus spoke up, looking to his brother for support.

"We don't like taking orders from the Indian," Ned said.

"You take your orders from me," Johnson countered sternly.

"Now, you know what I mean, Colonel," Ned said. "Here we are stuck down here in the woods away from all the action, and we know that the Indian told you where to position the regiment."

"Maybe you'd rather charge across the meadow into the cannon," Johnson said.

"Now, Colonel—" Marcus began.

"Dammit, Colonel," Ned cut in, "it's just that we don't cotton to having our lives controlled by a savage."

Johnson's eyebrows drew together. "That savage you're talking about is my son-in-law," he said coldly. "He's a man who can sit down at George Washington's table anytime he wants to visit, and he knows more about strategy than you two will learn if you live to be a hundred. If it's action you want, consider this: you say we're way down here in the woods away from the action, but we're the southern flank. There's no one out there to our left. We're here to keep the Chickasaw from flanking the main force, and I guarantee we'll have all the action we want, and then some. Now, if you have any other complaints, let's just wait until after we kill a few Chickasaw to voice them."

Johnson went about positioning his men, leaving the Pierce brothers looking at his back. He cautioned his regiment to conserve their powder, wait until they had a good target before firing, and save their main firepower until masses of Chickasaw were charging toward the creek and the Cherokee. He noted that Marcus and Ned Pierce had chosen good cover and were prepared to fight side by side.

Two hundred men had been gathered well behind the tree line. Renno, noting that the sun was almost three hands high, sought out Danega. The older warrior had been praying to his ancestors and the

manitous. He was painted in the traditional Seneca
style, and his scalp lock was like Renno's own, in the
best tradition of the Seneca of old, as they went into
battle.

"All is ready," Danega said.

"Gather your men around me," Renno said, and
stood on a fallen tree as the warriors pressed close.
He looked at them, his face stern and serious. Then
he lifted his eyes to the sky, made a silent prayer,
and looked again at the proud, eager group of warriors.

"The cannon will make the sound of thunder, and
death will fly among you like iron hail," he said. "Do
not slow or turn back, for this is the only way you
can draw the lancers from the knoll. El-i-chi cannot
attack and silence the cannon until the lancers are off
the knoll."

A mumble came from the warriors, voices telling
him they were not afraid.

"They will be shooting at long range at first, and
the sounds will seem more deadly than they really
are."

"We will run faster than the shot!" a young warrior
cried out, and a rumble of defiance came from the
two hundred.

"You are brave, and you could race into the very
mouth of the cannon, this I know," Renno said. "But
many of you would die, and our purpose is to make
the Chickasaw and the Spaniards die."

"A man on horseback is just a man," said a warrior.

"The man on horseback has the advantage in the
open," Renno replied. "Let us review your responsibility. First you are to burst from the trees with

much noise and make it seem that you intend to charge directly up the knoll to the cannon. This should bring the lancers into the field. Instead of staying to engage them in the open meadow, you are to fire and take as much of a toll as you can and then retreat, staying beyond the reach of their long lances. Draw the lancers toward you, and as they charge, you are to show fear and fall back into the trees."

"How does a Seneca show fear?" asked Dawida in a loud, derisive voice. Laughter followed Dawida's question.

"You could scream like a white woman seeing a snake," Renno said with a smile.

A young warrior near Renno squeaked in falsetto, to the accompaniment of much laughter.

"Show false fear by running," Renno said. "Run like the wind to stay ahead of the horses. Draw the lancers into the trees where you can. Among the trees, the horses will not be such an advantage. You and the Frontier Regiment will then send the Spaniards to their death."

"We will obey," Danega said, although the thought of running was repugnant to him. He had never run from an enemy is his life.

As the men moved forward, Renno's every impulse was to go with them, to lead the charge, but he sadly turned away. His responsibilities were far too great to allow him to indulge his heartfelt desire to be among the first to engage the enemy.

Renno waited until Danega's force was near the creek, ready to begin their charge. He could only trust that El-i-chi and Colonel Johnson were in posi-

tion. He knew that Rusog was ready. To Rusog fell
the task of making the Chickasaw think that the
entire Cherokee force was on the move. He looked
at Danega, who faced the west proudly, raised his
musket, and fired, then followed the shot with a
mighty Seneca war whoop. Off to his left the whoop
was picked up. The war cry swelled toward the south
and became predominantly Cherokee. From the woods
behind the creek a force of warriors rushed forward,
their muskets ready. As Rusog's force reached the
creek and began to cross, Renno held up his hand to
hold Danega's force temporarily in check. Danega,
his men at his back obediently waiting, watched
tensely.

The first Cherokee warriors splashed through the
muddy creek and through the scattered cottonwood
trees on the western bank, then were out in the
open. From the opposite tree line, too far away to be
effective, musket smoke rose, and the flashes were
followed by the low thunder of detonating powder.
Still Renno held his hand upraised.

Neither El-i-chi, nor Ena, nor Se-quo-i saw, or
had the honor of killing, the three scouts sent out by
Oklatumpa on de Rojas's orders. They saw only the
scouts' scalps hanging from the belts of El-i-chi's
strike force. El-i-chi's men gathered in the woods
just to the north of the grassy knoll, with El-i-chi
waiting tensely for the signal to capture the cannon.
This signal would be massed musket fire coming
from the Chickasaw as Rusog made his charge. When
he heard it, he motioned for the entire force to begin

to move. He himself went first, with Ena close behind him. When he could see the knoll, he saw that
the lancers were no longer in the same positions as
sketched out by Ena. His heart leaped in concern.
Now, unless Renno's plan worked, he and his strike
force would have to fight the dismounted lancers
before engaging the Chickasaw guard camped behind the knoll. All of the men, Spanish and Indian,
were alerted. They had muskets in hand, ready to
fire. Their fire, El-i-chi knew, would take a terrible
toll on his outnumbered force. He sent Se-quo-i back
to Renno with a report.

When the youth reached him, panting, to deliver
El-i-chi's message, Renno had other concerns on his
mind. Absently ordering Se-quo-i to the rear, he
turned his attention back to the field of battle before
him.

As Renno had expected, the Chickasaw were not
of the disposition to wait patiently in the trees to
allow the Cherokee charge to reach them. Rusog's
lead warriors were no more than a quarter of the way
across the meadow when the Chickasaw, having exhausted their initial loads of musket, abandoned those
weapons for the more familiar bow, tomahawk, and
knife and started streaming from the trees to meet
the Cherokee.

Guy de Rojas saw too that the Chickasaw were
abandoning his carefully laid plan. He yelled out an
angry curse when the Chickasaw broke discipline
and ran to meet the Cherokee charge. But still there
was no action around the cannon. Perhaps, the

Spaniard was thinking, the pale-skinned chief did not know the danger of the cannon, the destruction they could wreak. He quickly gave orders to the gunner to train the big guns on the charging Cherokee. They would be firing at maximum range and could only fire balls, but the sound and the balls thudding and rolling around the meadow would have an effect.

It was only when Renno saw the great puffs of smoke and then heard the roar of the cannon that he dropped his hand with a war cry and sent Danega's men charging across the shallow creek. He could distinguish the Seneca whoops from those of the Cherokee. He ran behind them to the tree line and watched them leap and splash through the waters of the creek. It took precious minutes for the cannon to be redirected from their longer-range fire as Rusog's first line met the countercharging line of Chickasaw. Tomahawks gleamed in the sun, while balls from the diverted cannon were crashing into the trees. The inertial force of the solid shot made limbs snap with a sound like the firing of a musket, and leaves and twigs rained down. The next salvo sent balls among Rusog's charging men, but Renno saw only one man fall. Meanwhile, Danega's men had left the creek behind them and were advancing, whooping, across the open meadow.

On the mound, de Rojas felt renewed respect for the enemy's pale-skinned leader, whose plan had been simple but effective. The charge of a large Cherokee force had, in effect, isolated the cannon because the Chickasaw, always eager to fight and accustomed to a freewheeling style of combat that gave emphasis to the deeds of an individual, were flocking to the center of action. Warriors all up and down the line congregated, or tried to mass, to meet the Cherokee charge, which obviously was being made by a limited number of the enemy's force.

There was still no sound, no sign of the enemy to the north. De Rojas ordered his gunners to change the direction of their fire to concentrate on the small force of men who were rushing toward the knoll. That took a few minutes, and again the gunners overshot, the balls crashing into the cottonwoods along the creek.

Actually, de Rojas and Renno faced the same basic problem—the lack of discipline of Indian warriors who in the past had gone to war in small groups. The problem was more critical for Renno because of the superior numbers of the Chickasaw. He knew full well that even if his men lived up to their boastings in an all-out, hand-to-hand battle and each killed two or three of the enemy, the losses to his men would be severe. There would be many lodges in mourning, and with most of its warriors dead, the Cherokee nation would be left almost defenseless.

Renno did not want victory at that price. It was only right, and fitting, for there to be mourning women after a war party, but he did not want mourning on the scale he envisioned should Rusog lose control of his men, who, in their confidence and eagerness, would continue to charge and face the superior Chickasaw force.

De Rojas, on the other side, had to shout and

gesture with his sword to keep the young Oklatumpa from leading his men toward the initial Cherokee charge. Then the Spaniard had to threaten the Chickasaw to keep them from leaving the cannon to meet the charge of the smaller force, which was obviously targeted against the cannon.

Danega and his son, Dawida, ran side by side at the forefront of their group. Each of them saw the frenzied activity of the gunners on the knoll and knew that within seconds they would face the deadly rattle of grapeshot. As they ran, they saw the lancers swing into a line to face them, and Danega whooped, happy to see that they had indeed captured the attention of the mounted men, as Renno had planned.

In the widest part of the meadow Rusog had been in the front when Cherokee met Chickasaw in hand-to-hand battle. Knives, tomahawks, and a few war clubs swung and flashed, with Cherokee and Chickasaw curses and insults being shouted by hoarse, excited voices. The heavy, rank smell of fresh blood came to Rusog's nose as he slashed past an overhand blow from the leading Chickasaw warrior, felt his tomahawk impact bone, and saw a spurt of arterial blood from the enemy's neck. Even as the enemy fell, Rusog was drawing back for another blow. He whooped in derision as a Chickasaw warrior, trying to find a place to meet the small point of the Cherokee charge, killed one of his own tribesmen by shooting an arrow into a charging Chickasaw's back.

Roy Johnson paced in front of his men and caused them to hold their fire as Rusog's charge drew Chickasaw from the trees, for the range was too long for effective shooting. But as the blood-hungry Chickasaw to the south of the meadow disobeyed de Rojas's orders and began to stream out into the open with great whoops and brandishments of weapons, Johnson leaped to his own firing stand and gave the signal to fire. His men were trained to fire in sections, so that men were loading as the other two sections discharged their weapons, giving the effect of almost continuous fire. The effect was withering on the Chickasaw, whose backs were to the regiment at first. As warriors began to fall, there was great confusion and shouts of dismay. Then some organization became apparent as war chiefs shouted orders. Many Chickasaw continued to run toward Rusog's charge, but others turned and whooped their way directly into the face of the regiment's musket fire, only to fall in bloody heaps.

And still, El-i-chi saw, the lancers held their position, and still the Spanish officer was able to keep the guard force of Chickasaw on the mound around the cannon.

"We cannot wait longer," El-i-chi said. He was about to order his men to charge both the lancers and the Chickasaw guard force when the cannon roared. He saw men in Danega's attacking force stopped in midstride by the devastating blow of grapeshot.

When the first four rounds of grapeshot rattled through Danega's charging men, there was a low growl of anger and surprise, for at least ten men were cut down as if by a scythe, but then Dawida whooped and increased the pace forward, yelling for the others to take advantage of the reloading time of the cannon.

Guy de Rojas awaited what he felt was an inevitable attack from the north. He estimated that only about five hundred men were involved in the hand-to-hand battle in the meadow, and that another two hundred were charging the hill. That left a large portion of the enemy unaccounted for. But where were they?

The men charging the hill were spread out. De Rojas admired that, for it told him that the pale-skinned chief knew about cannon. The second barrage of grapeshot stopped only six men, and he knew that the gunners would not have time for more than one more volley before the enemy warriors began to charge up the hill, so near that the cannon could not be effective against them. He looked to the lancers. They were eager and ready, over one hundred of the finest men in New Spain, eager to use their skill against the charging savages. He saw that Cortez was watching him intently. He raised his hand, pointed toward the charging warriors, shot the hand out in front of him in an emphatic order. He heard Cortez bellow the order to charge, his voice a bit strained and high from his excitement. The horses responded to order and spur, leaping to race down the slope.

"They come!" Dawida yelled to his running father. "They come!"

Danega's lead men were more than halfway across the meadow, which was about a quarter of a mile wide at that point. As the lancers thundered down from the top of the knoll, Danega halted and raised his hand. The men ran to form a line on either side of him. They had been carefully instructed, as they had waited there in the shelter of the trees, and they performed well: each man had a loaded musket; the lancers charged in a ragged line, with some horses outdistancing others; Danega waited until the lancers were well within range, then whooped a signal. Taking quick aim, he fired, and around him an effective line of fire blasted. Horses screamed and fell, and the line of lancers wavered, with men toppling from horseback.

"Arrows!" bellowed Danega.

Men slung muskets and seized bows, and the distance closed between the lancers and the warriors. Hooves thundered, and the sharp metal points of the lances lowered and gleamed in the sun of a perfect spring day.

El-i-chi saw that his moment had come. He checked to see if Ena was obeying what had been half order, half appeal. She had positioned herself well, seated in the V crotch of a large tree. Several quivers of arrows hung around her.

El-i-chi gave the signal with a Seneca war cry, the cry of the Bear Clan, and his men burst from the trees to bring startled whoops from the Chickasaw who encircled the cannon. El-i-chi did not have to worry about the lancers, who were charging Danega's group, now well past the slope at the front of the knoll. Around the mound where the cannon sat, it would be a fairly evenly matched battle.

Having drawn the Chickasaw's attention, El-i-chi's men knelt to have better aim and loosed their one

volley of musket. Chickasaw fell before them. The
enemy on the far side of the mound were scampering
to join those who faced El-i-chi's renewed charge. At
the top of the mound, beside a now-silent cannon,
stood a bearlike white man. El-i-chi directed his
charge toward that white man, met a howling Chickasaw head-on, parried a downward plunge of the
Chickasaw's tomahawk, and buried his own blade in
the Chickasaw's throat.

For moments, the Seneca and Cherokee attackers
had the advantage, making a solid, concentrated front
against only that portion of the Chickasaw guard
force facing the woods to the north. That early advantage saw disproportionate losses to the defenders,
the entire force to the north falling before the determined charge before the others could rally and form
to face El-i-chi.

De Rojas, knowing now that his worst fears had
come to pass, cast a quick look down the slope. The
lancers were about to engage the enemy there in
close quarters. There was no chance that the lancers
could turn—he had no way of giving them that order
in the bedlam of noise—and come to the defense of
the cannon. He jerked his twin pistols from his belt
and faced the charge. He scored a hit and saw a
warrior pitch backward, then missed with the other
pistol. In a rage he yelled to Oklatumpa, who had
been on the southern side of the mound, to get his
men in position quickly, but his voice remained unheard in the medley of war cries from both sides.

Rusog was caught up in that state of wild emotions
that is war. He knew the joy of victory as he killed,

as his tomahawk took yet another Chickasaw life, and the whoop came to his lips. He leaped to face still another enemy. He knew that all around him men were dying, many of them his own, but the way his charge had been formed made it impossible for the Chickasaw to engage all of his superior numbers. The enemy had reacted exactly as predicted by Renno—all of the enemy warriors trying to reach that point where Rusog stood, his body red with the blood of the enemy.

"You must watch closely, my brother," Renno had stressed. "When the enemy sees that he can flow down the flanks of your attack, that is the time."

That time was near. From his position, Rusog could see clearly that the Spanish lancers had been drawn from their defensive points. He heard a volley of shots from the mound on which sat the cannon, and he began to yell at the men who struggled on either side. "Fall back! Fall back!" he ordered time and again, making his steps backward rather than forward and seeing the men fighting on his sides follow his lead. Now the Chickasaw, seeing the enemy in retreat, redoubled their efforts, swarming in massed numbers, although only those in the fore could strike or be struck. Rusog's tomahawk flashed and smashed and left a trail of bodies as he backed slowly toward the tree line, and as the mass of Chickasaw swarmed to the action, their flanks were exposed to the deadly fire of the Franklin Frontier Regiment.

At the grassy knoll, El-i-chi's initial charge had taken a heavy toll, and Guy de Rojas was yelling as he reloaded, as he screamed, unheard, for the lancers to forget the charge across the meadow and return to defend the mound. As Oklatumpa led the balance of his force farther from the mound, de Rojas continued to scream in vain, peppering his orders with profanity. He was in a nearly insane rage, seeing, once again, the same lack of organization that had caused the Chickasaw's severe defeat on two previous occasions.

From her perch in the large tree, her own body protected against fire by the thickness of the tree trunk, Ena sent arrow after arrow winging toward the Chickasaw. Her accuracy was so good that two times out of three her arrows struck home, sometimes fatally. She was yelling a war cry as the Chickasaw countered El-i-chi's charge and the fighting men became so mixed that she could no longer choose a target for fear of hitting one of her own. She leaped down from the tree and ran in a circle to gain the rear of the battling warriors and began to send her well-aimed arrows into the backs of the Chickasaw. Twice she sent an arrow zinging toward the white man, and once she felled a Spanish gunner.

"Now," Renno was saying to himself as he watched the charge of the lancers. "Now, Danega."

"Arrows," Danega had ordered, and a wall of sharp-tipped missiles flew toward the oncoming cavalry charge, some striking horses, and the terrified and pained screams of wounded animals added to the din of battle. Lancers fell, but not enough. Their light armor deflected arrows, and now the charge was only yards away.

"It is time to run, Father," Dawida urged as he loosed another arrow and shouldered his bow to seize his tomahawk.

"Lead the men, my son," Danega responded calmly, tossing aside his bow and musket and holding his tomahawk.

"It is *you* who lead," Dawida replied, his eyes on the frothing, pounding horseflesh bearing a wall of long lances toward the line of Cherokee and Seneca.

"I have never given my back to an enemy," Danega said.

"Then we stand together," Dawida said with finality.

"No," Danega said heatedly. "The blood of my fathers must not die here." Dawida was Danega's only son and had yet to father a boy. "I order you, my son, to lead the men back to safety."

Dawida's every instinct told him to stay at his father's side, but he too had felt the ache of responsibility. The sachem had trusted him, had given him specific orders to follow. The lives of the men in the meadow depended upon his decision, for he knew that if he stood with his father, the others would also stand—to be skewered on the lances of the cavalry.

"Fall back! Fall back!" Dawida yelled, and the call was passed down the extended line in two directions. Men turned and began to run full speed back toward the woods.

Danega stood unmoving. First one and then another of the fleeing warriors, looking back over their shoulders as the rushing horsemen neared, noticed Danega's lack of action, halted their flight, and hurried back to stand in line with the old warrior.

"No, Danega," Renno breathed. "No, do not do it."

And yet Renno understood. Danega was of the old breed. A Seneca never turned his back on an enemy. And even as he knew that Danega and the few who stood with him were doomed, Renno's heart lifted in admiration. Danega's stand would become a part of Seneca lore, and the legend would live long.

"Spread out," Danega told the few who stood as the cavalrymen picked targets and adjusted the angles of their lances. The Seneca danced, putting space between them.

Cortez, the young officer in command of the lancers, saw the gray-haired warrior standing bravely, poised on the balls of his feet, and selected him as a target. The charge would carry the troop over those few who faced them, and then it would be bloody sport, sticking the fleeing men in the backs with the lances and then using sabers. A saber blow from the back of a running horse, if delivered with good timing, could send a decapitated head spinning freely off the shoulders.

Cortez had never been in action before. His enlistment was in the best of family traditions; he had had the best of training and was eager to prove himself in combat. He leveled his lance, dropped the tip to take the aging Indian in the chest, and leaned forward in the saddle.

As the lance seemed about to hit his chest, Danega pivoted, letting the lance slide past him. He leaped high, swinging his tomahawk as he was in midair, the momentum of the speeding horse adding force to the blow that took the young officer on the upper part of his thin chest armor. Deflected by the armor, the tomahawk blade flew upward, so that the officer's lower jaw was severed from his face and he fell heavily, life's blood spurting. The man following Cortez caught Danega as he landed off balance, his lance entering between two of Danega's ribs to pierce the heart and penetrate the entire torso, emerging on the other side. The force of the hit jerked the lance from the rider's hands. The warrior who had stood next to Danega caught the lance as the dying war chief fell, wrested it from the body, and leaned the end of it into the ground, so that its sharp tip was upraised and caught the breast of an onrushing horse. The horse's momentum drove the lance deep before it splintered, and horse and warrior died together as another lance caught the warrior full in the stomach.

Renno, much saddened, knew that Danega and those who stood with him had bought time for the main body of the attackers, who were streaming for the tree line as fast as they could run.

De Rojas saw the rout of the men in the meadow and was heartened, for now, he knew, the lancers would come charging back to relieve the hard-pressed guard force of Chickasaw.

But the lancers were without their commanding officer. Their appetite for killing was high because they had seen comrades fall to the initial musket and arrow fire. A few had bloodied lances and sabers, and the bloodlust was upon them as the Indians fled before them. One man was apparently maddened— the lancers could not know about the moment of

mirth when Dawida had asked how a Seneca showed
fear and Renno had laughingly suggested that he
scream like a white woman seeing a snake—so that
he alternated high-pitched falsetto screams with gust-
ing laughter as he ran.

The lancers spurred their horses and, weakened
by heavy casualties, concentrated on catching the
fleeing warriors before they reached the trees along
the creek.

Renno was ready for them. Soon after Danega's
strike force had streamed out into the meadow, Renno
had motioned his second line of men into position.
He himself would partake in this action. He thought
fleetingly of Emily and that she would be home soon,
with their son. He then focused his attention entirely
on the battle.

"Do not fire, men!" he yelled as the fleeing warriors began to leap the small, muddy creek and enter
the main mass of trees. "Hold your fire!"

The cavalry charge had been a magnificent sight.
From Guy de Rojas's point of view, it was impressive, for the men were well trained in tactics, if not
experienced in action. He knew that the lancers had
time to turn, charge back to the knoll, and turn the
tide in the battle in which the Chickasaw guard force
was being bested.

Then he realized that the fools were not going to
turn. "Sons of dogs!" he screamed—unheard by the
lancers. "Turn, you sons of whores!" he bellowed, as,
their ribbons streaming from gay polished helmets,
the lancers leaped their steaming horses over the

muddy stream and raced after the fleeing warriors into the forest.

De Rojas knew then that all was lost. He turned to see two gun crews fleeing south, toward the Chickasaw masses, while the other two crews tried to tend the bodies. "Destroy your guns," de Rojas roared. He himself ran to a gun and began to pour a huge amount of powder down its muzzle. Around him were the wild war cries, the screams of the dying, while yet another pale-skinned warrior led a determined push toward the cannon. De Rojas frantically tried to pack the muzzle of the cannon with debris, so that when the oversized load was fired, the gun would explode, but arrows began to come agonizingly close to him as Ena found a position near the fighting where she had a direct line of fire. Another artilleryman went down with a gurgle as an arrow lodged in his throat, and de Rojas, cursing, turned to flee. He was not willing to give his life in this useless cause of defeat. Oklawahpa still had thousands of Chickasaw warriors, and de Rojas had to get to their commander before he did something foolish, like send all his forces charging into the woods.

Guy de Rojas had no false pride. Wanting to live to fight another day, he began backing down the hill toward the south. He saw that the Chickasaw were overwhelmed, that it was nearly over, and the pale-skinned warrior in the lead was dealing death with knife and tomahawk. As de Rojas turned to run full speed, he saw a Chickasaw detach himself from the hand-to-hand combat and run swiftly toward him. It was Oklatumpa. So now this brave young warrior was deserting his men, who were at least fighting to the last.

"Go back and fight, you cowardly cur," de Rojas yelled at Oklatumpa, who was now nearing him.

"The word must be given to Oklawahpa," Oklatumpa panted.

"I will give that word, coward," de Rojas said, drawing his sword and impaling the young warrior with a swift move. The blade dug deep, and Oklatumpa's forward momentum caused it to emerge on the back side of his body, and he was dead even as de Rojas wrenched the blade out of his falling body and, sword in hand, ran as fast as his legs would carry him.

As the lancers penetrated the woods, yelling their victory and their blood excitement, they were met by painted demons who fell on them from the trees.

Renno let the lead horsemen pass his position, then flung himself from his perch on a limb to land heavily, his weight forcing a lancer from the saddle to tumble to the ground. Then it was but the work of a moment for Renno to use the Spanish stiletto to slash the man's throat, and then the great medicine ax was in his hand. A lancer, yelling defiantly, charged through an opening in the trees; Renno danced under the slash of the saber and broke the lancer's leg with a powerful blow of the ax, causing the man to lose his seat and fall heavily. His life ended with one blow of the ax, and immediately Renno was looking for other targets. Out of the corner of his eye he glimpsed a grim-faced Dawida agilely twisting and turning with the exertion of wielding knife and tomahawk. And then it was done: Renno saw his own warriors quickly scalping the fallen Spaniards, and horses with empty saddles running through the trees.

Renno, satisfied that the entire cavalry force was dead or dying, ran to the open, looked up toward the grassy knoll to see El-i-chi charge to the guns, catching a fleeing Spaniard in the back of the neck with his tomahawk. Farther down the meadow Rusog's force had reached the trees, and a withering hail of fire from the Frontier Regiment's muskets caught the charging Chickasaw and decimated their ranks to a fearful point. The entire meadow was piled with the dead, and now the Chickasaw charge faltered, slowed, and reversed itself, but still the fire from Roy Johnson's regiment added to the fatalities.

On the mound, El-i-chi signaled for Roy Johnson's two white artillerymen to be brought forward. The men had not been risked in the battle, having been ordered to stay in the protection of the northern tree line. Now they came forward, quickly inspected the cannon, cleared the gun de Rojas had tried to destroy, and soon had instructed Indians in how to load and carry shot and ball. A roar came from the throats of the guns and the throats of the victors as the cannon, now turned toward the woods where the Chickasaw were congregated, were fired.

Far to the south, a group of Chickasaw—no more than twenty of them—managed one last charge, maddened, perhaps, by seeing the number of Chickasaw dead on the field. Rusog and several of his men met the Chickasaw and quickly dispatched them.

All was quiet now except for the steady boom of cannon as the captured guns sent balls crashing into the woods over the heads of the stunned Chickasaw force.

Chapter XI

N ever had Oklawahpa seen so many dead men.
Never had he seen Chickasaw warriors run from
a fight. He had moved forward near the meadow so
that he witnessed personally the last futile charge of
a small number of his men and saw them die to a
man. Meanwhile, the cannonballs were crashing
among the trees. Actually, the cannon fire was taking
only a small toll, a man killed or wounded here and
there, mostly by flying wood splinters. But even one
man was too many to lose to the cannon, for de Rojas

had assured Oklawahpa that the fieldpieces would
make for swift victory.

Oklawahpa's every fiber told him to gather his
men and lead a charge against that enemy that had
taken so large a toll. The Chickasaw dead must be
avenged. He was in a glowering, black mood when
he saw Guy de Rojas run up to his camp. De Rojas
was panting.

"This is the way the great European generals fight?"
Oklawahpa roared, waving his arms at a group of
wounded men, then toward the blood-soaked meadow.
"You said we would combine Spanish and Chickasaw
tactics. It is not a Chickasaw tactic to lose, so we
must have been fighting with Spanish tactics alone."

De Rojas held his temper. "All is not lost, Great
Chief," he said. "We still have superior numbers."

"No more!" Oklawahpa retorted with a strong slash
of his hand through the air. For a moment de Rojas
feared that the chief was giving up on the war al-
together. "No more will we fight as you say, hair-
face," Oklawahpa went on, using a term of contempt
for de Rojas that, up to this point, he had used only
in de Rojas's absence.

"Now we will fight like Chickasaw," Oklawahpa
said, motioning his junior war leaders toward him.
"Now we will meet the enemy as we have always
met him, not with mounted lancers. Not with cannon. We will meet him man to man, and we will slay
him. Before the sun starts to fall down the sky from
its highest flight, we will sweep across the meadow
in all our numbers."

"The enemy will shoot you from behind trees,

from the treetops, from behind every rock and bush," de Rojas warned.

"Tie this hair-face to a tree," Oklawahpa ordered.

It took six Chickasaw braves to subdue de Rojas, and then it was possible to tie him in a standing position to a large tree only because he quit struggling. He glared at Oklawahpa. "Thus you give up your dream of a Chickasaw empire," he said.

Oklawahpa spat in his direction, vented a shrill war cry, and trotted toward the meadow. The Chickasaw had never lost a war. And they had won their wars man to man, without fancy tricks or strategy. So would it be now, and thus would the Chickasaw dead be avenged.

As soon as the lancers were killed so swiftly among the dense trees, where they could not bring their lances to bear or maneuver, Renno had moved forward to the next phase of his plan. First, there were some loose ends to secure. He sent Dawida and the remainder of his force of men to join El-i-chi on the grassy knoll to prevent the cannon from falling back into enemy hands. Next he detailed several men to round up the lancers' horses, which represented a great value and were a legitimate spoil of war. He sent a messenger to Rusog with a request for an estimate of losses, and within minutes the youth was back with a jubilant report.

"The war chief of the Cherokee sends word that the Cherokee failed in the boast that they would kill two Chickasaw to every Cherokee lost," the runner cried breathlessly. "Instead, the Cherokee killed three for one in the meadow."

"And how many of our own were lost?"

The youth frowned. "Great Chief, the women and children will mourn for over two hundred."

Soon Rusog joined Renno and the other senior war chiefs. Rusog was still on fire inside, unable to sit still. He kept leaping to his feet as Renno talked.

"Victory," Rusog kept saying. "Victory."

"It was costly," Renno reminded him. One of the older war chiefs nodded glumly. "El-i-chi has lost half his force. Danega is dead, and twenty of his men with him. To win, the Chickasaw has only to keep giving us these victories that cost us so much."

"Rush him now," Rusog yelled, "while he is licking his wounds. He sees the six hundred who lie scalpless in the meadow. He sees the pile of dead in front of the guns of the Frontier Regiment, and the dead on the knoll. He dies as the iron balls fall into his camp. His spirit is broken, my Brother. Let us hit him now, and we will drive the few who live running in fear back toward the big river."

"My brother has fought well," Renno said soothingly. "All have fought well. But the Chickasaw still number as many as the drops of dew on the morning grass."

Rusog made a vulgar gesture in the direction of the enemy.

"Rusog, we must still be cautious as we reduce the enemy's numbers. We must keep him guessing." Renno spoke the names of four young war chiefs. All four leaped to their feet expectantly. "Each of you will select thirty men. You will then move rapidly to the enemy flanks, two groups to each side, where you will seek out isolated pockets of Chickasaw. You will strike heavily, kill as many as you can on the first blow, and then you will pull back to probe and strike again. It is important that you get into position as quickly as possible, for it is my guess that the Chickasaw will fling himself at us in all his numbers within a few hours."

"I would go with the men who strike from the flanks," Rusog said.

"Rusog, you are a rock of strength around which the power of the enemy swirls and flows without effect," Renno said. "You and I will be here, in the trees. We will meet the great enemy charge, the two of us and the greatest force of our men."

"He will not charge," Rusog said. "He is beaten, and unless we move swiftly, he will pull far back and have time to lick his wounds. Then it will be harder to kill him."

Renno stood in silence for a long moment. He let his blue eyes, in which glittered the cold light of war, shift from face to face among his war leaders. "If I am wrong and the enemy has not made a move when the sun stands two hands high above the western horizon, I will hand over the cloak of leadership to Rusog, and then he can punish the beaten enemy."

"No such talk," Rusog growled. "It is just that I have tasted enemy blood, and the fire is hot in me. There will be no talk of Renno's abandoning the cloak of leadership, for you are our great sachem in war."

"Go, then," Renno said. "Impress upon all that we must not be as eager to die as the Chickasaw. We will hold our positions. We will fire from good cover. We will fire and fire again, with musket and with bow, and then we will meet the enemy thus." He let the great medicine ax make a slash in the empty air.

The gunners under El-i-chi's command had begun to work more smoothly, and now all four of the cannon were firing solid shot into the forest, where the Chickasaw lurked. Oklawahpa had ceased to worry about the cannon. He had moved his great force, thousands strong, as near to the tree line as possible. He had given stern orders to keep assigned positions during the charge, not to bunch up in an effort to meet the first countercharging enemy, as had been done before. His men were instructed to race all the way to the trees across the meadow and the muddy creek.

"There will be enemy enough for all," he told his men, the process taking time because he had to walk up and down the front and speak to individual groups of men.

All the while, Oklawahpa had been trying to keep one question out of his mind. Where was his son, Oklatumpa, who had been with the small force guarding the cannon? He had not asked, but he kept his eyes open, and he had now walked all the way to the south, to the last group of warriors on the southern flank, and he had not seen Oklatumpa. His anger toward the Spaniard had cooled somewhat, so he went back to where de Rojas was still tied to the tree and stood in front of the bearded man, his face unreadable.

"Untie him," Oklawahpa ordered. "Let him see how Chickasaw fight with their own methods."

De Rojas had scarcely been freed when, so near that the individual war whoops could be heard, a struggle broke out.

"Apparently the enemy is not waiting for your Chickasaw strategy," de Rojas said.

Oklawahpa headed for the fight on the run, found six dead Chickasaw. The enemy had not even taken time to scalp the fallen. He returned to de Rojas. "A nuisance raid," he said. "Come."

De Rojas belted on his pistols, sheathed his sword, lifted a musket in his right hand, and followed the chief toward the meadow. He was impressed, for the warriors were silent, tense, and ready, crushed together so that their charge would be in a tight mass.

"The pale-skinned one on the knoll will kill many with grapeshot," de Rojas told Oklawahpa.

"He will have time for no more than three volleys before we are into the trees and among them," Oklawahpa said. He stood and gave a yodeling war cry, which was picked up and relayed up and down the line. The undulating cry continued for long minutes. De Rojas knew that the purpose of that mass outcry was to awe the enemy, to let him know that there were many, many warriors, but he doubted that the pale-skinned chief would be much impressed.

In fact, the sound of the continuing war cry was impressive to those who waited under good cover across the meadow. After a few long seconds of it, a

Seneca gave his own extended, wailing war cry and soon every man on both sides of the conflict was yelling at the top of his voice.

Renno had taken his position among the finest of the Seneca warriors on the far right of his own formation. Thus he was facing the grassy mound where El-i-chi had more than one hundred warriors at his command. He knew that El-i-chi would be watching closely for a signaled order.

When the Chickasaw burst out of the woods on the other side of the meadow, Renno's heart leaped, and for one moment he was stunned by the sheer numbers of the enemy. They were coming at him in thousands. He whooped an order that was passed through the forces of the defenders. All was silence. The charging, yelling Chickasaw, the strongest runners among them beginning to outdistance the masses, cried out their insults and war whoops, but the defenders were silent, lest their own whoops give away their concealed positions.

With a swishing sound of death, grapeshot took its toll among the massed Chickasaw, and the wild whooping intensified. Once, twice, the guns fired, and more Chickasaw fell. And now the strong runners were paying the price for their swiftness as muskets spoke from the cover of the trees and the leading Chickasaw warriors fell. Each defender had time to fire, reload, and fire again. Then the defenders laid aside their muskets and sent flights of arrows. The result was to bridge the small muddy creek with Chickasaw bodies, and over these bodies more Chickasaw came leaping. And still the Cherokee did not break cover; they fired an arrow and fell back, drawing the vanguard of the Chickasaw force well into the forest, where the battle became man-to-man, hand-to-hand. So numerous were the Chickasaw that those who stood did not miss those who had fallen. And in the hand-to-hand fighting, Cherokee fell.

Renno, at the far right, saw his men decimate the charging line of Chickasaw with well-aimed musket fire and arrows. Se-quo-i, using his blowgun effectively, accounted for several of the enemy dead, and Renno's heart swelled with pride.

Although Oklawahpa had been careful to place his men along the entire length of the meadow, it was natural, during the charge, for the running Chickasaw warriors to close up toward the center so that the charging masses on the far right were fewer and those who reached the trees were actually outnumbered by Renno's Seneca.

Renno signaled to his men and led the way out into the open. He looked across the meadow and saw El-i-chi standing tall atop the mound. When he gave El-i-chi a family whoop and motioned with his hand, El-i-chi's force started to pour down off the mound. Renno then put both hands on the handle of his medicine ax and, giving the cry of the Bear Clan, rushed into the mass of Chickasaw who were crossing the muddy creek in an effort to close with the warriors in the forest. On either side of Renno the Seneca warriors formed strong flanks, and the Seneca were soon surrounded on all sides by more whooping Chickasaw.

Renno had established a rhythm. As he stepped forward with his left foot, the mighty ax swung, and time and time again the sheer power of the arms behind the blow and the weight of the supernaturally heated ax brought death. Then his right foot would step forward, and the ax would swing backhand. And just as it seemed that the Chickasaw would over-whelm Renno's band, El-i-chi's men smashed into the rear of the Chickasaw, and their flashing blades spread quick panic.

It was a sight El-i-chi would never forget: Renno, strongly built, a man in his prime, wearing only the deerskin loincloth of war and his moccasins, his broad chest running with sweat and blood, was the point of a line of smashing, slashing destruction. El-i-chi fancied he could hear the great ax sing of power and victory as it swung tirelessly, as warrior after warrior tested himself against the pale-skinned ax wielder and fell.

From the south, Roy Johnson saw the charge and wondered when it would be the turn of the regiment. His musket fire dropped more of the enemy during the charge, but the main body was too far to the north for his fire to be effective. He had men out watching his rear, for he knew that the Chickasaw was no fool. It was unlikely that he would rush head-on again into the massed fire of the regiment. But as the charge crossed the meadow and most of the Chickasaw disappeared into the woods, a new worry came to Johnson. He estimated that at least three thousand men had charged across the meadow, and even with their heavy losses, they would still outnumber the allied Seneca and Cherokee.

Johnson passed orders. The regiment left cover in the woods and marched in a line abreast into the open. "Pick your targets well," Johnson yelled. "Fire with care. And if they turn on us, run like hell for cover."

The men broke into a trot and soon came within range of the last of the Chickasaw to charge against the tree line. Without orders, the men of Franklin fell to their knees for additional steadiness in aiming, and it seemed to Johnson that each man found his mark.

Renno had incorporated El-i-chi's men into his own formation, and he was leading it along the creek, drawing Chickasaw into the woodlands. The ax shattered bone, opened skulls, and left dead men that Renno had to step over. As he worked toward the south, he saw Johnson's regiment moving, kneeling, firing, moving again.

Oklawahpa stood with de Rojas just beyond the protection of the trees on the western side of the meadow. The chief's face had not changed expression when the grapeshot had killed several men, nor when men fell so thickly that the muddy creek was bridged with their bodies. Now he saw a well-organized group of enemy warriors moving along his rear, taking a great toll, and the white men using their muskets to devastating effect. Not one of his war leaders tried to lead a charge to silence the muskets of the whites.

"This is not war," Oklawahpa sputtered.

De Rojas did not speak. Many Chickasaw had died in the charge, but it had begun with three thousand men. Perhaps Oklawahpa was right, and in their own element, fighting as the Chickasaw had always fought, they would be victorious.

But, Oklawahpa was thinking, his men were not fighting as they had always fought. Never before had such huge forces of warriors met in one spot. War was a matter for individuals, for small groups. War was for personal glory and advancement and fun. He did not know what was happening in the woods, but he knew, and voiced it again, that this was not war. This was slaughter, with men slaughtering men as they slaughtered the buffalo.

"I think we have them now," de Rojas said, listening to the distant cries from the battle among the trees.

In the trees, one Chickasaw warrior after another found himself alone, his companions having been killed as the Cherokee and Seneca fired from behind trees, rocks, and bushes. One man, then another, turned and began to make his way back toward the meadow. In the meadow a group of Chickasaw formed and made a charge at Renno's formation, only to be stopped dead by the terrible whooshing power of the medicine ax. The charge was quickly blunted, and the Chickasaw survivors, many wounded, backed away, holding weapons at the ready. Behind them Chickasaw began to emerge from the forest, many of them with fresh scalps dangling from their belts.

"To your left, Renno!" El-i-chi cried, as a group of

about a hundred Chickasaw came running from the trees to halt in confusion when they saw Renno's men in the open.

"Hold," Renno ordered.

The Chickasaw, silent, some clutching wounds, others giving signs of defiance, moved warily away, aimed for the open meadow.

"Let them pass," Renno said.

"Tell them to attack," de Rojas yelled at Oklawahpa when he saw that the returning Chickasaw were not going to fight that pale-skinned son of a dog who had become de Rojas's personal curse.

"If you are so eager for more blood," Oklawahpa said, "*you* attack."

It took a full hour for the retreating Chickasaw to cross the meadow in groups ranging from two or three warriors to more than a hundred at a time. Oklawahpa's heart grew heavier with each passing minute. From the trees across the meadow there still came the sounds of combat, an occasional war whoop, a musket shot, a scream of pain. And there in the open meadow, surrounded by warriors who looked as fresh as they had when the battle started, save for the blood spattered over them, was the pale-skinned one.

"I will speak to that chief," Oklawahpa said. One of his men quickly produced a medicine flag, and Oklawahpa stepped forward.

"Renno," El-i-chi said, pointing toward the Chickasaw chief who advanced under a medicine flag of truce.

Renno used the back of his hand to wipe blood and

perspiration from his forehead, lowered the great ax to hang in its sheath from his belt, stepped away from the group of warriors, and waited.

Oklawahpa stopped ten paces away. "You are a worthy opponent," he said.

"As Oklawahpa is worthy," Renno answered.

"You know my name, and yet I do not know the name of my enemy who has fought so well," Oklawahpa said. "It is time to talk. This is not war. This is the butchering of men. Come, we will go away from this field of death and parley."

"I think it fitting, Great Chief, that we talk our talk here, among the brave men who died for the ambition and greed of your Spanish friends," Renno said.

Oklawahpa looked around. He spat. "*That* for the Spanish," he said. "Yes, you are right. But first, warrior, grant me the knowledge of your name."

"I am Renno, of the Seneca."

Oklawahpa cocked his head. "But the Seneca are northern peoples."

"Now we are here," Renno said. "Our brothers, the Cherokee, share their hunting grounds with us, so we will fight to the last Chickasaw and Spaniard to protect our lands."

Oklawahpa had been examining Renno closely. He was smeared with the blood of his enemies and was still breathing hard from the effort of swinging the great ax. He was dressed as an Indian, but he had not the color of eye or hair that is Indian, and his tanned features were not Indian.

"The Spaniard said that this is the way the European chiefs fight," Oklawahpa said. "This great slaughter, this slaying of warriors from a great distance with the big guns. And you, you have cast a spell on our worthy enemies, the Cherokee, so that they, too, fight like the white man, killing from ambush, refusing to meet in honor. In the forest they fired and fell back, fired and fell back, leading my men deeper and deeper and still killing from concealment. Take your dishonor, white man, and go back to the land of the settlers with it and leave us to fight our wars with dignity and honor."

Renno laughed, and it was a cold, brittle sound. "You speak with a lying tongue," he said. "For where was Oklawahpa's honor when he plotted with the Spanish to kill every Cherokee and white man this side of the blue mountains?"

Oklawahpa lunged forward angrily. Renno took two quick steps to meet him and leaned into the face of the enraged Chickasaw. "If all the dead on this field were Cherokee and Seneca, you would not think the European way of war so shocking. If the lancers were alive and the cannon still killing your enemies, would you be here talking?"

"If it is more blood you want," Oklawahpa warned, "then you shall have it."

"Since Oklawahpa does not reach for his weapon," Renno said with cold arrogance, "I believe I hear only meaningless words."

"We are many," Oklawahpa said. "We are as many as the leaves on the trees."

"But look around you and consider. Do not the leaves fall from the trees in the chill of winter?

Count your dead, Chickasaw." Renno had been talking harshly, for he intended to give Oklawahpa the arrogant face of a victor, a face that left no doubt of the ability of the Cherokee and Seneca to win should Oklawahpa choose to reorganize his still-superior numbers and fight again. Renno could feel the doubt in Oklawahpa, even though the Chickasaw's face was now impassive.

"If you want to go on seeing brave warriors die for a Spanish plot that has already failed," Renno continued forcefully, "we have more room on our belts for Chickasaw scalps." He held up his hand in a peaceful gesture as Oklawahpa started to speak. "If, however, you care to talk over our differences Indian to Indian, without the interference of the white men from Spain, bring your wise men to the knoll where the cannon sit."

"We will talk," Oklawahpa said. He was thinking: *Yes, we will talk now, but in the future our tomahawks will do our talking for us. In the future when the Cherokee and the Seneca have gone back to their lodges in the east, we will send out our war parties as we have always sent them out, and we will, scalp by scalp, avenge those who have died here in this slaughter that is not war.*

Renno and his elders and war leaders sat on skins on the grass of the mound. They had been waiting two hours, for Oklawahpa had taken his time getting to the parley. When Oklawahpa and his war leaders approached the mound, Renno stood alone to meet them. Oklawahpa's face darkened when he saw that armed men were drawn up all around the mound.

"Does the mighty sachem of the Seneca fear that Oklawahpa and his chiefs will recapture the cannon?" the Chickasaw asked.

"Does the great chief of the Chickasaw think we are blind and deaf when he sends three hundred men there?" Renno pointed toward the north.

Oklawahpa was taken aback for a moment. He had surreptitiously sent the men out in small groups to congregate to the north of the mound, just in case. He had not expected to be found out in the maneuver, and his respect for this pale-skinned chief grew. "A hunting party," he explained offhandedly.

"And these warriors here," Renno responded, "asked for the opportunity to see the great war chief of the Chickasaw at close hand."

Oklawahpa nodded, then turned his gaze on Roy Johnson. "This was to be a parley between Indians."

"Colonel Johnson is a chief among the white settlers you and the Spanish planned to kill," Renno said. "Has Oklawahpa come to talk of peace or to complain like an old woman with the winter fever? Colonel Johnson stays. If you want to have your Spanish adviser present, we do not object."

"My Spanish adviser no longer advises," Oklawahpa said.

The enemies sat facing each other. The afternoon sun made long shadows. The smell of death was everywhere. In the meadow, warriors from both sides were collecting their dead, and occasionally the quiet of the late afternoon would be broken by a howl of mourning as a warrior discovered the body of a dead friend. On the mound Renno began the talk.

"Your political chiefs joined with the chiefs of the Choctaw and others to make a paper with the Spanish in Pensacola," Renno said.

Oklawahpa nodded, then spread his arms to encompass the land toward the river. "Here, this is Oklawahpa's land. The elders and the grand chief, they go to Pensacola. Oklawahpa does not go. It is true that the old chiefs made a paper with the Spanish. Oklawahpa did not."

"Are you not loyal to your leaders?" Renno asked.

"Oklawahpa and his people range free."

"Did Oklawahpa understand the full intention of the Spanish?" Renno asked. "Did he know that the intent was to slay every warrior and enslave the women and children of the entire Cherokee nation?"

Oklawahpa shrugged. "There is always grand talk before a war."

"Oklawahpa did not intend to destroy the Cherokee as a nation?" Renno asked.

Oklawahpa considered for a long time before answering. "I have always known that the Cherokee were too great to be destroyed totally."

"Yes," Renno said. "Since you have that knowledge, and it has been made more certain in your mind, perhaps we have a basis on which to talk."

Oklawahpa had been having second thoughts ever since he had agreed to meet with his enemy. His warriors had recovered quickly from the battle and were eager to fight again. His scouts had told him that the enemy, which had begun the fight with

smaller numbers, had suffered heavily. Now, in spite
of his arrogance, the Seneca sachem was showing
signs of wanting peace. Oklawahpa was going to find
out how badly Renno wanted the fighting to stop.

"The hair-faces from Spain give us many things,"
Oklawahpa said. "They give my warriors muskets
and fine blades. They give my women beautiful cloth
and utensils for cooking." He turned his face to Roy
Johnson. "Will the whites of the blue mountains
have weapons and gifts for the Chickasaw?"

Renno spoke before Johnson could answer. "We
did not come here to bribe Oklawahpa to stay alive."

Oklawahpa leaped to his feet. "You go too far, pale
one."

Renno stood. "The Spanish have used you," he
said harshly, his eyes impaling those of the Chickasaw.
"They have played with you as a cat plays with a
mouse. With my own eyes I saw them building a fort
in the heart of the Chickasaw nation, at Chickasaw
Bluffs. Against whom are the guns of that fort aimed?
Are they aimed at the Cherokee, far to the east? No,
they are aimed at the backs of the Chickasaw. Had
you done the job they bribed you to do, Oklawahpa,
when your warriors returned to Chickasaw Bluffs,
they would have faced those guns. Once you had
furnished the blood and the power to win this land,
the Spanish would have then taken it from you. That
is their history."

Oklawahpa heard, in spite of himself, and the words
made sense, for he himself had questioned the need
of a Spanish fort in the most secure area of the
Chickasaw nation.

"Speak on," Oklawahpa said.

"From the east, there will be no white invasion of your lands," Renno said. "We and the settlers of Franklin are allied. It will be up to you to prevent white invasion from the Spanish. The Spanish have already won one great victory."

Oklawahpa lifted his eyebrows in question.

"Can you call this a victory for the Chickasaw?" Renno asked, indicating the bloody field. "Can we truly call it a victory for either side, with so many brave warriors dead? And for what? Spanish dreams of conquest?" He shook his head sadly. "No, this is a Spanish victory, for his wish is to see all Indians dead or in slavery to him."

Oklawahpa nodded.

"You, Great Chief of the Chickasaw, will dismantle the Spaniards' fort on the river. You must deny him the right to establish forts in Chickasaw lands."

Oklawahpa sat down again. "And if the Spanish send a great army?"

Renno laughed. "Then Oklawahpa has the kind of war he likes, for he can fight the Spanish in the traditional Chickasaw way."

"And if the Choctaw come with him?" Oklawahpa asked.

"Ah," Renno said. "We, on our part, will see that the Choctaw do not attack the Chickasaw through our lands. There is talk of building a strong fort at the shoals of the river that runs south into Choctaw lands."

"We need no help in protecting ourselves from the flat-heads," Oklawahpa said.

Renno did not point out that it had been Oklawahpa who had first mentioned the Choctaw. "You would not object if we build such a fort, along with the Franklin whites?"

"If the threat of the flat-heads moving north dismays you," Oklawahpa said, "build your fort."

"Good. Now we will make a paper. Colonel Johnson, you will please write what we have said here."

"Wait," Rusog said, standing. "I have heard nothing from the great chief of the Chickasaw that guarantees he will not make war on the Cherokee."

Oklawahpa looked at Rusog with disdain. "You may put into the paper that the Chickasaw nation will never again march against the Cherokee."

Renno let a mirthless smile cross his face. He took the oratory stand again. "The war chief of the Chickasaw has stated that never again will the Chickasaw nation march against the Cherokee. This is good, and it shall be written on the paper. What I am about to say will not be written, except here." He tapped his heart. "When Oklawahpa states that the Chickasaw nation will not march, I see this huge army that has been gathered, the combined fighting force of all the Chickasaw. I think Oklawahpa promises only that this total war will not happen again. Oklawahpa has indicated that he does not like that kind of war, so he agrees only not to have the type of mass encounter of the past few days. I think he does not rule out war parties, am I right, Oklawahpa?"

"Young warriors are not always easy to control," Oklawahpa said. "The traditions—"

Renno stared at Oklawahpa coldly before speaking

in a low voice. "We Seneca have been a warlike tribe. We have fought the French, the early colonists, the British, and many Indian tribes. We have lately fought on the side of the white colonists in their great war of freedom, and we have been fighting for too long. Our Cherokee brothers have also been fighting for too long. We will not play the ancient game of coup with you, Oklawahpa. This I say, and this I swear: if you cannot control your young warriors, if even one small war party kills Cherokee or Seneca, *our* entire nations will move, and the results will make today's battle seem tame."

Oklawahpa glowered. "You state that there is no victor here, and yet you lay down terms as if you are the victor."

"I have sworn," Renno replied. "Now, there are other things. The cannon—"

"The cannon are ours," Oklawahpa said. "They were given to us by the hair-faces."

"The cannon will be destroyed," Renno said.

Oklawahpa knew that it was bargaining time, and there was precious little to bargain for. Then he remembered the fine Spanish horses. Many of them had been killed or wounded, but there still would be many of them left alive.

"If the Spanish come," Oklawahpa said, "they will be on horseback. The Chickasaw have few horses. We must be able to meet the Spaniard on his own terms."

"You would teach Chickasaw warriors how to fight with saber and lance?"

"With horses, we could match his mobility on the

flat plains near the river," Oklawahpa said. "You, in your forests and your hills, have no use for horses."

Renno caught a quick wink from Roy Johnson. They had discussed the horses, and they had known that Oklawahpa would have to have something, some semblance of victory.

"What Oklawahpa says makes sense," Renno said. "We will share the horses with the Chickasaw."

"This is generous," Oklawahpa replied, "but when the Spanish come, will you bring warriors mounted on your share of the horses to meet him? If we are to destroy the Spanish fort and meet his anger, we need horses."

"He has a good point, Renno," Roy Johnson put in.

"The horses are Oklawahpa's," Renno agreed, nodding his head.

"And from the whites," Oklawahpa went on, "we need muskets."

"We have no muskets for you," Renno countered.

"Perhaps the whites of Franklin are weak and need the Indian to protect them?" Oklawahpa said slyly. "You ask that we make an enemy of a powerful friend who gives us many weapons and many gifts. Is the medicine of the white Spaniards more powerful than that of the whites of Franklin? If I am to become an ally of your whites, I must know if they are strong or weak."

"The whites of Franklin were to the far south today," Renno said. "Count your dead here."

"Still, I must know," Oklawahpa persisted, for a solution to one of his problems had come to him.

Under guard, back in his camp, was the Spaniard. What to do with the man was his problem. He could not let him go back to the Spanish and tell them that Oklawahpa had betrayed them, and yet he did not want the Spaniard's blood on his hands, just in case the Spanish were stronger than they seemed to be. It was good to keep one's choices open. Perhaps, in the future, he would want to parley with the Spanish again.

"We will let the spirits show which of the white tribes is stronger," Oklawahpa said. "In my camp is a Spaniard. He is strong, much man. You will pick the bravest and strongest of your whites, and the spirits will govern the outcome. If your white wins, then we will know that his medicine is strong, and Oklawahpa will be his friend. The Spanish fort will be destroyed, and the Spanish will be kept out of Chickasaw lands."

"So be it," Renno said.

A mutter of excitement worked its way down from the mound and into the groups of warriors.

"Who will be your champion?" Oklawahpa asked.

"I," Renno said. "For although I am Seneca, the blood of the whites runs in my veins."

At first Oklawahpa thought to protest, but he was silent. He had never seen a man larger or stronger than de Rojas. If de Rojas killed this pale-skinned one who was Indian and yet not Indian, then he would still have to find some way to get rid of de Rojas, but it would give him no little satisfaction to see this one, this Renno, lying in his own blood, his light brown hair decorating a Chickasaw lodgepole.

"So be it," Oklawahpa said.

Chapter XII

The time of the wild strawberries had come and gone. The women and children of the Cherokee and Seneca village, as well as men too old to be part of the combined war party, spent a part of their days working their garden plots. Peas, beans, potatoes, cabbage, pumpkins, melons, and, of course, maize were growing well. Soon the new potatoes would be ready for digging, and they would taste very good with stewed rabbit or venison. Although the hunting had been left to those too old or too young to go into battle, there was no shortage of meat, for game was plentiful.

There was little mention of the absent warriors. It was as if those left behind felt that mentioning them might bring the attention of the evil ones upon them. There had been no word from the west since Emily had been escorted home.

Emily knew that each passing day brought closer that time when a runner would arrive with news, and she prayed daily that the news would be good. Meanwhile, she had her day-to-day chores. Little Hawk's burned hand had healed without any disfigurement except for scarring. His use of the hand seemed unimpaired. Emily had been shamed by the accident, for no one in memory knew of a serious burn from an open fire to an Indian baby, and she told herself that she had to be more open to the wisdom of the Seneca. However, it was difficult for her not to think of Little Hawk as a white baby. His skin was fair, just beginning to be browned by the sun. He loved being outdoors with her, and he played happily in the dirt when she worked her garden plot.

The days of spring were good days and would have been perfect had Renno been with her. As she went about her life, watching Little Hawk developing so rapidly, it seemed incredible to her that the man she loved could be in mortal danger at any given moment of the day or night.

Ah-wen-ga and Toshabe, sharing and sensing Emily's concern, made it a point to be cheerful and to spend a lot of time with her and the baby. Toshabe had taken responsibility for the Chickasaw maiden Holani, who was neither slave nor tribe member. Toshabe had been stern with Holani when it was needed, but she had not used the lash on the girl even when she felt that it would improve Holani's character.

Holani worked well. She enjoyed being out in the open, kept Toshabe's garden plot free of weeds, and did her share of water carrying and wood gathering. It seemed that Holani had accepted her fate, and she was given more and more freedom until Emily accidentally discovered a cache of parched maize, a stolen tomahawk, and a doeskin blanket. Emily had not been intentionally spying on Holani; it had just happened that she noticed that Holani quite often made a detour on the way back from the garden plots and wondered, idly, what the girl was doing.

Emily saw great beauty in Holani and thought that she would make El-i-chi a good wife if she could only accept her situation. Once she came upon Holani in the woods between the village and the garden plots to find the Chickasaw girl seated on the ground weeping silent tears. When Holani realized that she was not alone, she leaped to her feet and tried to dash away the tears.

"I didn't mean to intrude," Emily said.

"There is no privacy for a slave," Holani said in a sullen voice.

"But you are not a slave," Emily said.

"Can I go free, then? Can I go where my heart leads me?"

Emily had no answer for that. She knew that this kidnapping of women was a time-honored custom, and she knew women of the tribes who had become Cherokee or Seneca in that way. They had adjusted and indeed were often more fiercely partisan in favor of their adopted tribe than those born to it. Yet somehow it did not seem right that a young girl could be taken from her home and family and be expected to forget them.

"I will be your friend," Emily told Holani.

"Slaves cannot have friends," Holani said. She then turned and ran.

Perhaps, Emily thought, as she saw Holani take her detour late one afternoon on the way back from the fields, the girl simply goes out of the way to be alone for a few minutes. It was concern, more than curiosity, that led Emily to follow her, because she pictured Holani in some small clearing, weeping alone. She would make one more effort to comfort the girl.

Holani had chosen a beautiful moss-grown glade beside the stream for her private place. Little by little, almost grain by grain, she had been building up a supply of food. The tomahawk had been stolen from a young would-be warrior. She had stored her cache in a leather pouch buried under a stone and was examining it, gloating over the fact that she now had almost enough food to last as she made her desperate run toward the west and home when she looked up and saw Emily standing at the edge of the glade. She seized the tomahawk and leaped to her feet, raising the weapon threateningly.

"You don't have to hurt me if leaving is all you can think of," Emily said.

Holani was confused. She had been discovered. The white wife of the sachem of the Seneca would tell the old women, and they would beat her. At that moment she felt that her only chance was to use the tomahawk on Emily and begin her escape. But somehow she could not do it. She lowered the tomahawk and sat down, her head hanging.

Emily walked toward the girl and sat down beside her. "I didn't think you hated me enough to hurt me," she said.

Holani shook her head. "You have been kind."

"So have Toshabe and Ah-wen-ga."

"Ha!"

"You don't realize how completely you are accepted here," Emily pointed out. "Had you been chosen by an ordinary warrior, you would have been given to the single women in the women's house, where you would have been a slave, to cook and clean for them, and to be beaten. It is sad, but that is one of the truths in life, and there is nothing you and I can do to change it, Holani. However, you have been chosen by the brother of our sachem, by a warrior who has the blood of the greatest leader of all, and even if it means that you have been taken from your home and your family, you are fortunate."

"That warrior killed my family," Holani said.

"Did you see him kill them?"

"No."

"Perhaps it was not he, then."

"The same," Holani said. "They are dead."

"Many others are dead by now," Emily said. "Seneca and Cherokee and Chickasaw, and it is because the Chickasaw wanted war, wanted our lands."

"So it has always been," Holani said.

"If you accept that bloody custom, war, then why

can't you accept a custom that has grown out of it and resign yourself to being a good Seneca?"

"I am Chickasaw."

"And I am white," Emily said.

Holani looked up quickly. It had never occurred to her that Emily, too, might have come to the Seneca as a kidnap victim.

"But I was not forced to be the wife of a Seneca," Emily said. "I chose it. I chose freely to marry Renno, and it is a good life, Holani. It can be good for you, for El-i-chi is a good man and will be a great warrior. Your place as his wife will be one of great honor."

Holani was weeping again, silently.

"Give him a chance," Emily urged. "He will be gentle with you. In that brief time I saw him with you, I saw a light of love in his eyes."

"But I cannot love my enemy," Holani said.

"You can't as long as you consider him your enemy."

"Would you ask me to forget my heritage?"

"No. You don't have to forget. You can combine the good things of Chickasaw heritage with the good things of Seneca tradition." She took Holani's hand. At first Holani tried to jerk her hand away; then she relaxed.

"El-i-chi is not cruel," Emily said. "Nor would he want to live with a wife who hated him. Forget this idea of trying to run away. You know that it would then become a matter of honor with the Seneca, and that they'd have to send warriors after you. Forget it, and wait until El-i-chi returns. He will then, in the Seneca way, pay court to you. See if your opinion of him does not change, and if it does not, I myself will beg him to return you to your people."

"Why would you do that?" Holani asked.

"Because you are young, and beautiful, and a human being," Emily said. "I would love to have you for a sister, Holani, for I've never had a sister."

"You will not tell the old women about this?" Holani said.

"I won't tell if you'll promise me you won't run away."

"I give you my word."

"You'll wait until El-i-chi returns?"

"I will do as you ask," Holani said. "But I can never be the wife of my enemy."

Emily rose and pulled Holani to her feet. "I think you should come to live with me until the men return."

"If you want me."

Holani said nothing, but she walked side by side with Emily back to the village and was respectfully silent as Emily requested and received Toshabe's permission to take the Chickasaw maiden into her own house.

"Renno," Roy Johnson said, "I don't like this at all."

The sun had been up for almost an hour, and from first light, men had been gathering on the opposite sides of the meadow. The dead had been removed. Their bodies awaited the respective customs of their people. But morning dew had wetted the blood-soaked grass, and a stench of death was in the air.

"They are massed there, and we here," Johnson said, "only a swift charge apart. If a fight breaks out, we'll be at a disadvantage because they still outnumber us."

"Rusog has given orders to all to be alert," Renno said. "If the Chickasaw loses his head and attacks, we will not meet him in the open but will fall back, as we did before, and punish him from cover."

"And you? You'll be there in the center of the meadow?"

Renno shrugged. "My fate is here," he said, extending his strong hands, "and in the hands of my ancestors and the manitous."

Guy de Rojas had been summoned to Oklawahpa's shelter as soon as the chief returned from his parley with the enemy. He knew that he was in an uncomfortable position. All his fellow Spaniards, except those few who were back in Chickasaw Bluffs building the fort, were dead. The Chickasaw insistence on traditions and their refusal to listen to him had cost them over a thousand dead. Surprisingly, he had been given back his weapons, and he told himself that he would sell his life dearly if it were Oklawahpa's intention to kill him.

Oklawahpa met him with food, drink, and hospitality. De Rojas had heard that some sort of peace had been agreed to, but he asked no questions, biding his time, knowing that Oklawahpa would eventually tell him what had happened.

The Chickasaw ate and drank in silence. De Rojas ate well and held his tongue. When Oklawahpa spoke, it was not on the subject of de Rojas's interest. "I would know how my son died," Oklawahpa said.

For a moment de Rojas considered telling the truth—that he himself had killed Oklatumpa as he tried to run from the scene of battle, but de Rojas was not yet dead, and as long as a man is alive, he does all that is necessary to remain alive.

"He died bravely," de Rojas lied. "Ten warriors lay dead at his feet before he was overwhelmed."

"Now his scalp hangs at the belt of one of them," Oklawahpa said. "All your boasts and promises were lies, Spaniard. What did your European lancers do with their great horses and their long sticks? They killed a few warriors in the open field, and then rode stupidly into the woods to be dragged from their horses like children."

De Rojas said, "Who has the right to brag about yesterday's battle? Can the Chickasaw be proud?"

Oklawahpa's face tightened. "So you are still filled with big talk."

"All is not lost, Great Chief," de Rojas said, but he was thinking mainly of how he could extricate himself from his dangerous position as a veritable prisoner of the Chickasaw, for it was evident that Oklawahpa was trying to blame him for the Chickasaw's shame. "I will go to New Orleans, parley with the great Spanish chief, and return with many men, with many guns and many horses."

Oklawahpa grunted.

"The great Spanish chief has more guns for the Chickasaw, more gifts for Oklawahpa," de Rojas said. He saw a glint of what he took to be interest in the chief's eye. "Before the coming of the cold, I will return with guns and men, and if Oklawahpa will listen to my advice, we can still have the Cherokee country all the way to the far mountains."

"My chiefs say the Spaniard is all talk," Oklawahpa said, "that the hair-faces know nothing of fighting."

De Rojas smiled. "Would any one of your chiefs dare to say that to me to my face, each of us with weapons in our hands?"

"We will not fight among ourselves," Oklawahpa said, "but you will have your chance to show that the Spaniard can fight as well as talk, if that is your desire."

De Rojas had a sinking feeling that he had been maneuvered into something, and the chief's next words confirmed it.

"The pale-skinned chief of the Seneca has issued a challenge for single combat," Oklawahpa said. "My young warriors clamor for the chance to meet him, but I think we can serve a purpose here. You are big, like a bear, and you are strong. By killing this Seneca, you can show your courage to my warriors, and they will be more inclined to cast their lot with you and the Spanish chief in the future."

De Rojas felt a flush of elation. "This pale-skinned one, he wields a great battleax?"

"The same," Oklawahpa said.

So all was not lost, de Rojas was thinking. "I will kill this pale-skinned one slowly," he said, "to show the warriors of the Chickasaw the fighting techniques of a Spanish warrior." Yes, yes, he was thinking, as his hopes soared again, that was an inspired accident, this placing of himself and that pale-skinned chief face to face. For it was that white devil who was most responsible for the failure of de Rojas's plans. It was his leadership that had cost many Chickasaw lives, all of the lancers, and had made it seem to de Rojas that all his dreams of being ruler of a Spanish empire in the midcontinent had been destroyed. But now . . . Now! He would make a very impressive fight. He would regain his standing in the eyes of the Chickasaw, and he would somehow get more men from the south, and next time there would be no pale-skinned leader to teach the Cherokee how to fight in very un-Indian-like ways.

A great cheer rang out as Renno strode toward the center of the meadow. He was accompanied by Roy Johnson, Rusog, Ena, and El-i-chi, the four he had chosen as his seconds. When Guy de Rojas emerged from the trees on the opposite side of the meadow, Oklawahpa and three Chickasaw war chiefs walked behind him. There was no cheer for de Rojas from the sullen lines of Chickasaw, but he walked proudly.

Renno's heart leaped in joy when he saw that this Spaniard he was to fight was indeed the same man who had mistreated his Emily. Each day during the fighting he had looked for the Spaniard but had never seen him, and now the manitous had delivered the man into his hands. He gave silent thanks as he halted ten paces from the Spaniard and took the man's measure. He was of a height to Renno, but thicker of shoulder and chest, and his thighs were the size of small oak trees. A powerful man.

El-i-chi was Renno's spokesman. He stepped forward, made a salute of respect to Oklawahpa, and said, "My chief, Renno of the Seneca, allows the Spaniard to choose the weapons to be used."

De Rojas wore his sword and two pistols at his belt, and he had donned his boots. Renno carried his full complement of weapons—bow and arrows, musket, the Spanish stiletto at his belt, his tomahawk, and in his right hand, the great medicine ax.

"We will fight in the ring of death," de Rojas announced loudly, so that those Chickasaw warriors nearest him could hear. This decision drew whoops of approval from the warriors.

"So be it," said El-i-chi.

A Chickasaw chief produced a small leather pouch of flour and, under El-i-chi's watchful eye, outlined a circle twenty paces across. Once the circle was outlined in white, Renno and his seconds moved to the south side of the circle, de Rojas and his seconds to the north. De Rojas began to remove his weapons, placing his sword and the two pistols just outside the circle. El-i-chi walked to de Rojas's side. The Spaniard was wearing buckskins. He reached under the loosely hanging shirt to add a large knife to his weapons lying on the grass outside the circle and raised his arms to allow El-i-chi to feel with his own hands that there were no more weapons concealed. Satisfied, El-i-chi rejoined his own group, where Renno, wearing only a loincloth, had placed his weapons carefully outside the circle.

It was Oklawahpa himself who reminded the combatants of the rules. "You will meet in the center of the circle, armed only with tooth and claw," he said. "If you are thrown or pushed outside the circle by your opponent, you must reenter the circle. You may reach for your weapons at any time, but you must not step out of the circle to get them. If you do, the opponent's seconds will kill you."

El-i-chi escorted Renno to face de Rojas and Oklawahpa in the center of the circle. "He is big," El-i-chi whispered. "You must stay beyond the reach of his arms."

Renno was silent. He kept his eyes unblinkingly on de Rojas, noting the way the man moved. The Spaniard moved forward until they stood a pace apart, eye to eye, but with the bulk of de Rojas making Renno look quite slim.

Oklawahpa said, "It begins on my signal and not before."

Then Oklawahpa and El-i-chi walked slowly back toward their respective positions. For a long moment Oklawahpa held his hand raised. Renno still stood, arms crossed. De Rojas stood with his hands at his sides, but Renno noted that he had shifted his weight to his left leg.

With a whoop, Oklawahpa let his hand fall, and Renno's arms dropped even as he saw de Rojas kick with his right leg, sending the heavy boot directly toward Renno's crotch. Renno leaped high, over the kick, and sent out his own foot, bare for better footing on the grass, to connect solidly with the Spaniard's stomach. De Rojas grunted and leaped backward, crouching, as Renno landed and quickly regained his balance, then crouched, beginning to circle de Rojas to the left.

It was soon evident to everyone that Renno possessed the quickness while the Spaniard had the greater strength. Once again Renno's foot flew so quickly that de Rojas could not dodge, and there was a grunt as the foot sank into de Rojas's belly, but Renno knew that the man was in very good condition, his stomach muscles hard, and that his two early blows had done no damage. He knew that it was going to be a real fight when, with a quickness that surprised him, de Rojas landed a blow to the side of his head that sent him off balance, causing him to have to reach down with one hand to keep from falling. De Rojas tried to follow his momentary advantage with a kick with his booted right foot, but Renno recovered, shifted his body, caught the foot in both hands, and lifted, sending de Rojas toppling onto his back with a crash.

Renno threw himself, thinking to land with his knees in de Rojas's stomach, but the Spaniard rolled away and lashed out with a kick that caught Renno on the thigh with such force that for a moment it numbed his entire leg.

Renno leaped to his feet, dancing away from the Spaniard, who was also on his feet and charging, his fists swinging. As Renno was being pushed toward the edge of the circle, he lowered his head and charged, butting his head into de Rojas's stomach, sending the heavier man backward and down with Renno atop, Renno's hands reaching for the Spaniard's throat. For a moment it seemed that Renno would succeed, but then de Rojas brought up a meaty arm, pounded an elbow into Renno's forehead, and dislodged him. Renno lashed out with a balled fist and felt de Rojas's nose flatten under the blow; then he rolled away to escape the clutching, powerful arms and, again on his feet, saw that de Rojas's nose was spurting blood.

De Rojas moved in with slow deliberation, willing to take quick blows to his ribs and stomach in order to press forward, trying to get his arms around Renno so that he could use his strength to break Renno's back. Once he landed a blow to Renno's stomach that sent the air gasping out of Renno's lungs and caused him to fall back for a moment to recover, and then, with a roar, de Rojas charged, caught Renno in his bearlike arms, and lifted him from the ground, squeezing with all his power. Renno, knowing that he must escape the clutch of those powerful arms, did two things simultaneously. He buried his hands in de Rojas's thick hair and jerked the man's head up and back; he also lowered his own head and, pulling de Rojas's face toward him and butting at the same time, felt his forehead smash against teeth, felt teeth give, and heard de Rojas roar in pain. But still the wind was being crushed from Renno's lungs by de Rojas's bearlike arms.

Again and again Renno pounded his forehead into de Rojas's face, but still the relentless pressure continued; it was only when Renno managed to whip one leg up to knee de Rojas in the groin that the grip was broken with a roar of pain from de Rojas, enabling Renno to stagger away. Blood poured from de

Rojas's mouth and nose. He used the palm of his hand to wipe blood away, began to move forward again. In spite of the loss of blood, he seemed tireless. Renno kept his distance, flickering out with his fists or trying to get in a damaging kick, but de Rojas kept advancing relentlessly.

Renno felt his foot slip out from under him as he stepped into a slick spot of blood, and though he immediately tried to recover, he was seized in de Rojas's iron grasp and felt the air and life being squeezed out of him again. He called on the last reserves of his strength, smashed his right elbow into de Rojas's chin, and saw the big man's eyes glaze. He struck once again, and the huge arms released him and de Rojas stumbled away.

It was time for the finish, Renno felt. It had gone on long enough. His ribs ached from the powerful blows and the clutching of those huge arms. He moved toward de Rojas quickly, and the big man sat down suddenly, as if dazed, but even as he fell to the ground, his hand was moving toward the loose top of his boot, and as Renno charged, to finish it, de Rojas jerked a small pistol from the boot top, aimed, and fired just as Renno leaped.

Renno felt a smashing blow at his right shoulder, felt the force of the blow turn his body in the air, and fell heavily as de Rojas rolled away and ran toward his weapons, lying outside the circle.

When El-i-chi saw de Rojas bring out the concealed weapon, he started to raise his own musket, but then Renno was leaping through the air, the pistol fired, and El-i-chi saw Renno's body jerk with the impact of the ball.

In that moment, Guy de Rojas came near death as Oklawahpa lifted his own musket, but Oklawahpa was thinking that if he killed de Rojas for his dishonorable behavior, the Cherokee and Seneca might want more revenge, so he was paralyzed for a moment as de Rojas dived for his weapons. In his dazed and rather frightened state, the Spaniard missed the pistols and found his hands clutching the sword. He turned to see Renno on his knees, holding his right shoulder. Blood was oozing through Renno's fingers. The sword would do.

De Rojas had forgotten everything except the pale-skinned devil who had hurt him. His teeth were loose in his head, his nose was broken, his lips battered, and he ached in every muscle from the devil's blows. The sword would do to finish off this pale-skinned devil.

A roar of protest had gone up from the watching Seneca and Cherokee, and Roy Johnson knew that it would take very little to send the Cherokee and Seneca charging across the meadow. Johnson began to level his musket at de Rojas as the Spaniard was moving toward Renno, who was still on his knees. But El-i-chi put his hand on Roy Johnson's arm and said, "Hold." For Renno had leaped lightly to his feet and was running swiftly toward his own weapons. He outdistanced de Rojas, reached out with his left hand, for his right arm was numb and useless, and seized the haft of the great ax, whirled, and leaped away from a wild swing of de Rojas's sword.

Oklawahpa breathed again. Renno's seconds would have been within the code had they killed de Rojas with their muskets, but since they had not, the battle had to go on.

In his pain, fear, and anger, de Rojas was swinging wildly with his heavy sword. Once, it contacted the head of the ax, and sparks flew with a metallic clang. He soon realized that frenzied slashings were not going to win the day, so he told himself to be calm, to stalk, to thrust, to use the sword to parry the blows from the ax. The fact that Renno was having to use the ax in his left hand gave de Rojas all the confidence he needed to press the attack.

The great ax felt good in Renno's hand. Its weight was the weight of a friend, and he could almost feel the heat generated by that supernaturally created head. And yet he knew that he had to end the battle soon, for he was losing blood rapidly. He studied the thrusts of the Spaniard's sword, avoiding them either by swift movement or by parrying them with the ax, and then he saw that when de Rojas was preparing to thrust, he signaled the movement by setting his left leg. He waited for his chance, saw the left leg set, and moved toward de Rojas instead of away. Whirling, spinning past the thrusting blade, he raised the great ax and sent it thundering down.

A gasp went up from the warriors of both sides as the great medicine ax cleaved the skull of the Spaniard, split it open, and continued to cleave until de Rojas's entire head seemed to explode and part. In the silence that followed, de Rojas's body toppled and thudded to the ground. Renno lifted the great ax and made one complete turn, the ax held high.

"The Spaniard's scalp is yours, warrior," Oklawahpa shouted.

"My honor will not be soiled with the scalp of such," Renno answered.

"He was dishonorable, a coward," Oklawahpa agreed, spitting in the direction of the body.

"Will Oklawahpa now live up to the terms of the paper we have made?" Renno asked. He was beginning to feel a bit light-headed. Blood still pumped from the wound in his right shoulder.

"It will be done," Oklawahpa said, "for at least among our old and familiar enemies, there is honor."

Renno felt the world begin to dim. He turned and forced himself to walk proudly to where his friends waited. Ena, her face tight with concern, made a quick examination of the wound. "The bleeding must be stopped," she said.

Roy Johnson handed her his kerchief. "Press this tightly against the wound," he said. "El-i-chi, help me."

Renno put his hand on Johnson's shoulder. "I will walk," he said.

Holding the kerchief against his wound, he walked toward the muddy creek and felt as if he were walking a few feet above the ground, not on it, but he held himself erect until, well within the forest, Ena guided him to a bed of brush covered with skins, where he could rest and close his eyes. He did not wince as Roy Johnson examined the wound.

"It's a clean wound, Renno," Johnson said. "The ball went all the way through. No bones broken."

"The bleeding is almost stopped," Ena said a bit later.

"There is something I must do," Renno said.

"You will do nothing but rest," Johnson said. "Our doctor will be here in a few minutes."

The "doctor," a man without formal medical training, was also Knoxville's best barber. He agreed with Roy Johnson's opinion that it was a clean wound, and he was much impressed when, with a red-hot iron, he cauterized the two open sides of the wound without so much as a moan from the white Indian.

Runners had been dispatched to take news of the victory to the home villages—among them the fleet-footed Se-quo-i, who was at last agreeable to leaving his leader and mentor, Renno, now that the fighting was over. The Chickasaw had faded into the western forests, each village group returning to its own area. The Frontier Regiment was marching toward home, along with large numbers of Cherokee. Renno spent a night and a day resting, and then he could wait no longer, for he had a promise to keep. He waited until his concerned keepers were sleeping, then slipped quietly out of the camp.

The night was a splendor, the sky white with the lights of the stars, the moon not yet risen. His right arm had regained its feeling, but his shoulder was very sore. He moved at a swift walking pace, and it took him past midnight, past the time of the moon, to reach the stream where he had been led by the spirits of his ancestors. The same crooked tree was there, and the cool, clear waters of the stream whispered past its roots.

Renno stood, the great ax in hand, and prayed to the manitous. The great stone was warm in his hands. Slowly, carefully, he removed the bindings that held on the handle, and then, the stone cradled in his palms, he waded into the shallow water. It felt good and cool on his feet and legs. He bent, placed the stone reverently in the position, among the roots of the tree, where he had found it.

"I have kept my promise," he said, "and I have returned the stone to its resting place." He waited, but there was only the sound of a distant whippoorwill and the hoot of an owl. Still he waited, asking for, praying for a further sign. The stars were dimming, the sky lightening, when he finally decided that it was time to return to the camp.

For one brief moment he considered recovering the great stone, for it had been powerful medicine in the battle for the very survival of the Cherokee and his own people. It would be good to be able to show the great ax to his son in future years, and to see that great weapon of death swung by a strong young warrior who had sprung from his own loins. But he had made his promise, and he would keep it. He stood, stretched out his arms to the dimming heavens, and gave thanks, and as he stood, arms lifted, he heard a rumble of thunder from a clear sky, and with a sudden blast of light and heat, a bolt of lightning shot down from the cloudless sky to strike the shallow water at the exact point where the stone lay.

The great ax, he knew, was no more, but had he not received another powerful sign?

"I am awed and pleased," he whispered, "that my ancestors and the manitous favor me so. I will always strive to deserve it."

Chapter XIII

The homecoming was joyful for many, but never had the allied tribes suffered the loss of so many dead.

As he came from his lodge to greet the returning warriors, Loramas's face was filled with pride but also tinged with the gravity of the loss of men; Ahwen-ga, too, was solemn as she stepped from Loramas's side to greet Renno. Toshabe came next to welcome her son, and finally Emily—only the greatest self-restraint keeping her in her place as last in line to honor the returning hero.

Behind Renno came El-i-chi, Ena, and Rusog, and their reception was nearly as warm. Ena submitted with reasonable grace to worried reproaches from Ah-wen-ga and Toshabe; they had heard from Emily an account of her return to the battlefront against Renno's explicit orders. But El-i-chi's ready defense of his sister's conduct while under his command, as well as Rusog's readiness to forgive his headstrong wife, cooled the heat of her mother's and grandmother's scoldings, and the matter was soon forgotten in the atmosphere of general welcome and homecoming.

Rusog, noting that his father, Wegowa, was absent, inquired after him. Loramas gravely explained to his grandson that Wegowa's illness, which abated for a time, had taken a turn for the worse; to his great regret, Wegowa had not been able to join the welcoming party.

Because of the distance involved, and the time of year, it had proven impossible to return the bodies of the fallen to their families for proper and respectful ceremonies and treatment. At Loramas's order, the two tribes' medicine men and elders organized a joint fast of mourning, with appropriate singing and dancing, to commemorate the dead, who had been buried so far from the lodges of their loved ones.

At the forefront of the mourners was Dawida, whose father, Danega, was singled out by Renno for special mention at the ceremony honoring the fallen. With eyes glistening, the young warrior attended to every word of Renno's dignified eulogy, and there was a murmur of general approbation among all present when Renno concluded his lengthy account of Danega's glorious deeds.

In the days that followed, Renno's shoulder healed well under the tender and fussing ministrations of Emily and her herbs and salves. Little Hawk pleased Renno very much with his progress toward crawling, and Renno spent peaceful evenings with the boy sitting and playing atop his chest, cooing and reaching for Renno's bright hair, trying to sample the taste of the beautiful hilt of the Spanish stiletto. This last worried Emily, although the stiletto was sheathed and Renno was watching closely. But she had her man back and was happy. He did not scold her when she told him of Little Hawk's accident with the fire, saying only, "My wife, there is a reason for all Seneca traditions."

The good fruits and vegetables of early summer were ripening, and Emily's cooking had built Renno's strength back to near normal. He had begun to exercise the damaged muscles of his right arm when Roy Johnson, accompanied by his wife, Nora, rode in from Knoxville and asked for a tribal meeting; Roy had news.

Nora was delighted with her grandson, and she and Emily were content to remain in the lodge, cuddling and playing with Little Hawk, while the men came together with alacrity to hear what Roy had to say.

"My friends," Johnson began when the elders and chiefs were gathered, "we stood on the battlefield alone against the Chickasaw, but to my pleasant surprise our neighbors to the east, in Georgia and North

Carolina, have not been idle. I am happy to report
that we will not have to concern ourselves with fighting the Choctaw. He, like the Chickasaw, has decided that a treaty with Spain is much like going to
sleep with a rattlesnake."

"The Choctaw," said Rusog gruffly, "will be friends
with whoever pays him most."

"Perhaps," Johnson said, "but if the cost of his
friendship is paid by the established states, can we
not still benefit?"

The impending treaty with the Choctaw, to Emily's dismay, took Renno from her once again. First, it
required another trip west, for it was desirable to
have Oklawahpa's Chickasaw involved in the large
conference. That, and the trip south to Hopewell, on
the Keowee River in South Carolina, consumed the
summer. Renno sat next to Roy Johnson in the parley that brought together two states, a would-be
state, and the major Indian tribes of the area, and his
opinions were well heard. The Choctaw nation made
a treaty of perpetual peace and friendship with the
United States. Oklawahpa would not commit himself
to such a binding treaty, but he knew the strength of
the peoples to the east of him, and he was content,
with his splendid Spanish horses, to do his raiding on
horseback on the western side of the Mississippi
among less-determined tribes than the Cherokee and
Seneca.

Of all the warriors who came back from the great
battles of the west, none returned with more anticipation, nor with more increase in his status as a

warrior, than the younger son of Ghonkaba, El-i-chi.
Even as he was greeting his family and urging Emily
to induce the wounded Renno to rest, his eyes strayed,
seeking and not finding the slim form of his Chickasaw
wildcat. It was Emily who, after a joyful greeting of
her husband and a few minutes of privacy with Renno,
took it upon herself to tell El-i-chi that Holani had
left Emily's lodge not ten minutes before the main
body of returning warriors began to pour into the
village.

"How is she?" El-i-chi asked Emily, not quite able
to meet Emily's eyes.

"She is in excellent health, brother," Emily said.
"But if you're asking if her attitude has changed, I'll
have to say yes and no. She has ceased to give us
trouble, but she has not resigned herself to being the
wife of a Seneca."

El-i-chi drew himself up proudly. "She has no
choice."

"I don't wish to seem to correct so brave a war
leader as my husband's brother," Emily said, "but
may I speak as your sister?"

For all his deeds in battle, El-i-chi was still scarcely
more than a boy in years. He grinned and said,
"Sister, in the matter of women, I will listen to you
with humility and great eagerness."

"She is a young girl, far from home," Emily explained. "She came to us with her heart full of hatred, with the knowledge that her family had died,
and she's not even sure you didn't kill one or more of
them yourself. In spite of this, she has come to love
me, El-i-chi, and so I know that she is capable of

love. You must be gentle with her, and you must
speak softly to her. Tell her of her beauty—"

"My tongue sticks to my teeth when I try such
words," El-i-chi said.

"Try hard. Don't rush her. She has great pride,
and she is a young woman of great spirit. If you can
win her, she will be a worthy wife for a great warrior
and a future chief. But be patient."

"It appears, since I cannot find her, that I have no
choice but to be patient," El-i-chi said.

"If you take the path to the garden plots and turn
toward the creek on the old trail, you will find her,"
Emily said.

So it was that El-i-chi, having taken time to do
nothing more than speak a few hurried words of
greeting to his mother and grandmother, quietly disappeared from the scenes of reunion and mixed celebration for the victors and mourning for the dead and
made his way toward the garden fields. He turned
down an old trail that was almost overgrown but
showed signs of the passage of someone with small,
dainty feet, and approached the creek with a silence
that was habitual for him when he was in the forests.

He heard her before he saw her. She was singing a
sad Chickasaw song of mourning in a minor key. And
with her soft voice there was the sound of running
water and splashings. El-i-chi crept closer, keeping
to the cover of a stand of dense, low-growing cedars,
and his heart did a flip-flop in him when he saw
Holani's doeskin skirt and shirt hanging on a bush by
the side of the creek.

The creek was small, clear, and shallow. Near

Holani's private glade, where she was allowed to spend some time alone, a depression had been scooped out of the sandy bed of the shallow creek by village maidens who used that spot for cooling themselves and for bathing. The hole was just deep enough to come to Holani's waist, so that as El-i-chi peered through the cedar boughs his breath caught in his throat, for Holani's body, visible to him from the waist up, was a thing of such beauty that he could not breathe for a moment.

Holani splashed water over her bare breasts and shoulders and rubbed herself vigorously. El-i-chi had a sudden hope that she was bathing, cleansing herself in preparation for greeting him, but the sadness of her song belied such a hope.

For a long time El-i-chi watched, feeling guilty, but helpless to take his eyes away. Then Holani slid down into the water, sat there with the water to her neck, and began to swim. The hole was large enough for her to take about three strokes before she reached shallow water, where El-i-chi saw flashes of brown flanks and rounded bottom when she turned. Tiring of swimming, Holani shoaled herself, lying with shoulders and back out of the water, her rounded rump protruding from the shallows, her legs covered with water. She stayed in that position so long that El-i-chi thought she had fallen asleep. He had a tremendous urge to touch her, to speak to her, to tell her of her beauty, but he was uncertain as to how to approach her. In the end, his boyishness came out in him. He slipped to the creek in total silence and eased himself into the water as quietly as an alligator stalking a water bird, so that the first Holani knew of his presence, she was being jerked into the deeper water by her ankles.

Holani screamed, and then the water closed over her head, and she surfaced, prepared to fight for her life. She saw El-i-chi, and he was laughing loudly.

"It is only I, El-i-chi," he said, "not some wild creature."

Holani had been at home in the water from the time she was a toddler. The sudden fright he had given her roused her Chickasaw anger, and she launched herself at him and bore him down, so that he took a great swallow of water as he tried to laugh. He had to fight off Holani's weight in order to lift his head to cough and gasp for air. Then, before he could regain his breath she was on him again, and he was sure that she was actually trying to drown him, for she put her entire weight on his head and bore him down. So skillful was she in the water, and so weak had he become from taking a swallow of water and losing his breath, that he had begun to see white spots before his eyes before he broke free from her and crawled, coughing and gagging, into shallow water.

Holani ran. She seized her clothing from the bush as she passed, and did not attempt to put it on, for El-i-chi was recovering and, still coughing up water, had started to turn after her, love for her not the foremost item on his mind.

"What's this?" Renno gasped in surprise when a naked maiden hurled herself through the door of his lodge.

"Oh," Holani gasped. She had forgotten that Emily's husband would be home. She stepped quickly into her skirt and threw the shirt over her head and was pulling it down when El-i-chi burst through the door.

"Here, here," Emily said as El-i-chi launched himself across the cooking fire toward Holani.

"Help me," Holani cried as she dodged El-i-chi's lunge.

"Stop it, El-i-chi!" Emily yelled.

"Dignity, warrior," Renno gasped, for he had become convulsed with laughter as he saw El-i-chi, eyes wide in anger, miss the girl and fall to the floor.

"She tried to drown me!" El-i-chi yelled as he dived again, trying to catch Holani's ankles. Holani seized a heavy cast-iron skillet from Emily's cooking area and, as El-i-chi's hand closed on her ankle, struck him such a blow that the skillet rang and El-i-chi's world went black. Holani carefully put the skillet back on its hook and, leaping lightly over El-i-chi's body, ran out the door.

"Brother," Renno said, holding his wounded shoulder as he laughed and El-i-chi regained consciousness, groaned, and tried to sit up, "do not make me laugh, for it hurts."

"Where is that wildcat?" El-i-chi moaned.

"Patience, brother," Emily counseled as El-i-chi staggered out the door, holding his head.

Others had witnessed the flight of the naked Chickasaw maiden and the close pursuit of El-i-chi and had heard the laughter and the loud clang of the skillet from inside Renno's lodge.

"There," a warrior said to El-i-chi as the young

man emerged. The warrior pointed to the trail leading to the east, toward the mountains. El-i-chi ran. The trail was well traveled, so that he could not distinguish her sign at first, but then he saw, in the dust, the outline of her bare foot. He paused to listen, and just as he stopped, he heard her running footsteps ahead, and then they stopped too. He trotted forward.

He saw a bush move beside the trail and prepared himself, and it was well he did, for as he drew even and was ready to turn and leap into the bushes after her, he had just time to duck a hefty swing of a dry, hard tree limb. The limb whisked over his head, brushing his hair, and then he threw himself into the bush, felt his arms close around Holani's legs, and they tumbled to the ground together to roll in a wild melee of arms and legs until El-i-chi, with his superior male strength, finally controlled the situation by sitting astride Holani's stomach while holding her arms with each hand.

"You're getting me wet," Holani said after a moment of panting silence as he glared down into her wide, angry eyes.

"You tried to drown me," El-i-chi said.

"Next time I will," she warned.

"I have a knot on my head that aches like fire."

"Next time I will hit you harder."

"You are a crazy woman."

"I am Chickasaw, and I will never marry you," Holani yelled, trying to free her hands so that she could scratch out his eyes.

"In all honesty," El-i-chi said wonderingly, "I am having second thoughts about *that*."

"Good. Let me go back to my people," she said.

"Had you attacked any other warrior that night when we raided your village, you would be dead."

"Then I would not be a slave," she said.

"You are not a slave, but a fool," El-i-chi said heatedly, but the contact of her slim, soft-hard body beneath him was reminding him of his nature, and he ached to touch the smooth skin of her throat, the fullness of her lips. He pulled both her arms above her head and grasped her wrists in his left hand to free his right, and with his finger he gingerly touched her cheek. She turned her head swiftly and tried to bite his finger. He laughed.

"Are you so angry, then?" he asked. "Is there no tenderness in you for the man who wants you to be his mate?"

"There is only shame that I am not strong enough to fight you better," she said.

"So beautiful," El-i-chi said, stroking her throat, then moving his hand to the mound of her breasts that was flattened under her tautly stretched shirt. Holani tried to shrink away and, unable to move, spat into his face. In quick anger, El-i-chi spat back, and she spat and he spat until both of their mouths were dry, and Holani, in frustration, burst into tears.

"I hate you, I hate you," she gasped, shamed by her own weakness that caused her to weep. "I will make a knife of dry cane and kill you in your sleep."

El-i-chi was still very much aware of the warmth and softness of her body as he straddled it. And he

saw that she had made combs for her dark, long hair
in the Cherokee fashion, of wood and bone. One of
the combs was about to fall out. He pushed it back
into the dark hair and let his hand rest there for a
moment.

"I'm going to turn you loose now," he said.

"Thank you," she said.

He readied himself, released her hands, and tried
to leap away, but not quickly enough. Her fingernails slashed across his upper arm and left trails of
red.

"All right," he said, standing, glaring down at her,
"enough is enough."

The change in his expression frightened her, in
spite of herself. She tried to skulk away on her hands
and knees, but he seized her by both ankles and
jerked her to him, the movement hiking her skirt to
expose her shapely thighs.

"I have offered you the status of the wife of El-i-
chi, son of Ghonkaba, for I am the son of a great
chief. I have offered you my love, and I get almost
drowned. I get hit over the head with a skillet. I am
kicked and scratched and spat upon. So. I now believe you truly do hate me, but I also think that you
are a child, and before I leave you to do as you
please—go back to your Chickasaw home or not—I
am going to show you how bad children are treated."

When she realized his intention, she fought with
renewed strength and determination, scratching, kicking, and biting. But he, too, was angry, and he was
hurt, for he had thought of her longingly so often
during the days when he was away. He sat flat on the

ground, and heedless of her biting, kicking, and scratching, he positioned her across his thighs and ripped her skirt to expose her bare bottom. He felt a moment of deep loss as he saw that squirming female anatomy, but then he raised his hand.

"Hate me for this, child!" he yelled as his hand cracked down onto brown flesh. A white mark was left and then there was the steady sound of his hand, and she was weeping and screaming and trying to dig her teeth into his thigh. He knocked her head away roughly, making her see stars for a moment, and then he was applying his hand again and again, and her fury turned to hopeless shame and then exhaustion. She lay there sobbing weakly for a few more licks, and then he pushed her roughly away and stood. She rolled onto her knees, and when she looked up, his heart melted, for her eyes were swollen with weeping.

"Now," he said, "go or stay."

"I will go," she said through sobs. "I will go now without food or without clothing, since you have ripped my skirt."

"It is one with me," he said coldly. "However, you have my permission to go into the village and repair your skirt and have Emily give you some food before you go."

He turned and stalked toward the village, not looking back. He heard her sobbing and knew she was following, and then all was quiet, and he turned just in time to leap aside as she jumped for his back and went tumbling into the dirt of the trail.

"By the spirits," he said, "I will send you on your

way myself, or I may not survive you." He jerked her to her feet and clung to her arm all the way back to the village.

They received many amused looks as he led her to Emily's lodge, for her skirt hung from her waist by one narrow band, exposing her pert rear with each step, and he had scratches on his cheeks and arms, and her exposed rump had been definitely reddened by his palm.

Emily, hearing the commotion outside, came to the door.

"Sister," El-i-chi said, "honor me by helping this she-devil fix her skirt. Then give her food, and I will send her on her way back to her people."

Renno was sleeping. Emily had closed off his sleep shelf with a blanket. "What happened?" she whispered as she led Holani into the lodge, helping the girl hold her torn skirt together.

"He beat me," Holani said. "I will see him dead."

"With his fist? With a stick?"

"Worse," Holani replied. "As a child, with the flat of his hand, here. See, I am all red there."

"He beat you as a man driven to desperation," Emily said. "Are you determined to go?"

"He has told me that I am free to go," Holani said.

Emily had threaded a large needle with a fine leather thong and was making temporary repairs on the skirt.

"I will miss you," Emily said.

Suddenly Holani burst into tears. Emily finished the stitching together of the torn skirt and put her arms around Holani. "I will miss you, too," Holani said, "for you have been as my sister."

"You don't have to go."

"He says that I must."

"If he knew you wanted to stay, he would not tell you to go," Emily said. "Did you almost drown him?"

Holani giggled through her tears. "I didn't really mean to."

"Tell him that."

Holani stiffened. "Never."

"When will the Chickasaw be ready?" El-i-chi yelled from the door.

"Be quiet," Emily said. "How can a wounded man get any rest with you two carrying on so?" She went to the door and stepped out. "She doesn't really want to go, El-i-chi."

"She has me fooled, then," El-i-chi said, rubbing fingernail grooves on his arm.

"Were you tender?"

"How can one be tender with a female mountain lion?"

"Did you tell her of her beauty?"

A musing look came to El-i-chi's face. "I did," he said wonderingly. "I did, at least once."

"And?"

"She spat in my face."

"And what did you do?"

"I spat back."

Emily giggled in spite of herself, getting a picture of the two young people spitting into each other's faces.

"I think," Emily said, "that you have made an

impression. I don't approve, mind you, of a warrior laying hands to a woman, but in this case, perhaps it was justified. I *think*, if you'd speak to her, if you'd tell her you are sorry you beat her and that you will not beat her again—"

"The lesson of fire, if not learned the first time, must be repeated for a child," El-i-chi said. "Perhaps I will have to beat her again."

"Next time I will not be caught unprepared!" Holani yelled from inside the lodge. "Next time I will have a cane sliver hidden in my clothing, and I will—"

"Emily," Renno called out, "this courtship would be amusing if it weren't so noisy."

"See, now you've awakened Renno," Emily scolded, reaching inside to drag Holani out. "Now, both of you, behave yourselves. Holani, you know you don't want to go. Your family is dead. You're one of us now. And you, El-i-chi, tell her you will not beat her again."

"I will not beat her again if she does not try to kill me again," El-i-chi said.

"I will," Holani said, spitting into El-i-chi's face, drawing a spewed return from El-i-chi.

"Are you doing this because you wanted me to see how you did it the first time?" Emily asked in some disgust, as the two stood face-to-face, hands on hips, and spat themselves dry.

"Now are you both quite finished?" Emily asked, as they glared. "If so, walk together to the creek and wash yourselves. You are both filthy as boys who have been rolling in the mud, and spittle is not enough to clean your faces."

"I will," Holani said. "I will go to my own place.
You go to yours."

"It is no more your place than mine," El-i-chi said.
"I will wash where I please."

Holani kicked, narrowly missing El-i-chi's crotch,
and he crouched, a look of anger came onto his face,
and he moved toward her. "You are acting like a
child again," he said.

"No," Holani gasped, her eyes going wide as she
saw his intentions. She ran like the wind toward the
garden plots, El-i-chi in swift pursuit. As they disappeared, Emily heard Renno chuckling. He had come
to stand in the door.

"I think the worst is over," Emily said.

"Somehow, as your mother would say," Renno
told her, "I don't think theirs is a marriage made in
heaven."

"Perhaps it will be," Emily replied.

"If both survive the courtship," Renno said. "Do
you suppose, now, that I might be able to sleep?"

"I have a feeling that those two will be gone for a
long time," Emily said, taking Renno's arm to lead
him to his bed.

Holani gained the forest and was still leading when
she reached her private glade. She halted here, near
the creek, and prepared to fight, once again, with
tooth and claw. El-i-chi skidded to a halt when he
came upon her.

"Don't touch me," Holani said.

"No," El-i-chi said. "I will never touch you again
in love or anger, for I truly have had enough."

For a moment there was a smile on Holani's face; then her face puckered.

"What on earth is wrong now?" El-i-chi asked, as tears formed and rolled down her cheeks.

"I am sad to leave my sister, Emily," Holani said.

"She is my sister," he said. "The wife of my brother."

"But I have come to love her, and she me," Holani said, "and she bade me call her my sister."

"Thinking, no doubt, that you would show some sense and marry me, her brother."

Holani turned and walked to the mossy brink of the stream, jerked off her clothing, jumped into the deep pool, and washed the residue of El-i-chi's spittle from her face.

"If you care to wash, I will not use my superior strength to drown you," she said.

"That is so kind of you," El-i-chi said, wading in, dousing his head, and scrubbing his face. She stood facing him, her breasts proud, young.

"Had a warrior spoken for you?" El-i-chi asked.

"Many young men wanted me," Holani said, lifting her chin proudly.

"I can believe that, for you are beautiful."

Holani formed a scathing reply on her tongue, but for some reason she could not understand, she was silent and let her eyes fall modestly.

"I will not be the cause of your leaving," El-i-chi said. "I accept that you do not want to marry me. Stay. I will not trouble you further." He waded from the pool and, without looking back, walked away. For a long time Holani stood, her eyes on the spot where he had disappeared into the trees. Then she sighed, remembering how straight his back and shoulders had been as he walked away, seeing the special paleness of his sun-browned skin, the proud, eaglelike gaze of his eyes.

She caught him when he was halfway to the village, and he turned, crouched as if to protect himself from yet another attack.

"Perhaps," she said, "we can be friends."

El-i-chi remembered Emily's advice and smiled. She had told him to be patient.

"Friends do not try to kill each other," he said, grinning. "Perhaps we should make a paper of peace between us."

She drew herself up angrily. "Is my word not good enough for you?"

He held up his hand quickly. "Your word is good. I accept." She came to walk by his side. It was all he could do to keep himself from touching her, but he *would* be patient.

In the days of the summer's dying, when the air was clean and free of summer's moisture, runners went out to all outlying villages. The elders of the two tribes, observing that the Seneca and Cherokee were at peace and that the harvest had been abundant, had decreed a ceremony both to honor the season and to bestow thanks upon the two young and powerful sachems, Renno and Rusog, for their victory over the Chickasaw and the Spaniards.

Days were spent building a special pavilion, an open structure roofed against possible rain on the day of the ceremony, and the village population swelled as the outlying peoples came to make camps nearby. For days there was dancing and feasting, and then the oratory began. Each minor chief had to have his turn, each village elder had to add his praise for the two strong young leaders. Even Wegowa, still ill and barely able to walk, was on hand to offer his own words honoring his son and Renno.

Then Loramas rose to speak, after which Ah-wen-ga, with Casno standing beside her, intoned the sacred Seneca words of thanksgiving, until both Renno and Rusog were sated with ceremony and wanted little more than that it be over.

Emily watched proudly, Little Hawk sleeping contentedly in the carrier on her back. She noted that the Chickasaw woman, Holani, had trouble keeping her eyes off the slimly handsome El-i-chi, who was bedecked in the finery of a senior warrior, and she smiled. All was right with her world.

For several days following the feast Renno found himself besieged with callers eager to pay their personal respects and to consult him on matters of tribal business. Renno graciously received every visitor and listened closely to the matters presented to him.

He was particularly touched when, following a formal call by Loramas, Wegowa appeared at the doorway of his lodge. Though still suffering the effects of his relapse—and, it was rumored, unlikely to survive another winter—Wegowa had come to congratulate Renno on his recent victory and offer good wishes for the future.

Rising from his seat as Wegowa entered, Renno protested that he would gladly have come to the older man, had Wegowa summoned him. But the older chief, smiling, shook his head weakly and declared that it had been his firm wish to come himself to call on the Seneca sachem. In a voice that trembled at times, Wegowa recalled the day when he and Renno's father, Ghonkaba, had first met in the forest. Each had fired an arrow at the same deer, at the very same time, as if in omen of the future community of purpose between Cherokee and Seneca, the singleness of mind and heart that was to prevail between the two peoples.

The older warrior talked on for a few minutes; then, because other callers were waiting, he clasped Renno's hand and, with a fervent final look into the youth's eyes, rose to withdraw. Renno moved to assist him, but the once-sturdy warrior impatiently waved away his help and in an instant was gone.

Renno was pleased when the next visitor turned out to be Se-quo-i. Whenever he had observed the youth during the battle against the Chickasaw, he had been pleased to see him acquitting himself with honor, a pleasure that had gradually gained the ascendancy over his fears for the youth's safety. Now, seeing the lad in person, he extended his arm for a warrior's clasp and motioned him to sit.

"I know that there are demands on your time, Sachem," Se-quo-i said, "so I will not take much of it."

"I am pleased to see you, my friend," Renno said. "The supply of time is our most abundant gift."

"It is a gift that brings me here," Se-quo-i said, "along with my desire to reaffirm my allegiance to the strong and brave ally of my people." He extended his hand, in which was a package wrapped in doeskin. Renno accepted the gift, which had a satisfying weight as he held it in his hand.

"The workmanship is a bit crude," Se-quo-i said with anxious eyes as Renno unwrapped the doeskin.

In Renno's hand lay a large medallion of silver. The round metal had been pierced and hung from a strong silver chain. On one side of the medal was a representation of a rearing bear; on the other a soaring hawk looked very lifelike.

"The totems of my clan," Renno said. "It is a great gift. The craftsman knows his work well."

"Thank you for your kind words," Se-quo-i said.

Renno smiled. "You work in silver?"

"It is an interest of mine," Se-quo-i said. "My father tells me that it is not work for a warrior."

Renno looked at Se-quo-i seriously. "My friend, a warrior needs only a strong heart and strong body. The manitous have blessed our tribes with warriors." He put his hand on Se-quo-i's arm. "And from my own knowledge, you need offer no apologies to anyone about your abilities as a warrior. However, we need more than warriors among our peoples. We need craftsmen, artisans, and wise men. I have often thought, Se-quo-i, about our conversation regarding the art of recording forever the lore and knowledge of a people. You, a young man, have deep thoughts. A warrior who has deep thoughts, and thus advances the welfare of his people, is of infinite value. Keep up your work in silver. Artisanship is a rare gift. And should you wish it, I shall gladly arrange to have my wife, Emily, teach you to read the words of the white man. Whatever you do, continue to think deeply, and perhaps your contributions to our peoples will be greater than that of the strongest warrior."

At last, the onslaught of visitors abating, Renno was granted time to indulge a growing urge to be alone, to contemplate, to roam the forests in solitude. He had much to consider. He thanked his manitous that he had served the tribe well in the crisis. He prayed that the spirits would grant him wisdom in the future. He prayed, also, for understanding of the restlessness that seemed to come to him in times of peace and plenty. Far from the village and toward the west, he killed a yearling buck and made a secure camp in an outcrop of rock on the side of a hill. An overhang protected his fire from a cool autumn rain, and there he contemplated.

The sign came to him on a late afternoon while the soft rain wet the forests. Leaves were just beginning to gain their color. Squirrels were busy storing their winter food. And the great black bear appeared not ten feet away from his fire, standing on its rear legs. He recognized this as the same bear that had been wounded by the dead Spaniard's ball so many months in the past, and he raised his hand in greeting. The great bear swung his head back and forth, seemed to gaze directly into Renno's eyes, then fell to his four feet and melted into the rainy forest. Still, Renno felt, it was a sign, and he continued his contemplation, remembering Danega, who had said that he would return to the traditional home of the Seneca.

Change. Was that what was needed in his life? He had seen so much change in his relatively few years that he had become a natural conservative, distrustful of change. Yet change seemed to call out to him, seemed to be the cure for the restlessness he sometimes felt. More and more of the Cherokee were beginning to build houses in the white man's fashion, felling trees, hewing timbers, using the plentiful timber of the forests to build permanent homes. But was permanency good for the Indian?

From the beginning of time his ancestors had lived well on the bounty of the wilderness, taking their main sustenance from the hunt. Now more and more whites were moving into traditional hunting grounds. The buffalo, for example, was now rare in the eastern forests, where once he had been plentiful.

Renno's thoughts returned again to Danega. The old warrior had talked about going home. Was it wise of Renno to think of his lodge near the Cherokee as his home? Because of the heavy losses in the Chickasaw war, there were now fewer Seneca. El-i-chi seemed determined to take a Chickasaw wife. Many of the young Seneca had married into the Cherokee tribe. He himself had married a white woman. Was he, a descendant of the greatest leader the Seneca had ever known, to preside over the gradual disappearance of those Seneca who had fought for the United States?

He longed for knowledge of the Seneca who had remained in the Northeast. How were they faring?

From reports coming through Roy Johnson, he knew that white expansion was pushing into the Ohio territory. Was there pressure on the traditional lands of the Seneca by white men who wanted to settle there?

Now he was the leader. He had taken his place in the tradition of his ancestors, the original Renno, the brave Ja-gonh, and great Ghonkaba. Would he be worthy?

He prayed for wisdom, for a sign to tell him the best course to follow, not only for himself and his own family but also for the Seneca, the Cherokee, and that portion of the tribe that still lived in the Northeast. He sat beside his fire, burned to embers, and listened to the night sounds. A feeling of peace came to him, a feeling that was not sleep. His eyes were open, his mind alert, but he seemed to be drifting out of himself; in his mind's eye he could see himself seated there, a man tall and sturdy, a man whose skin was bronzed, but paler than that of an Indian, and before that seated man there appeared one, two, three spirits, spirits of equal tallness and sturdiness, of bronzed but pale skin.

"My fathers," the seated warrior breathed in reverence. "Renno, Ja-gonh, Ghonkaba."

The spirits were silent. Each extended a hand in blessing. The seated warrior bowed his head in gratitude, and two of the spirits faded, leaving Renno's father, Ghonkaba, standing alone. Ghonkaba's spirit wore a great bearskin robe, and the head of the great bear rested atop the spirit's head, making it seem, at times, that the spirit had two heads.

"You have done well, my son," the spirit seemed

to say, although there was no sound, only words forming in the head of the seated warrior. "The spirit of our people has been well entrusted to you. Face the trials of the future with the same wisdom and bravery you have already shown."

The spirit faded into the mists of the night, and Renno was alone, his eyes open, unblinking, still caught up in that spirit state that was neither waking nor sleeping, and then a cold wind blew, and the mist of the night swirled around him. He stirred, reached for a blanket, and wrapped his bare shoulders against the chill.

A sound from the forest alerted him. He cocked an ear, and the sound came again, the faint jingle of harness, the muted sound of the hooves of many horses, the clank of armor. He shook his head, for the sound came and went with something less than reality. But he could put pictures to the sounds, for he had heard those sounds as the Spanish lancers rode before they had been killed in the forest.

Well, it was a night for ghosts, for the sounds did not wax or diminish, but simply ceased, and he knew that it had been a sign. . . . But of what? Were the trials of the future, those hinted at by the spirit of his father, to involve the Spanish again?

He stretched, his body exhausted by the spirit encounter, and made his bed in the shelter of the overhang. He was confident. With the support of his ancestors, with the help of the manitous, he would, somehow, prevail.

Afterword

Baron de Carondelet, governor of Spanish possessions in the southeastern area of New Spain, was
receiving a guest. De Carondelet was not in the
mood to receive any guest, much less a lean, spare,
cruel-beaked monk who was a member of the su-
preme council of the Inquisition. De Carondelet would
much rather have been in the bedroom of his French
mistress, but the Dominican priest was a powerful
man, with credentials from the king himself.

After ceremonious greetings, de Carondelet es-

corted Father Sebastián to a cozy sitting room, and
the priest accepted a glass of wine.

"You live well," Father Sebastián said, looking
around at the richness of the apartment.

"It is necessary to maintain the trappings of civili-
zation in this savage land, lest one lose one's human-
ity," the governor replied.

"When I left Spain," Father Sebastián said, "the
king was most anxious for news of developments
along the middle Mississippi."

De Carondelet had feared that would be the subject of the monk's questions. He shook his head.
"First one must gain an appreciation of the vast
distances in this wilderness," he said. "Second, to
understand the difficulties, one has to see that river
for oneself. If we could send ships up the river—"

"I take it that things have not gone well," Father
Sebastián interrupted.

"Two men survived the battle to reach New Orleans," de Carondelet said, spreading his hands. "The
strength of the Cherokee was greatly underestimated.
The Chickasaw himself betrayed us."

"So all were lost?"

"All," the governor confirmed. "And we have not
the strength to march men overland in sufficient
numbers. It is my recommendation—"

"We will come to that when it is time," Father
Sebastián said with a wave of his hand to silence de
Carondelet. "The problem is, Governor, that you
pamper the savages. You must take a page from the
book of the conquistadors. It is impossible to deal
intelligently with heathen savages. First, their souls

must be turned to the true God, and then and only then can one trust them."

"And if they choose to continue to follow their own gods?"

Father Sebastián made a throat-cutting motion with his hand. "Heathenism and idolatry must be purged from all the lands of New Spain."

"That, I take it, is your mission, Father?"

The priest nodded grimly. "But that is only a minor part of my mission," he said. He took a letter from the folds of his robe and handed it to de Carondelet. "You'll find that is a commission from the king, giving me the right to draw any needed weapons and supplies and funds, and a sufficient number of men to accomplish the main portion of my mission."

The governor scanned the document quickly and handed it back. "I am your servant, good Father," he said, hoping that the man was not too greedy, for the document gave him power to squander all the riches that de Carondelet had been able to accumulate.

"Now, as for your relationship with the Indian," Father Sebastián said, "you have not done well. The Choctaw have already betrayed the Treaty of Pensacola. As I have said, there is only one way to control savages. Well, two. Convert them, save their savage souls, and force them to act like white men, or make them slaves until they see the light or are dead."

De Carondelet wondered how well this grim priest would behave when he was alone in the wilderness, on the home grounds of the savages he would convert, kill, or enslave. He found himself both disliking and fearing this priest who carried a mandate from the king, and he hoped that Father Sebastián would go about his mysterious mission quickly, leaving him free to join his mistress in her comfortable home.

"This mission," de Carondelet said, "I am curious about it."

"You will know in good time, Governor," Father Sebastián said. "In good time."

And, far to the north, Renno, too, would hear, in good time, of the mission of the Dominican priest.

Coming in 1987 . . .

BOOK XIV IN THE
WHITE INDIAN SERIES

APACHE

El Oro del Diablo, the devil's gold. A treasure worthy of any man's fantasy, it sits in an abandoned mine, guarded by the grisly remains of murdered Indian slaves—tragic evidence of Spain's greed and cruelty in the New World. Evil Father Sebastian is sent by his Spanish king to retrieve the gold, but to do so he must outsmart Renno and his newfound English friends and allies, William Beaumont and Beaumont's lovely sister, Beth, who also hope to claim the golden horde.

During this epic journey, the white Indian faces great personal dangers: a mysterious seer who feeds Renno hallucinogenic mushrooms; the fierce Indian warriors of the Great Plains . . . and Beth Beaumont, who falls in love with Renno even as the white Indian's wife lies dying after childbirth.

Surmounting every obstacle, the white Indian and his small group race across the Southwest to save the gold—and the Southwestern Indians—from Father Sebastian's Spaniards, the most heartless conquerors history has ever known.

**FROM THE PRODUCER OF WAGONS WEST
AND THE KENT FAMILY CHRONICLES—
A SWEEPING SAGA OF WAR AND HEROISM
AT THE BIRTH OF A NATION.**

THE WHITE INDIAN SERIES

Filled with the glory and adventure of the colonization of America, here is the thrilling saga of the new frontier's boldest hero and his family. Renno, born to white parents but raised by Seneca Indians, becomes a leader in both worlds. THE WHITE INDIAN SERIES chronicles the adventures of Renno, his son Ja-gonh, and his grandson Ghonkaba, from the colonies to Canada, from the South to the turbulent West. Through their struggles to tame a savage continent and their encounters with the powerful men and passionate women in the early battles for America, we witness the events that shaped our future and forged our great heritage.

☐	24650	White Indian #1	$3.95
☐	25020	The Renegade #2	$3.95
☐	24751	War Chief #3	$3.95
☐	24476	The Sachem #4	$3.95
☐	25154	Renno #5	$3.95
☐	25039	Tomahawk #6	$3.95
☐	25589	War Cry #7	$3.95
☐	25202	Ambush #8	$3.95
☐	23986	Seneca #9	$3.95
☐	24492	Cherokee #10	$3.95
☐	24950	Choctaw #11	$3.95
☐	25353	Seminole #12	$3.95
☐	25868	War Drums #13	$3.95

Prices and availability subject to change without notice.

Bantam Books, Inc., Dept. LE3, 414 East Golf Road, Des Plaines, Ill. 60016
Please send me the books I have checked above. I am enclosing $_____
(please add $1.50 to cover postage and handling). Send check or money —no cash or C.O.D.'s please.

Mr/Mrs/Miss _____

Address _____

City _____ State/Zip _____

LE3—9/86

Please allow four to six weeks for delivery. This offer expires 3/87.

★ WAGONS WEST ★

A series of unforgettable books that trace the lives of a dauntless band of pioneering men, women, and children as they brave the hazards of an untamed land in their trek across America. This legendary caravan of people forge a new link in the wilderness. They are Americans from the North and the South, alongside immigrants, Blacks, and Indians, who wage fierce daily battles for survival on this uncompromising journey—each to their private destinies as they fulfill their greatest dreams.

☐	24408	INDEPENDENCE! #1	$3.95
☐	26162	NEBRASKA! #2	$4.50
☐	26242	WYOMING! #3	$4.50
☐	24088	OREGON! #4	$3.95
☐	26070	TEXAS! #5	$4.50
☐	26377	CALIFORNIA! #6	$4.50
☐	24694	COLORADO! #7	$3.95
☐	26069	NEVADA! #8	$4.50
☐	26163	WASHINGTON! #9	$4.50
☐	22925	MONTANA! #10	$3.95
☐	26184	DAKOTA! #11	$4.50
☐	23921	UTAH! #12	$3.95
☐	26071	IDAHO! #13	$4.50
☐	26367	MISSOURI! #14	$4.50
☐	24976	MISSISSIPPI! #15	$3.95
☐	25247	LOUISIANA! #16	$3.95
☐	25622	TENNESSEE! #17	$4.50

Prices and availability subject to change without notice.

Buy them at your local bookstore or use this handy coupon:

Bantam Books, Inc., Dept. LE, 414 East Golf Road, Des Plaines, Ill. 60016

Please send me the books I have checked above. I am enclosing $_____ (please add $1.50 to cover postage and handling). Send check or money order —no cash or C.O.D.'s please.

Mr/Mrs/Miss_____

Address _____

City _____ State/Zip _____

LE—9/86

Please allow four to six weeks for delivery. This offer expires 3/87.